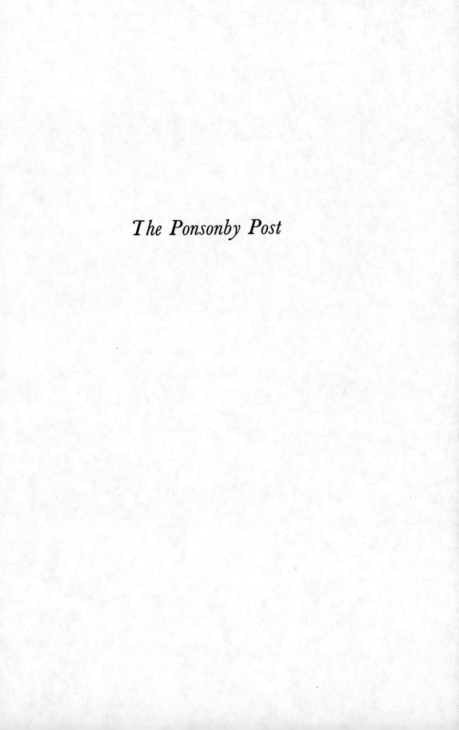

The Ponsonby Post

The Ponsonby Post

Bernice Rubens

St. Martin's Press,
New York

First published in the U.S.A. by St. Martin's Press in 1978
Copyright© 1977 by Bernice Rubens
All rights reserved. For information, write:
St. Martin's Press, Inc., 175 Fifth Ave.,
New York, N.Y. 10010.
Manufactured in the United States of America

Library of Congress Cataloging in Publication Data

Rubens, Bernice.
 The Ponsonby post.

 I. Title.
PZ4.R8913Po 1978 [PR6068.U2] 823′.9′14 78-3998
ISBN 0-312-62987-7

For Mark Goldberg

Prologue

It was when Ponsonby saw the brand new Family Planning Clinic at the end of a dirt-track in the middle of the Javanese countryside, that he decided that something had to be done. And quickly.

'How do the women get there?' he asked his guide.

'They don't. The road, if you can call it that, is mainly swamp.'

'What about the staff?'

'Americans, mostly. They use a helicopter. Land in the field behind.'

'What do they do all day?'

'Play backgammon with intra-uterine devices.'

Ponsonby didn't find it funny. He hadn't been in the job long enough. Victor, his guide, had been working for the United Nations for over ten years, and had long since lost the blithe zeal of his apprenticeship. Now for him, as for most of his colleagues, he had landed a cushy number, with a surfeit of servants, sundowners and *sati*, and his only fear was that he might be promoted to head office back home in New York.

Ponsonby was English, and he felt it keenly and with pride. Victor's cynicism did not surprise him. He was, after all, a foreigner. In Ponsonby's book, integrity was found only amongst his own kind, and perhaps with the odd Swede or two, though he had to admit that since coming to Java he had found that amongst his own countrymen a sense of probity was in short supply. Come to think of it, most of them had been here as long as Victor. Well, it wasn't going to happen to him.

The United Nations Organization was approaching its twenty-fifth birthday. Yet again it was time for assessment. Hitherto, these annual reviews had been cursory, undertaken with reluctance, in the fear and shame that there was precious little to assess. But after a quarter of a century, an evaluation of its work could no longer be a mere formality.

In the tall building in New York, the executives were forced to face up to certain unpleasant facts. Their costly attempts to stem the world population explosion in the Third World had made little impression. The natives still bred like flies. Their investments in fertilisers, pesticides and new strains of rice had paid off even less. Starvation and malnutrition were widespread. Their forays into the field of education were a fiasco. Illiteracy seemed merely to be on the increase. Only a handful of the local officials could read the statistics of those of their people who couldn't. In fact, the more honest amongst the UN examiners had to admit that all their twenty-five-year-long aid programming had been able to achieve in the Third World was a higher consumption of Coca Cola and a gentle gnawing away of cultural patterns. So happy birthday of them all. Something had to be done.

The call went out for Ponsonby. 'Make a start on Indonesia', they briefed him. 'See what's going wrong.' A tall order, but not tall enough to daunt Ponsonby. He was known for his success in tackling the most insuperable problems, in wearing down the most intransigent opposition. His record had been staggering. In the space of two short months, for example, he had managed to persuade a rather conservative and greedy dental association to sponsor the fluoridation of a sample water supply. He had launched a campaign against the manufacture of synthetic fabrics, producing incontravertible proof that the wearing of nylon next to the skin was directly connected with the increase of mastectomy, and numerous skin diseases. A Ponsonby investigation sent shivers through the Stock Exchange. Many brokers heartily wished him dead, and there was a sigh of relief throughout the well-heeled land when Ponsonby took upon his broad and honest shoulders the manifold problems of the Third World. As his plane took off for Djakarta, shares rose, and speculators breathed easy. Never was a man wished a more hearty *bon voyage*!

He had been in Java for six weeks. He had travelled the length and breadth of the island, and every square inch of UN interference told the same story. Futility. Intention had been honourable enough, and in some instances, heroic, but most projects had failed because they had been conceived in a vacuum. Educational schemes, for example, had been launched with no research into the availability of books or teachers; agricultural innovations had been bravely introduced with no regard to transport facilities. In the main street in Djakarta, the branches of the UN umbrella were housed almost next door to each other. Yet no one knew what the other was up to, and cared even less. During his stay on the island, Ponsonby had visited universities, and had found newly built modern libraries without a single book, prestige laboratories without skilled teachers. In hospitals he had found doctors too intent on the study of heart-transplant to bother to master the treatment of their door-step diseases of bilharzia and yaws. In the villages he had found farmers with their granaries packed with bales of well-meaning deliveries of pesticide and fertiliser, unused and gnawed by rats. At each delivery the farmer would shrug his shoulders. He would have used them, grudgingly, it is true, but he would have tried them had he been able, but instructions on the parcels were written in German. In the fields, the tractors and modern farming equipment rotted away for want of maintenance skill, and now this brand new family clinic without any means of access. For Ponsonby, it was the last straw. He went home and made out his report.

As far as he could see, there was only one solution. The appointment in each developing area of the world, of a link man, whose job would be to liaise between the various concerned authorities. The solution was so obvious, that it almost embarrassed Ponsonby to put it forward. So he dressed it in executive phraseology, giving it a far more sophisticated reasoning than the simple solution merited. His report took him two weeks to complete and it stretched to one hundred and twenty pages. The sun was setting as he typed THE END in large capitals. From his hotel window in Djogjakarta, he could see the fumes of Mount Merapi smouldering on the volcano's crown. He would take a walk, he thought, across the fields to the little village of Kota Grede where he would visit the village chief with whom he had become friendly. He would say his goodbyes, and then return to the hotel to prepare for his departure.

The path to the village ran through the tobacco fields, giddy with their cloying sunset scent. He first had to skirt a rice-paddy, and then to cross a fallow field before the tall tobacco plants came into view. At the end of the field was a sculptured land-mark, common enough in most villages in Java, the giant Massey-Ferguson combine harvester, or FAO folly. It looked rather beautiful, Ponsonby thought, a stubborn silhouette, immobile against the setting sun. He considered, that as a piece of sculpture or as a children's climbing frame, it belonged more under the aegis of UNESCO than of the FAO. Inside himself, he blessed its stillness.

So he was pretty well clobbered when the thing began to move. Jerkily at first, and then at great speed. In the 735 thousand square miles of the Indonesian Peninsula, it was probably the only tractor that was field-worthy, and poor, honest and decent Ponsonby had to be in the line of fire. It was heading straight towards him.

One of the last earthly sights that flashed past Ponsonby's pebble lens, was that of Hamil, the medicine-man's boy from the village, screaming the terror and the joy of his involuntary power, as the proud and unwanted machine mowed down the bewildered Ponsonby, shredding him like a cabbage-grater. The poor devil had died in the name of Development. Thus Progress does make ribbons of us all.

With due ceremony, they gathered up the bits and pieces of him, and laid them to rest in the English cemetery in Bandung. On his tomb, they put the simple legend :

George Ponsonby 1923–1969
'There is some corner of a foreign field,
That is forever England.'

The natives who sought out its translation, concluded that such jingoistic arrogance just about summed up the chauvinistic attitudes of the so-called developed world in general, but they took some consolation from the fact that poor old George was supplying them with the only kind of fertiliser that they found acceptable.

In the head office in New York, the Ponsonby Report was read with due respect and awe, and unlike the thousand and one other reports, commissioned from all corners of the world, it was taken seriously. They decided to act forthwith on his suggestion of a Liaison Officer, and to honour him and his memory they called the appointment the Ponsonby Post.

Chapter One

Only a month till the Queen's Birthday Honours, and still no word. Too late for this lot, Hugh Brownlow supposed, as he had supposed prior to each title hand-out for the last five years. Ten years ago he had taken a highly powerful job with the Arts Council. They had sworn to him then that it would lead to a knighthood. Well, it was still leading, and seemingly getting nowhere. This time he would have to change course. There must be easier roads to rank.

He was close on fifty, and he was wearing well. He had those well-bred good looks of vintage Englishmen which improve with age. He had married late, in his fortieth year, a slip of a girl, half his age, Belinda, blessed and beautiful. His daughter Emily was almost seven, and beautiful too. As a family group, they had made the centre spreads of most of the glossy magazines of Europe, entertaining in their Georgian quarters in Mayfair, or riding to hounds from their manor pad in Hertfordshire. Yes, he considered he was well and truly blessed, but the rank eluded him. He couldn't understand it. Since his tenure at the Arts Council he had done much to foster interest and encouragement in all cultural pursuits. He loved the company of writers and painters, and he held them all in genuine admiration. In his regional excursions, he had fought the local councillors who wondered why artists couldn't go out and do a decent day's work like anybody else. He shamed them into financing theatre groups and experimental workshops, and because he personally had plenty of brass, they respected him. He liked his job and he was good at it. In his official capacity, he had attended many a royal occasion. He moved in the right circles. He knew the right people. He concluded that he was simply on the wrong wicket. He would have to look elsewhere.

People like Hugh Brownlow don't *look* for jobs. At the very

5

most, they rumour their availability. But not, Heaven forfend, in any positive sense. He would let it be known that he was not disinclined to consider certain offers, that he was not uninterested in a change, that, given the right circumstances, etc. etc., he might not show indifference. Such was the manner of his job application.

Its method was equally noncommittal. A word dropped in the ear of his broker, a hint or two whispered in his club, and above all, and by far the most successful channel, through the steam of a Mayfair Turkish bath. Here, he could afford to be perhaps, a little less negative, for embarrassment was quickly vaporised.

Through this ethereal network, this labyrinth of negative tender, word came to the ear of the United Nations' representative in London, and back through the grapevine of broker, club and sauna, came the hint that Giles of the UN was not disinterested in Brownlow's nondisinclination. For in the circles in which Brownlow moved, to offer a job was almost as humiliating as seeking one, and anything which fell short of this negative procedure was tantamount to whoredom on both sides. A discreet lunch was arranged at the Connaught.

Giles and Brownlow arrived simultaneously, each marvelling at the coincidence, though each had kept a look-out for the other. The Connaught was acquainted with both men, so the location offered no advantage to either. They sat down to their aperitifs as equals. Giles was a racing man. He owned a string of horses that he kept in Cambridgeshire. He hunted too, so there was enough conversation matter to take them through the artichokes (vinaigrette), the sole (Veronique), and the wild strawberries (imported). Over their brandy they played with the economic crisis, and the current political coup, and it was not until Giles was doing up the top button of his overcoat, and both men were politely ushered through the doors of the hotel, that Giles mentioned the Ponsonby Post for the first time. Between the second and the third button, he described the nature of the appointment. On the last button, he hesitated, not necessarily for dialogue, but in consideration of whether to do it up at all. Having paused however, he thought he might as well fill the silence, and turning to Brownlow, he said, 'Think it over, old man. You might find it interesting,' adding, for Brownlow's weakness was well known, 'Shouldn't be surprised a title'll go with it.' Then, in the only positive act he had made that day, he fastened the last button.

The commissionaire hailed a cab. Brownlow opted to walk back to his office, no doubt to think it over, and Giles settled in the back of the taxi having filled the Ponsonby Post to his satisfaction.

The Arts Council were sorry to see Brownlow go. They offered him a substantial rise, and suggested he might try to make do with a gong. But it was as Sir Hugh that Brownlow addressed himself as his bath-water was running out, and Lady Belinda it was who was showering in the bathroom next door. An OBE or whatever alphabet they had in mind, could never be an oral appellation. It was simply written down, and there was little satisfaction in that. And a rise in salary was of no interest to him. Instant knighthood, he decided, or quits. So quits it had to be. They left for Djakarta at the end of September.

Djakarta, like most Third World capitals, is pock-marked with monuments, rude fingers aimed at the sky. An obelisk here, a column there. Occasionally the monument honours a national hero, but in the ranks of patriotic devotion the turnover is very rapid. Very often the hero has fallen from grace, and possibly too, from the gallows, before his monument has been unveiled. And so to cover this contingency, monuments to human beings tend to be very high, so that the features, except from a helicopter, are quite unrecognisable, and the only item to be changed on the stone edifice is the legend, easily replaced by the name, rank and credits of the current favourite. Often, of course, national loyalties being fickle, a deposed hero may be reinstated. Thus the brass plaques are kept in cold storage for such an eventuality.

On his first day, Brownlow made himself known at the UN headquarters in Djalan Pregolan. They welcomed him formally, arranging a dinner in his honour. They presented him to the local dignitaries and generally gave him the grand tour. They did all the right things. But they were not pleased. The very notion of the Ponsonby Post was a slight on their efficiency. They were aware of many shortcomings in their organisation, and of a great deal of mismanagement. But it was, after all, even after twenty-five years, a trial and error business, and how could this handsome middle-aged Etonian, hot from his cushion on the

Arts Council, how could he begin to understand the infinite un-predictabilities of the Third World. Besides, he looked much too eager. They had discussed his arrival beforehand, and had decided to advise him to set up his headquarters in Djogjakarta in Central Java. There, centrally straddled between Surabaya and Djakarta, he could survey the whole territory. But most of all, he'd be out of their way. They rather liked Belinda though. She would have made a splendid addition to the numerous state banquets they were obliged to attend. Their own women, after years in a climate where the humidity was higher than the temperature, had lost their native bloom. They were bored, and boring too, and seemed to spend most of their time at the hair-dressers or at massage. An inordinate amount of time, especially at the latter, their men-folk thought. Certainly the skill of the Javanese masseur was bruited all over the Far East, and though stories abounded as to the nature of that skill, the husbands quickly turned a deaf and English ear. The wives, however, came to temporary life when Belinda arrived. All of them were experts, and they bombarded her with tittle-tattle and advice, bemoaning the fact that she had not brought out a governess from England. The native amahs were not all that trustworthy and most of them couldn't speak a word of English. And what would little Emily do for schooling?

'There must be schools in Djogjakarta,' Belinda said. They marvelled at her naiveté. 'But they don't speak English', and that was the least of their objections. 'Then we shall have to learn Indonesian,' Belinda said.

They saw the Brownlows off on the train to Djogjakarta, waving a last farewell. Governess-less, and intent on native education, bound for that one-eyed hick town where that inter-fering Ponsonby had met his untimely and fragmented end, they felt sure they were seeing the last of them. Back they went to the hairdressing salons and massage parlours, while their executive husbands in the FAO bypassed those husbands in the WHO who in turn ignored those from the UNESCO but who all united in a band to avoid the staff of the UNDP who were always hounding them. Brownlow had gone into the wilds, and God be thanked, communications were poor. By now he was well into the hinterland. That evening, as they settled on their patios, sundowners in hand, their bee-hived-lacquered wives, massage-throbbing alongside them, Hugh and Belinda Brownlow were taking their first language lessons from the sleeping-car attendant on the Djakarta–Surabaya express.

The train had been constructed in East Germany, a highly technological affair strangely at odds with the primitive and deprived landscape which it threaded. Outside, in the river which skirted the track, village women washed their bodies, clothes and cooking utensils, in the same water where they and their menfolk daily defecated. Inside the train the midnight movie was in progress, an American Western with Indonesian sub-titles. As his term of office progressed, Brownlow was to use that train frequently. Less and less he looked out of the windows dividing the 'them' from the 'us'. More and more the train epitomised for him the sad and distorted priorities of the so-called civilised world.

The sleeping-car attendant wished them 'Good night'. He would call them at four a.m. when the train would reach Djogjakarta. The Brownlows slept on a vocabulary of some thirty Indonesian words. They were dangerously on the way to going native.

They had been booked into the Ambarrukmo Palace Hotel. Like the cross-island train, it was an anachronism, a luxury rudely out of season. The Brownlows' suite of rooms, which were to be their permanent residence, were furnished in English style with the odd Dutch and Japanese antique, as a reminder of the country's colonised past, together with a portrait of the benevolent Queen Elizabeth II to impress upon the Brownlows that even their green and pleasant land was not in the clear. It was in this same hotel, on a lower floor, that poor old Ponsonby had written his last report, and across the paddy fields beyond the hotel swimming-pool, Mount Merapi smouldered still. Hugh and Belinda stood on the verandah and marvelled at the view. Most spectators on seeing such still and rumbling majesty, would have been lost for words, but would nevertheless have scratched and scraped for some inadequate vocabulary to describe it. The Brownlows, having resolved to speak only Indonesian, wouldn't have been able to find words anyway, but they were happy to watch and be silent. But each had the same English thought. They were a very long way from the Arts Council.

Emily was placed in the local school. The headmaster spoke a little English. He had been a prisoner of war during the occupation and his vocabulary was confined to concepts of survival. His words were material, relating to his body's needs; those pertaining to his spirit were uncatered for, except in his still Indonesian inner voice. He made Emily welcome, guiding her to a class of her own age, and pinning a circle of little girls around her, he left her to their gentle curiosity. Most of them had never seen a Western girl at such close quarters. A few younger children were in the kindergarten, but at Emily's age, they were usually shipped out to the American school on the outskirts of the town, carted to and fro in large limousines. Not for touching. Now they fingered Emily's dress, her miraculously blonde hair. Together they compared their physical attributes and within an hour, Emily knew each part of her body by new and distant words.

Belinda enrolled herself in a class of batik, not wishing to have time on her hands, and every afternoon she helped out in the hospital with auxiliary nursing duties. Meanwhile Hugh toured the area, familiarising himself with UN projects. Within a month, they were settled enough to throw their first party.

Even though they knew few people, and ill-assorted ones at that, the Brownlows were discriminate with their guest list. They considered the party a private one, and only those whom they liked were invited. The handful of UN officials in the area, together with their wives, did not qualify for the latter category. Djogjakarta is small, and the grapevine direct, so the non-invitees were early aware of the snub. They hadn't liked the idea of Brownlow from the start. Now they hated his person. One of them hastily arranged a dinner party for the uninvitees of their group, calling it an official UN function, and spreading the news abroad. Brownlow would have to learn, they decided, what kind of men he was dealing with.

But Hugh had not ignored the UN entirely. In fact most of the guests worked for the same authority as himself. But they worked in the field. They had bothered to learn the language. Their children went to the local school. They were deeply involved in the work they were doing, aware all the time that there was as much if not more to take as there was to give. Jan Horst was one of them. He was a Dutchman working for the FAO. He had lived in Djogjakarta for four years. He was one

of the first to persuade the farmers to use the new rice grain
which yielded a double crop, and to this end he and his family
had lived for two years in a village near by to experiment
themselves with the peasants. Their Indonesian was fluent, and
they had knowledge of dialects too. Bella Horst, his wife, was
Belinda's teacher. There was Mochtar Kayan, a painter, and
one or two poets, all of whom had spent spasmodic periods in
gaol under the changing conquering regimes. Brownlow's
chauffeur was there, a retired farmer himself, who knew most
of the head men of the villages across the centre of the island.
Some parents and teachers from Emily's school, and a few
hospital workers completed the party. Brownlow moved amongst
his guests. He was content. Occasionally the old title-need
gnawed at him, but somehow in Djogjakarta it seemed less and
less important. Belinda had settled well, and Emily too. He liked
the job and was confident he could do it well. But for some
reason, in the midst of all these bonuses, he was afraid. He
couldn't pin-point the fear. He knew it had no cause and he was
not a man to subscribe to premonition. Yet since arriving in the
country, he had had fleeting moments of panic. One night, his
first at the Ambarrukmo Hotel, he'd had a dream. He was in
the English countryside, and the colours were soft and gentle as a
Bonnington painting. He was picnicking with his family, playing
with Emily, and the whole dream was scored to their laughter.
Yet when he'd woken, he was sweating. The dream, for all its
joy, had assumed the quality of a nightmare, and fear gripped
him. Now, moving amongst his guests, he panicked again.
'Stuff and nonsense,' he whispered to himself, and without knowing why, he rushed to Emily's room to watch her sleeping.

Chapter Two

Every morning on his way to work, Brownlow would pass by a little shoe-shine boy plying a lively trade in the courtyard of the Sultan's Palace. The boy's name was Burhan. No one knew his family name. No one would have asked, any more than they would have enquired the surname of a pet. He himself was none to sure of his parentage. He remembers an assortment of wooden huts as his home, and numerous grown-ups around him, but he cannot connect his welfare with any one face in particular. When he was five—in his short life it seemed decades ago—he picked up the piece of rush matting on which he slept and walked out of the village. Nobody called him back. Indeed, few noticed that he was gone. He didn't know how long or how far he walked. But he remembered that they were planting rice in the wet paddies when he left, and by the time he reached Djogjakarta, the farmers were harvesting. He did not know his age. He had the appearance of a boy of ten, though he was possibly older. But he had the wit and the cunning of an adult. Within a few years of his arrival in Djogja, he had become the contact man for all the underground activities of the province. He was wholly innocent, and even though he was running from dope supplier to consumer, from one political cell to another, from call-girl to pimp and back again, he remained innocent still. His illiteracy was regarded as an asset. As a runner, he would carry written secrets from one hide-out to another, and he had little notion of the illegality and perils of his vocation. Occasionally he would be delegated to transact a dope deal, for he bargained with the skill of a hardened trafficker. And the ten or so lean years of him would slouch in an alley doorway, fingering the capsules of white powder in one hand, while with the other, he gently sucked his thumb.

He was in on the tourist racket too. The town was increasingly raided by tourists—the Borobodour and Prambanan Temples were just outside the city—and they came for the pickings on the package deals, looting the batik and Djogja silverwork. Burhan acquired the essentials of their language. Five basic words in every European tongue, was sufficient vocabulary for trading. Dollar, Lady, Man, Dope, Fuck. Armed with such an explosive lexicon, he rushed all over the city, catering for tourist needs. His reputation was far flung. If anybody in Djogjakarta wanted anything at any time, Burhan was your man. Shoe-shining was his gentle cover.

Every morning at eight-thirty, Brownlow would cross the courtyard to reach his office. Usually Emily was with him. Her school was on the way. Every morning Burhan would offer his services to Brownlow's hotel-polished shoes, and every morning Brownlow would regret that he had not saved them for Burhan. For the boy fascinated him. He'd picked up his story from various sources, for Burhan was widely known. His own organisation was often tempted to use the boy to gain information that might have been unobtainable through official channels, but his connections were known to be too dubious to take the risk. But Brownlow wanted to get to know him on his own account. He felt sorry for the boy. He pitied him his illiteracy, he regretted his lack of childhood. In an extravagant moment, he would have wished to pack the boy off to England, to have him fitted out at Gieves, and schooled at Eton and Cambridge, his own Alma Maters. As a UN official, Brownlow was very new at the game. A rescue mission fever burned inside him. Most of his colleagues had come out with the same zeal; most had lost appetite. Though there were some who had begun to understand that the so-called underdeveloped world could rescue much in *them*, could teach an art of refinement and culture that their own civilisation had long lost. But Brownlow was still green, and full of good works and the Simpson/Eton production excited him. But he knew it was not possible. All he could do was to let the boy shine his shoes.

He placed his hand-made shoe on Burhan's stand. Emily hung on to his hand. Though younger than Burhan, she was as tall, and their eye-lines were parallel. Between his brush-strokes, he looked at her, wide-eyed at her alien beauty. He polished as if his life depended upon it, until her reflection gleamed in his handiwork. Brownlow pressed a five rupiah note into his hand.

It was far too much for a shoe-shine, but Brownlow had the feeling that what had passed between them was more than a simple street valet service. Burhan smiled silently, then, looking at Emily, he donated one word from his meagre lexicon. 'Lady,' he whispered. He did not say it as he might have addressed an American blue-rinsed tourist, nor as he might have enquired the needs of some lonely commercial traveller. By some linguistic instinct, he heard the word as an object of man's devotion, and it was this sweet sound that he gave her. She giggled with the compliment, though she too sensed its worth. At the end of the courtyard, she turned back to look at him. He waved, with a small timid gesture, his shy fist clutched to his chest, his fingers wiggling. When school finished, he was at the gates, waiting. An oldish woman collected her, along with other children, and walked them across the courtyard. Burhan followed at a respectful distance. Occasionally Emily turned and smiled at him. Then, at the end of the courtyard, he stopped, and watched her out of sight.

Every morning thereafter he shined her father's shoes, waving to her across the courtyard. And every day he waited for her after school. Such was the manner of their early courtship, and the routine continued for some three or four weeks. Emily's first waking thought was Burhan. Every morning she tugged at her father's coat-sleeve, urging him to hurry, and Burhan would wait at his stand, his heart thumping. Then one day, one ordinary day, a mid-week day that celebrated neither Muslim nor Hindu nor Christian faith, Burhan wasn't there. Emily saw the empty stall from way across the courtyard, and she felt a pricking behind her eyes. Her father said nothing. On each side of Burhan's empty space, other shoe-shiners waited for trade. 'Burhan?' he questioned one of them. They shrugged. Brownlow squeezed Emily's hand.

'Maybe he's ill,' the word squeaked out of her like the cry of an injured bird.

'He'll be better tomorrow,' Brownlow said, and knew for some reason that he shouldn't have said it.'

He wasn't outside the gates when school was over, and as they crossed the courtyard, Emily kept turning her head. She awoke in sour panic the next morning, fearing that her father had lied, and when she saw the empty space in the courtyard, she looked at her father as if he were a stranger.

The Burhan-less weeks passed. Brownlow and Belinda hoped that she'd get over it. But each day she woke with hope and with fear, till one morning she decided that Burhan must be dead. She was too grieved to go to school, and Brownlow left alone, his brow furrowed. As he crossed the courtyard, he avoided the shoe-shine barrier. Then suddenly, in front of him, blocking his way, stood Burhan. He looked up at him, his eyes fever-bright. 'Lady?' he said. Brownlow put down his briefcase and in one large movement, swept the boy into his arms. Never in his life had he made such an open and spontaneous gesture, not even when Belinda had agreed to marry him, not even when little Emily was born. But now his joy was overwhelming. Burhan's reappearance had replaced Emily's trust in him. Had he not told her that Burhan would be there tomorrow, and though belated, tomorrow had finally come, and his daughter would trust him once again. 'Come,' he said, and taking Burhan's hand, he hailed a *betjak* back to the hotel.

The *betjak* driver, one of Burhan's friends, gave Burhan a knowing look, but not too knowing because it was generally understood that Burhan's contacts were private and often secret, and only when Burhan was alone or with other known friends, could one openly acknowledge him. Nevertheless, the driver made a mental note of Brownlow's face. Though he looked a kindly man, he was white, and resident at the Ambarrukmo, two qualifications not calculated to win over the natives' confidence. As they alighted at the hotel, Burhan raised his eyes skywards to the driver, conveying that he knew as little about it as anybody. Then he followed Brownlow into the hotel.

Burhan had never been inside the Ambarrukmo. He'd loitered outside often enough, passing and waiting for messages. Now his bare feet sank into the carpeted foyer, and through the plate-glass window he could see the pool. He had often taken messages in hour-long *betjak* rides (expenses paid) to the rich outlying districts of Djogjakarta where there were brothels lush and carpeted like this hotel. But no swimming-pool. He had seen baths though, sunken into marble floors, and men and women through layers of steam, and he suspected that some of the people in the hotel foyer had probably been there too. Certainly some of their faces were familiar. But they acknowledged Burhan no more than did the *betjak* driver, though no doubt they wondered what he was doing inside this place, and on whose behalf. Brownlow's face was noted. A few innocent enquiries at reception could, if necessary, establish the beginnings of a small dossier.

Brownlow guided the boy into the lift. He didn't know what it was, and he was afraid. He pressed his body snug into the angle of the wall, seeking safety in its shelter. He watched Brownlow press a button, and his stomach heaved as a warm jet of his fear trickled down his leg. He had never in his life been so afraid. He had undertaken perilous journeys over mountains and rivers, dodged police, bandits and rival messengers. And always he had trusted in Allah, for like any self-respecting god, Allah looked after widows and orphans. But Allah was no match against lift-buttons. He wanted to get out, because he smelt it as a trap, but it seemed illogical that the white man was trapped too, and by his own volition. He looked down at the pool of water at his feet. He was ashamed. Brownlow ruffled the boy's hair in a friendly attempt to convey to him that he had done nothing wrong. Then Burhan clutched at Brownlow's coat. White though he was, and from foreign parts, maybe his god had had button-training. Then, as if in answer, one door of the trap opened. Hanging on to Brownlow's sleeve, he followed him into the corridor. Then into a washroom, where Brownlow lifted him on to a stool, and washed and wiped him down.

'Lady?' Burhan said again.

'We go,' Brownlow said, pigeoning his English in the faint hope that it would be understood. Then down the corridor again to Brownlow's suite.

Burhan lagged behind when Brownlow went through the door. He now understood that Emily would be there, and he was suddenly shy. He felt his face flush with the realisation that he had entirely forgotten what she looked like. But as Belinda appeared in the doorway, he suddenly remembered. 'Lady,' he said, this time as a statement, to confirm that he knew why he was there. Belinda took his hand, and brought him into the drawing-room.

Through the open french doors, he could see her standing on the verandah, her back to the room. He hoped she would not turn, not just yet anyway, because that was how he often saw her, as he watched her chaperoned out of the square on her way home. He looked at her, preparing himself, though mindful that she would not have this advantage. He would have liked to use her father as a messenger, but not one of his five words could convey that information. He went over them in his mind. Dollar, lady, man, dope, fuck. Not one of them. They were each concerned with basic practicalities and had nothing to do with real communication. He looked at Brownlow pleadingly.

Then, as if Emily felt a change, she turned suddenly, and seeing Burham, she let out a squeak of delight mingled with disbelief, and she ran, not to him but to her father, hugging him for having kept his promise. Belinda, sensing the need for celebration, brought out cold drinks and cakes, and when they were sitting round the table, Emily tentatively touched Burhan's hand. She looked at her parents and silently they adopted him.

It was too late for Emily's school, so Burhan was invited to spend the day at the hotel. As Brownlow left them, he felt that he had already accomplished a good day's work.

The phone rang as he was going through the door. And once again, against the prevailing backcloth of calm and pleasure, he was needled by the old nightmare fears. He picked up the receiver. As he listened, he was glad that Belinda was in the other room because he knew his face registered shock. 'I'll come straight away,' he said.

As the car drove into the village of Harbobingangun, some fifteen miles from the city, he could see the scattered remains of the small Piper blocking the road. The landing had shattered its nose, and the tail still trembled mid-air. On one side of the plane he could make out the German markings, and the scrolled name, 'Fortschritte'. He made a note to find out what it meant.

The villagers stood on the side of the road, fearful of approaching the machine. They were sullen and angry, and when Brownlow stepped out of the car, Sastro, the headman of the village, who normally waited for him and bowed him into his house, did not go forward to greet him. Brownlow looked around for Weiner. It was he who had phoned him. Even on the telephone, his voice had been an accusation. Even though he was in charge of the airstrip, he would find some loophole where he could lay the blame. And blame there possibly was in some quarter, for until a thorough investigation was held, it was possible that the crash was no accident. Suddenly Weiner appeared out of the crowd, and approached Brownlow as if he were about to handcuff him. 'We'll go to the meeting-house,' Brownlow said coolly. 'We'll wait outside for Sastro.'

The two outsiders walked through the clearing to the village hall, and once there, they waited on the steps. From the road, Sastro watched them. In his heart he was loathe to be their host, but his duty was to the people in the village. They understood his conflict and those around him did not urge him to step forward. They waited. He would do what was right for all of them. Brownlow and Weiner waited too, the latter scuffing his feet on the steps, and clearly showing his impatience. 'Keep still for God's sake,' Brownlow was bound to tell him, because he knew that Sastro would not take a step forward to Weiner's present mood. He wondered why the man was tense. A closer look about his eyes suggested that he might have been crying. Weiner sulked and was still. Then there was a stirring amongst the villagers, and as if catching Sastro's mood, they walked slowly forward, escorting him to the hall. At the foot of the steps, he bowed slightly and let the two men into the hall. They were silent, while the women brought mint-tea and cakes, and Wan, Sastro's eldest son, was summoned from the family house. Today his father had forbidden him to go to Djogja, where he studied English at the Gadja Mada University. After this morning's incident Sastro had been sickened by all the alien inroads into his people's way of life, by all these do-gooding intruders who tampered with their faith in the name of progress. But he knew that such feelings were temporary. Brownlow was his friend, and so were many others in the Organization. But they were exceptions. A man like Weiner was the rule, and Sastro looked at him with undisguised mistrust.

'Tell me what happened,' Brownlow addressed Weiner, 'and allow time for Wan's translation.' He nodded to the boy. 'I want your father to join in our discussion. His advice, as you know, is for me the most valuable.' Wan translated and Sastro nodded with satisfaction.

'The FAO plane took off at eight hundred hours,' Weiner began. He waited for Wan's translation and his pause was insolent.

'Eight o'clock this morning,' Brownlow said. He wasn't going to be treated to any refuge in technological terminology. Often such language was used as a cover-up for guilt. 'I just want it so that we can all understand,' Brownlow said. Wan translated this too, and Sastro nodded his approval once again. 'Today is Thursday,' Weiner went on, 'and as you know, every Thursday is crop-spraying. The scheduled take-off of that plane is nine hundred—er—nine o'clock, but for some reason this morning, it took off early. When I got to the airstrip, the flight form and the time of take-off had been filled in. The crash occurred at nine-ten.' He paused. He was clearly under great strain. 'I saw to the removal of the body,' he said quickly, 'as for the wreckage, I thought it best to leave it. There will obviously be an investigation.'

There were many questions that Brownlow wanted to ask Weiner, but it would have been undiplomatic in Sastro's presence. But Sastro was entitled to some explanation. He had to be open with him. He turned to Weiner. 'Where were you at seven this morning?' he said. He had checked on Weiner's official hours. They began at seven.

'I was delayed on my way to the airstrip. I was late.'

'How late?'

'I arrived at eight-fifteen.'

'So there was no one at the strip when the plane took off,' Brownlow said. Weiner looked at Brownlow pleadingly. There was much to tell him, but not in front of this man. He got up. 'I'll see that no one touches the wreckage,' he said.

Brownlow understood and let him go. When he reached the door, he called after him, 'Weiner, what does Fortschritte mean?'

Weiner tightened his jaw. 'Progress,' he said.

Sastro was speaking to his son. Brownlow could tell from the few words he could understand, and from the rising inflexions of the man's voice, that Sastro was angry and determined. Wan turned to Brownlow. 'My father says that things must now be different here. After the accident some villagers were rejoicing. They sang and danced, and my father is ashamed. But those farmers, who were laughing, they never wanted the fertiliser and the pesticide and the new Bimas rice. They say that the gods have had their revenge. Now all the farmers will be on their side. They say that the fertiliser and all the strange powders are evil. They interfere with nature. And the gods are angry. Today was a sign. My father says that perhaps Merapi will be angry too, and pour hot lava on to the village. He orders that you take away all the powders, and all the machines and all the buildings, and let us live our life as we did before you came.'

Sastro got up. He'd had his say, and he saw no point in argument. He came over to Brownlow and took his hand. Then slowly and clearly he spoke. Brownlow's Indonesian was adequate to understand the old man's farewell. 'I do not wish to see you again,' he had said. He walked to the steps of the hall, where he stopped and spoke again to his son. Wan returned. 'My father says that you must take all your charity away, or the farmers will burn everything. He says too that you are his friend when you are not working. He would like tomorrow to play mah-jong with you.'

Brownlow smiled with relief. He liked Sastro. He had welcomed his own family to the village, and Emily was particularly fond of him. Moreover, as long any line was open, however tenuous, there was still a possibility that the villagers would allow themselves to be helped.

He had to see Weiner again, so he ordered the car to the air-strip. It was no more than a field. At the far end was a make-shift hut, Weiner's office, where airport business, such as it was, was handled. Brownlow stood at the open door and saw Weiner at his desk. His back was towards him, and from his hunched and quivering shoulders, he knew that he was sobbing. Quickly he withdrew, and walked around the hut, whistling softly to herald his approach. He gave Weiner time to pull himself together. When he approached the door a second time, Weiner was standing and sorting out some papers.

'Can I come in?' Brownlow said.

Weiner looked up and pushed a chair towards him. 'Did you know the pilot?' Brownlow said softly.

'Klaus Schmidt was a close friend.' Now he sobbed openly, and Brownlow, gathering the nature of the friendship went over to him and placed his hand on his shoulder. 'I'm sorry,' he said. 'I'm very sorry.' He shuffled around the room, while Weiner turned in a sad circle. 'Was there *anybody* here this morning when the plane took off? *Could* there have been?'

Weiner seemed grateful to talk. 'No, I'm the only one on duty.

Apart from paper work and the telephone, there's little to do. The planes are small and the pilots are very experienced. They take off on their own. There's hardly any air traffic anyway. Nothing apart from the spraying.' He had talked without pausing for breath. Now he gulped, realising what all the words had been about. While he had been speaking, the words were routine, and were wholly disconnected from the reality of Klaus's body spread-eagled under the trees. How still he had looked, Weiner thought, asleep almost, with no sign of hurt. Until he had lifted his body gently to his own, and seen his back, trellised with jagged metal.

Brownlow waited, not looking at him. Once before in England, he had been witness to a similar loss. A painter friend of his had lost his lover in a train smash. He too had poured out irrelevant words, till breathless, they had to curdle into sobs. I must let him weep, Brownlow thought. I must let him mourn. He got up to leave.

'Stay,' Weiner said. 'You're worried, aren't you? So am I. It doesn't add up, does it?'

'It's strange that the FAO plane took off so early,' Brownlow said. Then gently, 'When did you last see your friend?'

'Last night. Normally he'd stay overnight on a Wednesday, and in the morning, we would drive out to the strip together. But last night he didn't stay. He said he had to meet somebody in Djogja. He left about ten o'clock.'

'Did he seem worried or different in any way?'

'No. We were very happy together.'

Brownlow twiddled with the clasp on his briefcase. He needed to know a great deal more and he wondered how much more questioning Weiner could stand. 'Could I ask you something else?' he said.

Weiner nodded.

'You said something about a delay this morning. The reason you were late. What happened?'

'Well, I left the house a bit earlier than usual, in fact. I hadn't slept too well. I was upset that Klaus hadn't stayed.' He put his head in his hands. 'I loved him, you see,' he said, almost to himself. Then he shook his head violently as if to rinse it of the unbearable truth. 'I'd got about half a mile up the road,' his voice was suddenly gruff, 'and there was a tree blocking my way.

21

I couldn't by-pass it, and it was too big to shift on my own. I'd passed two boys on the road, so I waited for them. They seemed to be an awfully long time. When they reached the car, they offered to help, and together we shifted the trunk. I offered them a lift, but they wanted to walk, they said. Then in about another 200 yards, there was another tree. I was really late by now, and I had to wait for the boys again. After a while they reached me, and we moved it out of the road.'

'Have they been felling in the village?' Brownlow asked.

'They do, from time to time. But I've never come across a road-block before.'

'Would you recognise those boys again?'

'I've been out in this jungle for three years,' Weiner said. 'I'm sorry, but they still all look the same to me.'

In view of his loss, Brownlow let it pass. 'How old, about?' he said.

'Seventeen. Eighteen. You can't tell with them.'

It was clear to Brownlow that Weiner could give little more at that time. The man was faced with the sad truth of things; his mind was too shaken to stretch to probabilities. He was faced with the solid loss of a loved one, and seeking out someone to blame would have in no way modulated his grief.

But Brownlow was more uneasy than before. On his way back to Djogja, he tabled a number of questions in his notebook. There was clearly more to Klaus Schmidt than a crop-spraying pilot for the FAO. And those road-blocks were suspiciously well timed. In a few days, he would talk to Weiner again. Meanwhile he had to discover the cause of the crash. The investigation frightened him a little. He suddenly thought of Burhan, and he blessed him for his return.

The driveway of the hotel was blocked by police. When Brownlow saw them, the old fears returned. His first thought was for Emily. Almost simultaneously, he sensed that the presence of the police, so soon after the Klaus affair, was in some way, however tenuous, connected with the shattered Piper.

After checking, they let his car through. Isani, the Chief of Police, stood at the hotel entrance. He was a friend of Brownlow's, having a child at Emily's school.

'What happened?' Brownlow said.

In a low whisper, Isani told him. The body of a girl, so far

unidentified, though from the look of her and her clothing—
'you know', he said, 'those patched and frayed jeans', she was
American, and probably worked for the Peace Corps. Her body,
fully clothed, he was careful to add, was found in the tangled
thicket beyond the pool. As yet, no one knew how she had died,
or at what time, though the doctor, at a rough guess, had put it
last night, round about midnight.

'But I was swimming this morning. Before breakfast,'
Brownlow said irrelevantly. He felt suddenly cold and accusable.

Isani shrugged. 'Hope she isn't Peace Corps,' he said, 'or it'll
be a diplomatic incident. Though I'll lay a bet it wasn't one of
our people. They murder, it's true, but they're violent. They cut
and they maim. But there's not a mark on her.'

'Perhaps she had a heart-attack,' Brownlow offered feebly.

'At that age?' he said. 'And what would she be doing wandering alone in that place? There are snakes there. It's well known.'

Brownlow had no further explanation to offer. He went
straight to his rooms.

Belinda had drawn the blinds on the window that overlooked
the pool, and the balcony doors were closed. Burhan and Emily
were playing checkers, while Belinda worked on a batik. By the
feigned concentration in the room, he knew that they knew
about the turmoil downstairs.

'There's a dead body, Daddy,' Emily shrieked, running towards
him. 'Somebody was killed.' She was trembling with the excitement of it.

Brownlow sadly quietened her. He thought of the young girl's
mother, and he winced at her bewildered pain. How could she
be told? And who would have to tell her? Despite his pity, he
could not help hoping that the girl was an American as Isani
had supposed. At least the affair would be out of his jurisdiction.

But as it turned out, it landed fairly and squarely in his
province. An hour later, he was summoned to the Chief of
Police. 'The girl has been identified,' Isani said. He read from
a typewritten piece of paper. She was but a name now, in red
capitals, a heading with a nationality, a profession, and an
address. 'Patricia Forrest,' Isani read aloud, having painful
difficulty with the pronunciation. 'British subject.' He looked
at Brownlow, and shrugged a vicarious apology. 'Worker
for Voluntary Service Overseas. Attached to World Food

Programme, Djogjakarta. Only child, father deceased. Mother lives at Rose Cottage, Woodland Street, Virginia Water, Surrey.'

Inglenook and chintz, Brownlow thought, and bowls of cut roses on consoles. The mother absorbing her widowhood into good deeds, a garden party for the restoration of the village church, a flag day for handicapped children, and the evening hot cocoa by the fire, while reading the latest missive from the adventurous and virtuous daughter of whom she was so proud.

'She had had recent sexual intercourse,' Isani splintered Brownlow's reverie.

'She doesn't have to know that,' he said, almost to himself.

'Who?' Isani asked.

'Nothing.' He walked over to the window. Outside, in the street-market, a young girl sat, bud-like, in the centre of petals of fruit, and Brownlow was assaulted by a feeling totally alien to him. He wanted that girl; he wanted her with a cruel and violent need, a strangled need that cried out from his groin. 'How did she die?' He turned to face Isani, and he heard the echo of his voice. He had been shouting.

'Are you all right, Hugh?' Isani said.

Brownlow drew up a chair and sat by the desk. He leaned his head on his hand. 'It's a tragic business,' he said.

Isani poured him a glass of water. Brownlow drank, and the writhing worm inside him was slowly stilled.

'The doctor's verdict,' Isani was saying, 'was that she died of a brain haemorrhage, caused by a savage blow on the side of the neck. There was a big bruise,' he said, 'but it was covered by a polo-necked sweater. That's why I didn't notice.'

'What's it matter?' Brownlow said. He was utterly dejected. The fact of the girl's death was tragic enough, but the un-accustomed feelings it had aroused in him disturbed him profoundly. I do not know my own self, he thought.

Isani was handing him the typewritten sheet. 'The mother will have to be told,' he said needlessly.

'I'll take care of everything,' he said. He walked to the door. Then turning, he said, almost angrily, 'And what are *you* taking care of?'

Isani was a simple man. He did not understand his friend's sudden hostility, but he liked him well enough to ascribe it to shock. 'I have her friend waiting in the next room. She's very upset. My wife is with her. I shall talk to her shortly.'

Brownlow came back to the desk and shook his hand. 'I'm sorry,' he said. Then, almost pleadingly, 'Keep me informed, won't you.'

He went to his office. He wondered how he could best break the terrible news to the girl's mother. A cable was out of the question. It was too sudden, piercing the blue dawn on the Surrey hills. A telephone call, presuming that near one of the rose bowls, or standing under a doll's crinoline in the hall, there was a phone. No, no, he thought, as he heard the terrible words crackling over the long watery line, muffled into inaudibility.

'Pardon?' in a silvery voice.

'Dead,' I said.

'You really must speak up. I can't hear you.'

He decided to telephone Belinda's brother. He lived in Surrey, not far from Virginia Water. He was a good and kind man, and he would go gently in among the roses and stab her with their thorns. Gently, gently, Brownlow insisted to himself, though in what voice or what language could 'dead' be a gentle word? In what whisper or song or civil sigh could murder be a soothing tale. Were there degrees of 'dead'? Only a little bit dead, Mrs Forrest. Not much murdered, dear lady. But withal you will have no more letters, withal you will have no grandchildren, withal Mrs Forrest, she must be buried.

Brownlow shuddered as he remembered the sexual detail. He would not mention it to Belinda's brother. He would try to keep it between himself and the inspector. And the doctor, of course. He prayed, but with little faith, that it was not relevant to the investigation, and that outside a few people, it would never be known. In Mrs Forrest's crumbling church, the daughter of the village would be mourned as a virgin. She would lie beside her father in the small churchyard, and Mrs Forrest, as she Sunday-knelt, would wonder on the ways of the Lord, and she would pray to him in hushed and aching curses. Brownlow wiped the sweat from his face and forehead. He dialled the international operator.

Chapter Three

In his office down the corridor, Hermann von Henkel turned off his air-conditioner. Though the temperature was 102 degrees, and the humidity almost as high, it could never be hot enough for von Henkel. Wiping his forehead, he returned to his desk, and wrote out in salivating detail, the menu for his evening meal. He was thus indulging in his two great passions, heat and food. Von Henkel was in his late fifties, and he was wearing well. He was a terrible but regular tennis player, he ran, he went to a gym, he would indulge in any activity through which he could sweat like a pig and thus confirm the heat that suffused his body. And after his exertions he would eat. And eat and eat, until he sweated again. From time to time, between mouthfuls of food or missed forehand drives, he had to remind himself that he was an FAO official concerned with the distribution of fertiliser in the Djogjakarta region. But that only reminded him of why he had taken the job in the first place. It had offered him his two primal passions, his favourite cuisine, and a constant heat. He never felt the need to apologise for this dual appetite, rather he would explain it with utmost logic. He was more than entitled to his passions. In the war, he had reached the rank of colonel, and towards the end he had been taken prisoner and sent to Siberia to a Russian labour camp. For five long years, he had starved and he had frozen. And every day of his imprisonment he had sworn to himself that if ever he should survive, he would make it up to his poor and suffering body. He would warm it and he would fill it, and he would warm and fill it fine. It was for his body he did it, he would explain, even to those who were not interested. He himself, in his mind—'in meiner Sinn'—he would dictate each syllable—he had no need for it. It was for his body that had so faithfully and so stubbornly endured. He had to look after it. It was his duty as a German officer.

He pondered over his first course. Shrimps, crab or carp? The dribble fell on the paper and smudged the carp on which he decided. He would ask his driver to go down to the river. They were always fishing there and the carp was muddy and to his liking. He would have it cold with mayonnaise. He made a note to ring Ingrid. She was a great hand at mayonnaise. In fact his daughter was a great hand at everything, and often when he thought of her, of her flaxen plaits humped over her bursting breasts, he cursed the blood that ran between them. She was a tantalising seventeen, and played hostess for him. He loved the way she admonished the servants in front of guests. He loved her sense of everyone's status. He loved the way she tasted her food. He knew no one else who could suck her lips and belch with such finesse. Not even her mother who was now cooling her sensible heels in Berlin on the pretext that she was trying to sell the family house. But the house had been sold over a year ago, and still Hildeborg dallied. It wasn't as if she had friends there. She lived entirely alone and probably spoke to no one. But von Henkel knew why she stayed there. He, like so many other UN officials, was a humidity widower. Hildeborg just couldn't stand the climate. But he didn't mind. He had his Ingrid, and what's more, he had her all to himself.

He thought about his main course and decided on a chicken sati. Some flaky and saffroned rice would go with it and would nicely absorb the succulent and nutty sauce. He would wash it all down with one of his dry hocks, aged in his hoarded cellar. He still had a piece of weeping Emmenthal that a friend had brought from Singapore, and with that, he would drink a half bottle of claret. The dessert always presented a problem. In a land of such exotic fruits there were so many goodies to choose from. At last he decided on mangoes, laced with creme chantilly. With that he would drink his last bottle of Trockenbeerenauslese. He was almost weeping as he wrote it aloud.

He cursed the phone as it rang beside him. It was Brownlow, that interfering upstart who had come out of the blue to mark their exercise books like some spinsterish school ma'am. 'Von Henkel here,' as if giving an order. 'Could it wait five minutes?' he said after a pause. 'I'm in the middle of an important paper.' He put the phone down, cursing the interruption. For to think about a meal, was to von Henkel as pleasing as consuming it.

Every day of his post-Siberian life, he was doing the one or the other so that anything not related to this pursuit was an offensive interruption. He put down his pen and read the menu over. He would go to Brownlow when he was good and ready. He read it over so often that he was sated with the carp hors d'oeuvre. In its place he opted for perhaps his greatest weakness. Crab. His driver could by-pass the river and go to the market instead. He put his pen in his pocket and strode towards the door. He would give Brownlow a few moments of his gastronomic and gluttonous time.

When he entered Brownlow's office, he was disconcerted to see Stern there. He knew that Stern hated him, and though they had to work closely together, since Stern was in charge of the World Food Programme in the area, they avoided each other as much as possible. This was mainly Stern's doing. For his part, von Henkel had no animosity towards Stern. Indeed he would have wished to be his friend. They had things in common. Stern too was a climate widower, though his wife, as a practising psychiatrist, had more reason than humidity to remain in England. But Stern would have none of von Henkel, and for six million reasons. Stern had been born in Germany and he was a Jew. As a child of twelve, from a cupboard where he was hiding, he saw his parents jackbooted through their front door. His uncle had fathered him for a while, putting him to work in his factory where he made all-lead pencils. This uncle too was eventually taken to the camps, but not before he had quietly made up a small pencil stock substituting tightly rolled mark notes for the lead. Encased in a narrow plastic sheath, and stamped 'The Writers' Everlasting Friend', they were placed on all parts of little Hans's person, and down the sides of his suit-cases. At great risk to himself, his uncle had taken him to the railway station, and armed with the address of a benefactor, and cases of everlasting friendship, little Hans travelled to London. Later on, after the war, he was told about Dachau, and in the dark, and alone, he wept for his parents. His pencils had paid for his education and a degree in law. He hated von Henkel with a devout and enduring passion. He hated him for all that he stood for, but he hated him more for his obsequiousness, for his apologies, for his constant wooing for friendship. He did not look up as von Henkel entered.

Brownlow motioned the German to sit down. His entrance had interrupted no conversation. Brownlow had obviously been waiting for his arrival before he announced the reason for bringing them together. 'A terrible thing has happened,' he said. He spoke to his desk, as if it were all not true, as if he were talking some madness out of himself. 'A girl has been murdered. She was a member of VSO. She worked with the Food Programme here in Djogja. Her name was Patricia Forrest.' Then he looked up.

Von Henkel's face registered a manufactured shock, though the corners of his mouth smiled a little as it came into his mind that the sweet succulence of carp was due to the fact that it was a scavenger. On Stern's face, however, the sweat was pouring, though the air-conditioner was at full blast. 'Oh my god,' he said. 'She was working on my project. How did it happen? Who did it?' He was half-standing at the desk. Brownlow thought he might have loved the girl. 'Did you know her well?' he said softly.

Stern sat down again. 'No,' he whispered. 'I just saw her from time to time. She was a good worker.'

'What will happen?' von Henkel said, delighted with the prospect of sensation and scandal.

'They're investigating, of course,' Brownlow said. 'They will be round asking questions. I thought you'd better hear it first from me. I want you to collaborate with them totally and give them as much of your time as they need. It's a terrible tragedy, but I want it cleared as soon as possible. It is in the interests of the whole organisation that the murderer be found, and quickly. I'm in contact with her mother,' he said after a pause. 'I think perhaps we should think of some form of memorial.' He looked at both men.

'Yes, of course,' von Henkel said happily. 'I'll ask my Ingrid. She's very good at that sort of thing.'

She's had a good dress rehearsal, Stern thought and he turned his chair slightly to the window. 'My god,' he whispered, 'it's all so unfair.'

Brownlow wanted to end the interview before Stern, as he suspected, might elucidate what in his mind would have been fairer, and that no doubt would have been the deserving corpses of von Henkel and all his jackbooted contemporaries. He stood

up. 'Please call on me if you need any guidance,' he said. He
hesitated. He wanted to tell them about the crashed Piper, if
only to unburden himself. But he decided that the connection
between the two events was only in his mind and that it would
be unrealistic to suggest it to them. He saw them to the door.
Then back at his desk he rang the Police Headquarters in
Djakarta. They would send their experts to examine the plane.

He was tired. It had been a long and painful day. He would
go home, he decided, and tell everything to Belinda. Everything,
that is, but for the strange worm that had stirred inside him as
he looked down on the market-girl.

He crossed over the Square of the Sultan's Palace. Burhan was
back at his post. He had a customer, and solemnly he was
shining his shoes. As Brownlow passed, he saw that it was Richard
Stern, Hans's son, and he acknowledged him. The boy sneered
back but Brownlow was not surprised. The boy was known to be
a moody drop-out, and a constant worry to his father.

'How's Emily?' Brownlow said as he passed, ruffling Burhan's
hair.

'Lady's beautiful,' he said.

Brownlow walked on, his heart lightened. As he came to the
main road, he looked back, and he wondered why Richard was
shaking Burhan by the shoulders.

Chapter Four

Von Henkel had gone straight back to his office. The Forrest murder did not in any way affect him. Any other father, perhaps, would have made a split-second identification with his own off-spring, but such thoughts were beyond von Henkel's imagination. 'It's too bad,' was all he permitted himself as he walked back down the corridor. But there were more important things. He had to re-read his menu. He sat at his desk, slipping his hand down between his pants and his wrinkled skin. Nothing serious, he said to himself. Just comfortable and reassuring to keep it there. No more than that, he kept telling himself as he rubbed his fingers along his groin. He was sweating profusely; he was drooling over his lovingly inscribed supper; he was in all ways a perfectly contented man. So it did not please him when his door burst open without warning, and there, almost filling its frame, and wedged by one small suitcase (*Gott sei dank*, he thought, she's not come to stay) stood his flushed and portly Hildeborg. Quickly he slipped his erring hand on to his desk, but she had caught the gesture and knew it well and she sniffed with disgust at his continued habit. He got up to greet her, and as he crossed over, he thought dismally how his crab would have to stretch to one more serving, and a large one at that, for Hildeborg's appetite was as gargantuan as his own. He wished she'd had the good taste to arrive after supper. 'Why didn't you cable me?' he said, as he took her hands.

'I came on the spur of the moment,' she said. She sat down opposite him. Though she had never been an outgoing person, and one with little warmth, he sensed an added coolness about her. He watched her closely as she opened a large hold-all and took out a bottle of schnapps. She had even brought two small glasses with her, along with a jar of paté de foie gras. A packet of crackers too. She was thorough, was Hildeborg. She was not a stormtrooper's daughter for nothing.

Von Henkel looked at the mouth-watering goodies, and for a moment he decided that he loved his wife. She poured out the schnapps.

'What shall we drink to?' he said, lifting his glass.

'Our divorce.'

He put down his glass and eyed the paté. First things first. Then grabbing a cracker, he smeared it thickly with the relish, and loaded it in one piece into his mouth. He swallowed. Normally the great Strassburg delicacy would fill him with benevolence, but this time he felt little goodwill. How fat she is, he thought, and ugly too, with her pudgy hands and garlic breath. Who on earth could begin to want her. He laughed. 'Who is it?' he said. 'The Duke of Edinburgh, or a sixteen-year-old whose mother paid you to break him in?'

'He's your age,' she said coldly, 'and he's a Russian officer.'

With his hand, he dug into the paté, taking it all, and licking it from his fat fingers, one by one. But even this choicest of food could not keep down his rising spleen, and he took the empty jar and threw it at her. She dodged and coolly picked it up from the floor.

'I didn't expect you to be delighted,' she said. 'I came because I thought it would be fairer. I could have written,' she added.

'D'you know how I spent five years of my life?' he spluttered.

Yes, she knew that, she said. She'd heard about it often enough. She'd been bored to death by it. But that was *his* life and *his* problem.

The thought crossed von Henkel's small mind that he must kill her. What did she know of suffering? What did she know of hunger, that fat pig opposite him licking her fingers of paté crumbs. How dare she negate even one moment of his life with her selfish and wanton pursuits. Yes, I will kill her, he thought, but I must do it with cunning.

'Who is he?' he shouted. 'How did you meet him?'

Calmly she told him. When her mother had died she had left a small bequest to her own surviving brother who lived on the other side of the wall. Hildeborg had obtained permission to visit him, and to transfer the legacy. At the East Berlin station, she had met a Russian officer, who had guided her through the numerous permit offices and helped her skirt the impeding bureaucracy of the city beyond the wall. They had become friendly. He had a high position, and was able to get her permits to come and go as she pleased. He had asked her to marry him and to live with him in the East. 'You know, Hermann,' she said simply, 'it's nice over there. Really nice. It's just like Germany used to be before the war. And d'you know,' she went on chattily, 'I went to Buchenwald, you know, that camp where they said lots of Jews died. Well it isn't true, Hermann,' she said. 'I saw it in black and white. There weren't any Jews there. There were only Germans who were against the government.' She took another gulp of schnapps.

Von Henkel thought of Stern, and he wondered whether there were ever any Jews in Dachau, or in any of the camps they had at their tongue-tips. The Jews made a mountain out of everything. His Hildeborg was right. My god, he thought, we have so much in common. 'Won't you think about it again?' he asked. 'If it's Java . . .'

'I'm sorry Hermann,' she said. 'But I'm in love with him.'

He had to keep his cool. He wondered why all his anger centred on Hildeborg, and whether, had the Russian swine been to hand, he would have killed him instead. But no. It was she whom he hated, it was she who had betrayed his sufferings, his agonies. She had scoffed at them, pulped them, and now thrown them in his face. She would not live long enough to be forgiven. 'What about Ingrid?' he said.

'I think she'd better stay with you. She's very fond of you, and perhaps she wouldn't like the East. It can be very cold there,' she added.

The sweat poured from him and he wondered why he shivered. As he looked at her the bile rose in him. He didn't want her himself, but he would be damned if anyone else would have her. And he would be double-damned if he gave her up to a Russian officer.

'He's my age, did you say?'

'A little older.'

Then he blew. 'D'you realise,' he screamed at her, 'that he could have been the very man who starved me almost to death, who stood me out naked in the snow, who tortured me to within an inch of my good German life? You rotten slut,' he roared at her. 'You fat ugly bitch. Have you no respect for the past of your daughter's father?'

Hildeborg was a simple woman and she took a little time to work that one out. When she'd managed it, she shrugged. She found it all very boring. 'How is Ingrid?' she said.

He knew he was talking to a wall. The idea that such a monstrous wedge of flesh could love and be loved, seemed to him an obscenity. He pictured her with her Russian stud, the twin grossness of them lying a-bed. It was a long long time since he had seen his wife's body, but he remembered it as pink, like a nursing sow. And picturing it, he let forth a stream of obscenities that seemed in small measure to release his hurt. Because he *was* hurt by it, though he couldn't sort out where it pricked him most. She stared at him, dumb-founded, thinking that he was a very rude man indeed. 'You're not a gentleman,' she said when he was finished.

He looked at her. She was, without doubt, a wall.

She got up and picked up her case. 'I'd like to see Ingrid,' she said. 'I can stay at a hotel if you like.'

No, she musn't stay at a hotel, he thought. There must be no cause for suspicion. No one must ever know the real reason for her coming. He would think of something that would validly bring her to Java for a few days. He must keep calm. He must show no outward disturbance. 'I'm sorry I shouted,' he said. 'Of course you must stay with us. We'll have dinner together. Then tomorrow we can talk it over.'

She was at the door. 'I've made up my mind, Hermann,' she said. 'I know,' he said. 'I shall accept it. But we must discuss the practicalities.'

She smiled at him showing the gold-capped tooth that he'd paid out good money for a few years ago. He wondered how much it would fetch now. 'Let me call the driver,' he said. 'In any case, I have a shopping-list for him.' He had by now lost all desire for his meticulously planned repast. The fact that he would have to share it with that bitch and her Ivan Ivanovitch thoughts, robbed him of all appetite. But he would give it a chance. Perhaps later he would feel better. Picking up his shopping-list, he called for his driver.

Chapter Five

'You go so fast,' Richard called out. 'Can't we slow down a bit?'

'We must reach the hills before it gets dark,' Burhan said. 'We should have left earlier.'

They were trudging uphill, along a dirt-track. Burhan was way ahead, and he stopped, looking back at Richard with loathing. He didn't know why Richard wanted to go into the mountains or why he had to go so quickly. It was late afternoon when he had come to his stand. He had simply demanded that Burhan be his guide, and that he should ask no questions. He was to tell nobody anything, or Richard, quite simply, would kill him. That he made quite clear. He had offered Burhan 500 rupiah. A fortune. But Burhan was doing it simply for his life and a future with Emily.

He would have to spend the night on the mountain, because it would be too dark to make the return safely. Emily would have forgotten him, and he threw a whispered curse to the struggling figure below. He was worried about his friends' hide-out. Nobody but himself and a contact in the village knew of their whereabouts. Often he went there with messages, but he didn't know why they were hiding. He thought it had something to do with the government and politics, but he didn't understand anything about that. But he knew they would give him little thanks for bringing a stranger into their midst. Richard, having heard of the mountain men, had insisted on their shelter and no other. He and they, he knew, were beyond the law, so they had no alternative but to trust each other. Burhan realised that it was out of the question to take him to them. He would climb on and on, and say he had lost his way, or that his friends must have moved. He dreaded what Richard would do to him.

'When do we come to the flatland?' Richard panted.

'About an hour.'

Richard went on cursing, while Burhan tried to think of Emily. How could he explain his absence to her? Hitherto he had been answerable to nobody. He had come and gone as he pleased. Amongst his friends it was expected that he should suddenly disappear and turn up as unexpectedly as he had gone. Now he had a root, a pull-back, someone who had a right to ask questions, someone who could so easily dissuade his wanderings. They trudged on.

'How old are you, Burhan?' Richard said. He was trying to be friendly, but for Burhan friendship was not part of the deal.

'I don't know,' he said.

'But you must have some idea.'

'Ten, I think,' Burhan grunted.

'Have you ever had a woman?' Richard asked.

Burhan hurried ahead.

'You know,' Richard shouted after him, 'gone to bed with a woman. Fucked her.'

All the while, Burhan had been thinking of Emily, and now these terrible words had intruded on her image. He could never think of her in those terms, and Richard's question had smudged his vision and, in a way, had sullied her. He didn't answer.

'Come on,' Richard persisted. 'You must have.'

'Yes I did,' Burhan shouted back. He had to distance the matter of their talk from his pure and loved Emily. 'I did,' he said again. 'She paid me. She was an old woman. I did it for the money.'

'Didn't you like it?' Richard persisted.

'It made me sick.'

Richard laughed. 'You'll get used to it. I've had sixty-six women,' he said.

Burhan ran further ahead. He hoped that the distance between them would prelude further conversation. But Richard was suddenly silent. He was too tired to shout. It seemed he'd been walking uphill for hours. After a while he stopped and gathered enough breath to call after his guide. 'I've got to rest,' he said.

'I can see the flat,' Burhan called down to him. 'We can rest up there.' Richard trudged on. He wondered whether he ought to insist on Burhan carrying his rucksack. But he knew that if Burhan refused, he had nothing to threaten him with. He needed him to guide him to the hide-out. He wondered whether Burhan was trustworthy, whether in an unguarded moment, he might tell where he had taken him. 'Hey,' he shouted after him. 'You know I can kill you, don't you, or get somebody else to do it, if you ever tell where you've taken me.'

'I'm taking you to my friends,' Burhan lied. 'It is *them* I shall not betray.'

They rested on the flat. It was getting dark. The silhouette of Mount Merapi was bright in the half light. Not too far below, they could see the village of Harbobingangun. There was a small square of light on the road. Peering down they could make out four hurricane lamps framing a tangled mass of what looked like metal that glinted in the setting sun.

'What's that?' Richard said.

'Looks like a smashed car.'

Richard fumbled in his rucksack. One of his few innocent pursuits was bird-watching, and he carried his binoculars everywhere. He hung the strap round his neck and focused. Burhan watched him as he twiddled the knob. Then he saw his mouth drop open and his hands were trembling. He put the binoculars down. 'It's a plane,' he said. 'Go down and see what's happened.'

'But we have to reach the mountain before dark,' Burhan said.

'Fuck the mountain,' Richard shouted. 'Go down and find out, or I'll kill you.'

Burhan was frightened, not by the threat, but by his companion's trembling. He seemed almost on the verge of a fit. Burhan scrambled down the side of the hill. Richard waited. He was tempted to look again, but he was afraid. He felt his eyes sting. 'It's nothing,' he said aloud. 'Just a plane. Plenty of planes round here.' Then he stood up and saw Burhan slithering down the slope. 'Find out the name of the pilot,' he shouted after him. Then he regretted it. He hoped that Burhan hadn't heard. He sat down again and lit a cigarette. It would pass the time, but he had smoked it to the tip and Burhan still had not returned. He peered over the hill. It was much darker now, and even if Burhan had been climbing, it would have been difficult to see him. He tried his binoculars again. Now all they reflected were the four beacons of light. He shivered. Never in his life had he known grief. He had been sorry when his mother had decided to remain in England. He missed her and that had been sad. But by some instinct he knew that it was nothing to the pain that might assault him soon, and from which, he knew with absolute certainty, he would never in his life recover. His eyes were stinging again. He tried to hold back the tears. There was still the slight possibility that they need not be shed. It could be any old plane, any old plane, he screamed to himself. He wiped his eyes with his sleeve, and when he looked up, Burhan was standing there.

'It was a crop-spraying plane,' he said. 'It crashed early this morning. The pilot was killed. His name was Klaus Schmidt.'

Burhan had never seen a grown man cry before, and bewildered he watched Richard, as he cried aloud, his choking sobs echoing over the hills. Sometimes he shouted, 'No, no,' then he would sob again in such loud and heart-rending pain, as if his sore sorrow had grazed his heart. Burhan shifted from one foot to the other. Despite the inconvenience that Richard had put him to, and the enforced separation from his love, he felt that somehow his companion's sobbing had something to do with love too, and he felt very sorry for him. He put his arm round Richard's shoulder and comforted him. Richard clasped his hand, and Burhan felt the hot tears on his fingers. 'Let's move,' he said softly. 'It's almost too dark.'

Richard loosened his hand, and looked up at him. In the half light, Burhan caught the agony on the man's face, that reeked with the sour odour of despair.

'Let's go back home,' Richard said.

Burhan lifted him to his feet, and took hold of the rucksack. Then putting his arm round Richard's waist, he guided him down the track.

Chapter Six

As he and Emily reached the square of the Sultan's palace,
Brownlow was relieved that Burhan was in his place. His
absence would not have surprised him. The last he'd seen of him
the previous afternoon, Richard had been shaking Burhan by
the shoulder, and the gesture had seemed less than playful. All
night he'd wondered about it, and regretted that he'd not turned
back to investigate. So he was relieved to see Burhan firm and
beaming at his stand, and he gladly loosened Emily's hand as
she ran towards him. When he reached the stand he waited and
listened to their chatter. It was a mixture of both languages,
though Indonesian seemed to rate a higher score, though
Brownlow was surprised by the numerous and innocent addi-
tions to Burhan's basic lexicon. He was chatting away while he
cleaned Brownlow's shoes, while Emily told him that he must
come every day to the hotel to visit them. She looked to her
father for approval. He nodded. In the present unreliability of
events, he found their togetherness reassuring. He knew he was
in for a rough ride. What he had to do today, and probably
over the next few weeks, had nothing to do with the purposes
of the Ponsonby Post. He was now called upon to play the
detective, a role for which he had no training and even less
aptitude. 'You come whenever you can,' he said to Burhan.

In his office, he waited for the investigators from Djakarta.
A cable lay unopened on his desk. He would not have been
surprised if it would have announced another murder or some
like catastrophe, so he was delighted to see that it came from
one of his closest friends, Stuart Featherstone, an old colleague
from the Arts Council. He was on his way back from Bali
having organised an exchange dance festival, and he was
stopping over a few days to see Brownlow. Brownlow was
pleased, though he wished he'd arrived at a more convenient

time. He wouldn't even be able to meet the train. He'd be up in the village with the investigators. He decided to send Belinda. They'd always been very fond of each other.

When the investigators arrived, they left straight for Harbobingangun. There were three of them, all Javanese, who had been trained in Holland. They were silent men, and the drive to the village was long and unrelieved. A crowd of villagers gathered as the car drew up, and one of the men quickly dismissed them with a gesture of silent and severe authority. They dispersed, hanging round the edges of the field, watching them as they picked their way amongst the wreckage. Brownlow decided to go and see Weiner, and he took the car to the airfield.

He whistled as he approached the hut. Weiner came out and stood by the door. He looked even worse than he had the previous day, though he'd obviously made an effort to pull himself together. He even managed a smile of greeting.

'Could we talk?' Brownlow said. 'The investigators are down at the plane. I thought I'd come up and see you.'

They sat down at the wooden table. 'D'you know a girl called Patricia Forrest?' Brownlow said. The connection between her demise and the plane crash existed only in his own mind, and it frightened him. He wanted Weiner to confirm its improbability.

The German shook his head. 'Who is she?' he said.

'She's an English girl. Works for VSO.'

Weiner shook his head with a genuine indifference. He wasn't even curious as to why Brownlow had asked.

'Did Klaus Schmidt know her?' Brownlow tried again.

'He never mentioned her to me. He might have, but—well, you know . . .'

Brownlow nodded. 'She was murdered last night,' he said. He watched closely for Weiner's reaction, but apart from a slight shrug of the shoulder, he seemed barely to have heard. His own personal unhappiness was too crowded to allow room for concern over another.

'Where?' he said, without interest.

'In Djogja.'

Weiner shrugged again. It obviously did not occur to him that there was any connection with the death of his friend. Brownlow felt easier. 'D'you ever come to Djogja?' he said.

'I used to. With Klaus.'

'Why don't you come down one weekend?' Brownlow said. 'We're at the Ambarrukmo. There's a pool. My wife would be happy to meet you.'

Weiner nodded, without looking up.

'Please come,' Brownlow said. 'It's not good to be alone all the time.'

On his way back to the village, Brownlow made a detour through the road that Weiner took daily to the airfield. In the paddies the women were planting, and for a while he watched them, admiring the skilful symmetry of their rows. Then, from the dry perimeter, he called out to them, and asked if they had been felling trees in the village. One of the women crossed the water towards him. No, there had been no felling, she said. They never felled in the rice-planting season. It would be an ill omen on the crop.

Brownlow thanked her. Yet he felt little gratitude for the information. He was uneasy with the realisation that Weiner had lied to him. If he were to investigate the reasons, he would become further and further involved. It had nothing to do with the Ponsonby Post, he kept telling himself, and he made his way back to the car.

When he got back to the village, the men were waiting for him. They sat in the *Lurah*'s house, drinking mint tea. A large canvas sack was on the floor beside them, and one of them held it close as he drank. When they saw Brownlow, they stood up. 'We're ready,' one of them said. The sack was heavy, and the three of them had to share the weight. They would not let Brownlow help, nor the driver, and they insisted that the sack went inside the car, along with them.

They said very little on the drive back to Djogja. One of them commented on the height of the tobacco in the passing fields, but that was all that Brownlow could make out. He wanted very much to know about their findings, but he didn't know whether he was entitled to ask. He touched the sack tentatively. 'Quite a heap of evidence,' he said. Then, as casually as he was able, 'Did you find anything?' he said. Then, just as casually, as if they had been waiting to tell him if only he had asked, they said, almost in unison, 'It was sabotage.'

Chapter Seven

Von Henkel picked away at his crab with little appetite. He stared at Hildeborg, and hawk-eyed, followed each mouthful of her purloined share. Ingrid sat between them. She had been told. Hildeborg had spilt it out even as she had come in through the door. Ingrid had shown no sign of surprise or even regret. It was not going to disturb the pattern of her own way of life, so her attitude was one of indifference. She had never been very close to her mother, and there was even a small area of relief that they would now be rid of her. She was not even curious enough to ask why they were divorcing, or who, if anybody, had replaced her father. Perhaps she did not entertain such a possibility. So the red rag of the Russian officer did not figure in the discussion, a fact that needled von Henkel. It would have given him an opportunity for yet another xenophobic outburst.

The meal was eaten in silence. Nasah, von Henkel's chef, had cooked the chicken superbly. Von Henkel looked at it. The brown sauce oozed from the chicken wing, and the white breast was mottled with its stain like a slice of lightly varnished wood. The aroma was irresistible. Yet von Henkel could not relish it. His appetite had evaporated completely. He thought of the prisoner-of-war camp. He shivered with the recollection of the snow, that vast off-white carpet edge to edge with the surrounding hills. He felt the frost gnaw at his feet, and shrivel his nose and finger-tips. He felt the hole of hunger in the pit of his stomach, and the desperate need to fill it, slowly, ever so gently, and with much tenderness, like sprinkling a dry and delicate plant. Yet even this recollection, the actual physical pain of hunger, gave him no stomach for food. His only appetite was for revenge. He wondered when he could do it. And where. And how. And what were the snags, and how he should safeguard himself. He nibbled quickly at his chicken as a cover for his murderous thoughts. And as the white meat melted in his throat, and the juices stroked his inner cheeks, his thoughts wandered. As he continued eating, he found it harder to trace a thread in his thinking, and after one gulp of Chablis, he wondered what matter had been so disturbing him.

'Prost,' Hildeborg said, as she lifted her glass to him, and at once he re-gathered his criminal thoughts.

Ingrid rang the small bell on the table. She was ready for seconds. Her mother looked at her smugly, and had her mouth not been full at the time, she might have remarked on how naturally a daughter of her blood had assumed the hausfrau role. Nasah appeared promptly, and Ingrid directed him to her father. As Nasah passed the sweet-smelling tureen to von Henkel's left side, his appetite returned, and though his plate was far from empty, he piled it full. He decided to return to the serious business of eating, and that he would have eyes and ears for nothing else. He did however notice that Hildeborg refused a second helping. He was gratified that there would be more for himself, but at the same time he was disturbed at her unaccustomed lack of appetite. Certainly she was not ill. Never had he seen her in such ripe bloom of health. She therefore must be in love, and once again, he thought of the means of her disposal. Quickly he took another mouthful of chicken, and as he chewed and savoured the juices, he hit upon a plan.

He excused himself from the table, leaving his knife and fork star-crossed. He needed a clean handkerchief, he said. He felt a cold coming on.

'I'll get it, Vati,' Ingrid said, though making no move to that purpose. But he was already at the door.

Once upstairs, he went straight to his bedroom, and leaving his door ajar, he noisily opened the chest of drawers. Then he tiptoed quickly to Hildeborg's room. Her handbag lay on the bed. He was tempted to read the letters inside, but there was no time. He could manoeuvre that later. At present he was concerned only with taking all her money, her traveller's cheques, her passport, and health certificates. Without all these she would be grounded. He would hold her prisoner. He giggled as he envisaged the exciting possibilities of such a situation. She had never understood how he had suffered after the war. Now he would give her a like imprisonment. His had been snowbound, in freezing horror; hers would be a hell of heat and humidity. He made a mental note to disconnect what was left of the air-conditioning system in the house. Let her cook in Java till her red passion was over. He stuffed her freedom tokens into his pocket and hurried back to the dining-room.

'Hurry up, Vati,' Ingrid said. 'I'm ravenous for the cheese.' There was an urgency in her voice that suggested she hadn't eaten for many days. Von Henkel seized his knife and fork, and wolfed down the food with renewed appetite.

Nasah hovered until his master had finished. Then he set down the cheese board. Von Henkel rested, sipping his wine. He looked across at his wife and smiled with benevolence. She, grateful for his understanding, flashed him her gold-capped tooth. Von Henkel could barely control his glee. The more he thought about it, the more mightily pleased he was with his plan. He passed her the cheese. She shook her head wordlessly. Then, as Ingrid forked her slice, Hildeborg said, 'I must lose some weight,' and she blushed a little.

Oh you'll lose some weight, von Henkel thought, with the eternal sauna he'd arranged for her. He helped himself to the Emmenthal, and spent that course, and the dessert, in dreaming up little refinements of torture he could put her to. He imagined that after a week or two, she would knuckle under, and comport herself as a good German wife to him. Not in all ways of course. He did not want her going overboard with her duties. But perhaps she could cook occasionally. He had moments of longing for Sauerbraten and Kartoffelklöse. No one could make that dish as superbly as Hildeborg. Yes, there were many bonuses in his plan. He was smiling at his wife so affably that Hildeborg shifted on her seat with embarrassment. She suspected her husband's sudden generosity of spirit, and she decided to get back to her Stanislav as soon as was practically possible.

After dinner, Ingrid left for the club. Most evenings she went there for a swim or a game of tennis, and her father usually accompanied her. But this evening he chose to stay at home. 'We have a number of things to talk about, your mother and I,' he told Ingrid. It struck her that in all the long years her parents had been together, they had found nothing at all to discuss. Now, their separation had at last given them a topic of conversation.

Hildeborg was anxious to go to her room. She did not want to be alone with Hermann. His cordiality unnerved her. In any case, there was nothing to be talked over. Her mind was made up. She was asking for no financial support, and the arrangements of their Berlin home and its effects could be settled by correspondence. Ingrid was old enough to come to terms with her stepfather, and she was at liberty to visit them or otherwise. This too could be satisfactorily dealt with by letter. She need not even unpack. She would cable Stanislav, and leave on the next available plane from Djakarta.

'I'm tired, Hermann,' she said. 'I've had a long journey. I think I'll go to bed.' She was rather surprised that he made no protest. He nodded, and wished her a good night's rest.

He sat alone on the settee smiling to himself, twiddling his thumbs, eavesdropping on her progress up the stairs and to her room, timing her movements, the unpacking of her night-things, perhaps searching in her handbag for the keys. Patiently he waited for the shit to hit the fan.

He did not have to wait long. His timing was almost to the second. A pure scream came first, then it was laced with a jumble of words. 'I've been robbed,' he managed to decipher. 'Everything gone. Thieves, thieves. Oh Hermann,' she pleaded.

He went to the foot of the stairs. She stood in the doorway of her room, her open handbag hanging at her wrist, her eyes wide with the horror of her sudden dependency. 'The servants,' she screamed at Hermann. 'Search them. Go to their rooms. They've taken everything.' She began to cry, with a piercing wail, but a wail so cacophanous, it could break no one's heart.

'Sh,' he hissed with authority. He took his time going up the stairs. She wailed continuously.

'Shut up,' he yelled at her when he reached the top. He pushed her backwards into the room, and she landed on the bed, cowering.

'Why has it got to be the servants?' he shouted.

Still she did not understand. 'Who else?' she whispered.

He noticed that she'd found time to put a framed photograph on the bedside table. He picked it up. 'To my Beloved', it read. 'From Stanislav'. He studied the features carefully. Allowing for the passing of the cold war years, it could have belonged to any one of the guards who had, day and night, and in the cold, belched into his starving face. As calmly as he could, he put the photograph down. 'In Siberia,' he said, 'they took our photographs away. I had one of you. D'you remember? It was in a frame a bit like this one. Now I remember that they were a pair. My Uncle Fritz gave them to us when we were married.' He turned to face her. 'Is this the other one?' he said.

'No.' She had the sense to deny it. 'I bought it especially.'

'Liar,' he screamed at her, and she didn't have the sense to deny it again.

'They took my photographs away,' he said, 'but I shall let you keep yours. It will be a comfort to you perhaps, because all you're ever going to see of that pig for the rest of your life, will be his stinking picture.'

She got up from the bed. For a moment she'd forgotten the robbery. 'I'm leaving tomorrow, Hermann,' she said. 'I told you I'd made up my mind. There is nothing at all to detain me.'

'And how will you go?' he smiled. 'With what passport? With what money? And how will you go to Djakarta to get a new passport without money to go to Djakarta? And how will you go anywhere in fact, when you will be locked in this house until you come to your senses. And perhaps not even then,' he added, taking her passport and money from his pocket, and waving them in front of her. She boggled at him. 'You have a lot of money, Hildeborg,' he said, flipping through the notes. 'I will need it to help pay for your keep.' He put the notes back into his pocket. 'But as for this,' he said, slipping through the passport, 'I have no use whatsoever.' And he tore it out, page by page, and ripped it to pieces.

Hildeborg watched him, paralysed in disbelief. 'Swine,' she spat at him from the back of her throat. 'It won't stop me loving him,' she said. 'Never. I shall tell on you,' she screamed in desperation.

He went to the door, smiling. 'Who will you tell?' he said softly. She had no idea of course, but one way or another, she had to threaten him.

'So who?' he repeated.

'The United Nations,' she screamed.

He laughed. 'That's a good joke, Hildeborg,' he said. Then

he remembered a small detail from his own incarceration. At night, when the guards locked him in his cell, they would take away his shoes. And in the mornings, he would be shod for work. This nightly deprivation had been for him the definitive symbol of captivity. For a child, a state of bare-footedness can spell freedom. For a grown man, it is the code of bondage.

Her case was open on the bed. He rummaged through. Two pairs of shoes. Low-heeled, sensible, with a bunion-socket to each. He tucked them under his arm. Then stooping down, as if to worship her, he removed the slippers from her feet. She was too astonished to make any protest.

'*Bon voyage*,' he said, and he went out of the room, locking the door behind him. He instructed Moh, his house-boy, to sleep outside her door, and to restrain her if she tried to get out. 'She's ill,' he explained, pointing meaningfully at his head. 'Mad. Amok,' he elucidated. The boy's eyes sparkled. In Java you knew about such things. Then von Henkel picked up his swimming things and called his driver to take him to the club.

The bar was buzzing with the Forrest murder. Each member was his own detective, with different speculations as to how and why it had happened. Most, however, agreed on one point. The murderer had to be a Javanese. When Henderson approached the bar, there was a gradual withdrawal from that conviction. Henderson, an Australian working on the food programme, had married out. His wife, Threes, had been born in Sumatra and had graduated as a teacher from the Gadga Mada University in Djogja. She was wise, beautiful and loving, and Henderson's colleagues regarded him with a mixture of envy and disgust. They had cast Threes in the role of the United Nations token native, and the couple were thus inundated with dinner and party invitations, so that at least one place-setting visibly confirmed the Bill of Rights, whatever that might be. Nevertheless, there was a feeling amongst his colleagues that Henderson, good man that he was, had rather let the side down with his personal and practical alliance with the Third World. His mating had per-forated the notion of separateness, of the 'them' and 'us'. With his marriage he had declared that such separateness was assail-able. And the fact that the marriage was a good one, and already of ten years' standing, unnerved them all.

'Perhaps the murderer could conceivably have been one of

your lot,' Henderson said. He looked round the bar with disdain. 'One of us, perhaps.' He gathered his drinks and took them over to his table.

'Strange fellow,' Mantoni, another food adviser said. 'Never know which side he's on. Our lot. Your lot. What does he mean?'

Von Henkel had reached the bar and felt obliged to offer his contribution. 'All we're sure of is that the poor victim is one of us. It's impossible, therefore, that one of us should kill her.' It was the kind of statement that in Europe would have been a *non sequitur*. But let it travel, especially in the direction of the Third World, and it assumes a cloak of logic.

The men at the bar seemed to settle for that, and groped round amongst themselves for more details of the killing. But the grapevine, though speedy, was sparse, and little more was known about Patricia Forrest than the fact that her body had been found in the thicket.

And then a sure source of further information came into the club. Brownlow. The men at the bar were delighted, and also surprised. Brownlow was a rare caller at the club. He had put that elitist life behind him when he'd left the Arts Council. Besides, in his mind, the Athenaeum off the Mall in London was a far more tenable proposition than this exclusive venue dumped in the middle of such palpable poverty. There was something about the Athenaeum that over the years had earned its right to be there. He knew that this establishment had probably been in existence as long. But somehow it had never acquired a *raison d'être*. Over the colonised years, its walls had echoed with drink orders in Japanese, German, Dutch and English tongues. Now they were all shouted in the same place, and the only permanent members of the cast were the servants. For Brownlow there was something parvenu about the membership, something upstart in its coterie, a clique of which he wanted no part. But it was a convenient place to bring guests. There was always a game of backgammon going, or a rubber of bridge, and Featherstone, Brownlow's friend, was an addict of both. Belinda was with them too, and there was much calling from the bar to buy them drinks and bid them welcome. Featherstone was introduced all round, and a decent interval was allowed to elapse, covered in small talk and news from the old country, before

Mantoni aimed the hovering question. 'What news of the murder, Brownlow?'

Brownlow was prepared. 'It's out of my hands,' he said. 'The Chief of Police is dealing with it.'

'How did she die?' another insisted.

'I know no more than you do,' Brownlow said. 'Did you know her?'

'I'd seen her about,' Mantoni said. 'Nice girl. Knew her friend better, though. Veronica. She plays the piano rather well. Accompanies my wife.'

Any mention of Mantoni's wife was a conversation stopper. Louisa Mantoni was an excruciating soprano, and could be relied upon, with little persuasion, to give a rendering of anything from Schubert to Sullivan in any group of two or more that constituted a gathering. The Mantonis gave soirées specifically for this purpose. They were always well attended, because in his attic, Mantoni had equipped a miniature and illegal casino. The centre-piece was a large roulette table, and Mantoni himself, who was a man of private means, acted as banker. But before you could earn these splendid heights, you had to sit through Louisa's off-key 'Heidenröslein' or a painful 'Liebeslied'. The recital was usually tailed off with an experiment in the upper register that occasionally sounded like 'One Fine Day'. But the only butterflies in evidence were those in your stomach, as it fluttered with the certain knowledge that she would miss the last high C. The closest she had ever got to it was an A sharp. But a miss is as good as a mile, and the audience generously camouflaged it with their applause, as they trickled off to the attic.

'They lived together,' Mantoni was saying. 'Shared a flat near the university.'

'Of course we knew her,' another member said, a *habitué* of the Mantoni soirée. 'Didn't know she was a friend of the poor Forrest girl.' Now suddenly everybody knew Veronica, and thus had rubbed shoulders with the dead.

'Terrible thing,' von Henkel said, who though feeling nothing, felt he had to contribute a semblance of emotion. 'D'you think it was rape or something?'

'I doubt it,' Brownlow said quickly. He wanted to scotch that kind of rumour. It bred, and in no time, every male native would be suspect.

'Did I see your good lady this morning?' Pijoux said to von Henkel. Gerard Pijoux was an easy-going Frenchman, who worked in an office adjoining von Henkel's. He had felt the need to change the course of the conversation. It was an innocent enough inquiry and he was surprised at von Henkel's hesitation. Frau von Henkel had either shown up at the office or she hadn't, and von Henkel's mouth was so firmly shut, it looked as if he was refusing to answer. He had been caught off-guard, and his clear hesitation had made of his wife's appearance or otherwise, an important issue, a production, and the others at the bar were panting for his explanation. Von Henkel sniffed a malicious curiosity. 'I'm sorry,' he said, explaining away his hesitation, 'my mind was with the poor girl. Yes, of course,' he added, 'she arrived this morning. Totally unexpected. But then, that's Hildeborg.' He laughed. 'She's not too well, in fact,' he added quickly, giving himself a few extra days for cover. 'Jet lag, I suppose, and an awful chill.' He ceased ornamenting for fear he would reach pneumonia.

'I'm sorry,' they all murmured, though none were sorry at all. Hildeborg, in her rare appearances, had never been taken to very kindly by their circle. Not unkindly either. She was just a solid unavoidable Teutonic block. Von Henkel gulped his drink. He'd hoped to keep Hildeborg's presence quiet. But now it was out. That was inevitable, he supposed. He would now have to take her out occasionally, be seen with her, entertain even. However, he would keep a strong hold on her shoes.

Brownlow had settled Featherstone into a bridge game. Belinda had found some of her friends from the batik class. Brownlow checked that both were happily settled, then he turned to the barman and ordered a round of drinks. The crashed Piper nagged at him. He wondered whether any of them could shed any light on it. 'I've had an awful day,' he said, by way of introduction. 'There was a crop-spraying plane crash this morning.' He was not going to mention sabotage. He only wanted to cast his rod, hoping if not for a catch, then a tickle, a nibble, any slender thread that would rule out a connection between the two young dead. The members buzzed for more information. When? Where? How? 'Who was the pilot?' one of them asked.

'Klaus Schmidt.' Brownlow eyed them quickly and separately.
'Klaus?' Pijoux said. 'The young German? Richard's friend.
You know,' he turned to the assembly. 'Stern's son. The difficult
one.'

Brownlow went cold. He knew his face had paled and he
lowered it at the bar. What Gerard had said did not signify a
direct connection between Klaus and Patricia, but, since the girl
had worked with Richard's father, their two separate deaths
made Richard something of a common denominator. Brownlow
had a quick photo-flash recall of Richard shaking Burhan by the
shoulder. Brownlow shivered. It was threadbare evidence, but
deep in his heart, he knew that both murders crouched on the
doorstep of the UN.

He looked round the room. Many of his colleagues were there,
and all suddenly looked accusable. Henderson, von Henkel,
Pijoux, Mantoni. He looked over to the billiard table, where
Stern was known to spend much of his free time. 'Where's . . .?'
He stopped himself. Suddenly Stern's absence took on a meaning
of positive non-attendance, and his empty and customary pitch
at the snooker table, became a wide and gaping hole of
accusation.

Chapter Eight

The reason Hans Stern was not at the club was very simple. He was sitting on a bench in the corridor of Police Headquarters. He had been waiting for hours. Isani had called him on the telephone. 'I'd come over to your place,' he had said, 'but as you can imagine, I've so many people to see. You'd do me a great favour...' All very polite. But as far as Stern could see, no one else was waiting and the place looked none too busy. He was nervous and he shuffled his feet on the tiled floor. Then a door opened at the far end of the corridor. Weiner came out, his head erect, his jowls pale and sunken, a picture of disciplined misery. He nodded at Stern as he passed. The two men knew each other slightly, and Stern was suddenly ashamed to have been caught in such a compromising location. 'Just popped in to see Isani,' he said, hoping to convey that the initiative was his own.

Weiner nodded again. He was indifferent to Stern's social habits. 'Isani told me about the crash,' Stern went on. 'Any more news?' He wanted to detain Weiner a little longer. Sitting alone in that long and empty corridor made him feel like an accused.

'No. Nothing,' Weiner said. 'It was sabotage you know.'

'So Isani told me,' Stern said. 'A terrible business. Political, d'you think?'

Weiner shrugged. He had no point in caring.

'They'll be caught,' Stern called out as Weiner moved down the corridor. 'Mark my words,' he pleaded, but Weiner was gone, and Stern shuffled his feet once more.

After a few minutes, he paced the corridor. There was no one about. Then, thinking he might have been forgotten, he stood still and shouted, 'Isani.'

The door at the end of the corridor opened. The Chief of Police stood in the doorway. 'I'm terribly sorry,' he said, over-polite once more. 'Herr Weiner was here. The Piper crash, you

know. Come in Mr Stern. I'll get you some coffee.' He returned
to his desk, and dialled an order. 'Come in,' he called to Stern.
He drew up a chair. 'Make yourself comfortable.' It was a phrase
Isani had picked up during his police training in Australia. He
used it constantly, unaware of the irony with which, in his profession, it was often loaded. 'Make yourself comfortable,' he
would say to any caller, accused or otherwise. He would have
said it in all innocence to a man who was settling in an electric
chair. Stern sat down.

'Shall we wait for coffee?' Isani said. He obviously wanted no
interruption once he'd started on the business of questioning.
Stern shuffled his feet on the wooden floor. Isani fiddled in a
file. Both men scratched in their minds for small talk. Weather
was out. It was predictable and unchangeable. Always hot.
Always humid. The rainy season was either coming or it had
passed. In Java, not even very small talk availed itself of such
a topic.

'Richard well?' Isani tried.

'Wonderful,' Stern said. 'Much better now. Pulled himself
together, I think. Went through a bad patch. Misses his mother,
you know.' He said it all in one breath, over-protesting.

Isani let it pass. 'Children,' he said, and that was all. Then,
after a few moments. 'Where's that coffee,' and he started to
dial again. Then the door opened and a young boy brought in
a tray. Isani passed Stern a cup and took his own. There was
now no reason to delay any longer. 'Mr Stern,' Isani began.
'This is rather a delicate matter. You knew Patricia Forrest, of
course.'

'Yes. She worked in my section.'

'Did you know her well?'

'Well enough, I suppose. I knew her as a colleague.'

Isani looked him squarely in the face. 'When did you last see
her?' he asked.

'A few days ago,' Stern said, without hesitation. 'She came to
my office. We were working on a report.'

Isani took a long and loud gulp at his coffee. 'Are you sure
of that?' he said, putting his cup down.

'Certainly.'

Isani got up. 'I am very puzzled,' he said. 'I have been talking
to Veronica. Veronica Tidmarsh. D'you know her?'

'Yes,' Stern said. 'They were close friends. Both from Surrey, I think. In England.'

'I've been talking to her,' Isani went on. 'She told me that on the evening of the murder, Patricia went out saying she was going to visit you.'

'She might have said that,' Stern said quickly, 'but it's a ridiculous idea. I don't think she even knew where I lived. In any case why should she want to visit me?'

'According to Veronica, she visited you rather often.'

'According to Veronica.' Stern tried to say it lightly. 'It was probably one of the girl's fantasies.'

Isani sat down again. 'You were in Geneva a few weeks ago,' he said. 'A conference for the food programme.'

'Yes. That's right,' Stern said.

'You wrote Patricia a number of letters. I have them here,' he said. Slowly he opened the desk drawer. There was no need to bring out the evidence. His point had been made. There was a silence. 'Think about it, Mr Stern,' he said softly. 'Make yourself comfortable.' He poured himself another cup of coffee. He did not offer one to Stern. 'I know it's a delicate matter,' he went on, 'but all this, I promise you, is confidential.'

'Yes,' Stern said straight away. 'We were friends. All right,' he almost shouted, 'we were close friends.'

'And she was with you the night she was murdered?'

'Yes.'

'Was Richard at home?' Isani asked.

'Why do you ask?'

'I know he goes away from time to time. You've told me yourself. That he's a bit of ... er ... drop-out, I think is the word'

'That's right,' Stern said. 'He'd been away. He was in Bali. But he was back.'

'When did he return?' Isani asked quickly. 'The night she was ...? After she'd left your house?'

Stern hesitated. 'Yes,' he said. 'I mean, no. Richard came back just as she was leaving. He was totally unexpected.'

Isani noted Stern's hesitation. He was not fully satisfied. He made a note to investigate Richard's whereabouts himself. 'Now,' he said, 'I want you to answer another question, and I remind you again that all this is confidential. Patricia had had sexual intercourse before she died. It would help greatly in our investigations if we could establish who . . .'

'Yes,' Stern interrupted. 'We . . . yes . . .'

Isani looked at Stern. He was old enough to be Patricia Forrest's father. He wondered whether it was just that that had attracted her. He thought of his own daughter. And he prayed that he would live long enough to see her married. 'Why didn't you see her home?' he asked.

'I wanted to,' Stern said. 'I usually did. But she wanted to go on her own. You see, I hadn't seen Richard for so long, and he'd just got back. She thought we might want to be together.'

'Did Richard know about it? About Patricia and you, I mean?'

'No,' Stern said. 'No. I saw her to the gate,' he added quickly. 'She lived only a few minutes' walk away.'

'And the Ambarrukmo Hotel is in quite the opposite direction,' Isani said, almost to himself.

'Yes,' Stern agreed. 'She must have met someone on the way.' He looked up. Could he go now please, he thought. What more was there to tell? He'd adulterated, and on his own door-step. He had been discourteous in letting her go home alone. He had a drop-out, no-good son. A wife who'd chosen to leave him. A job he wasn't very good at, a past that forever haunted him. Could he go now please?

'That's all Mr Stern. Thank you,' Isani said. 'I'll be in touch.'

'Why?' Stern asked, and knew immediately that it was a very guilty question. 'Of course,' he added, 'I understand. I'd like to know how the case goes.'

As he watched Stern shuffle off down the corridor, Isani had the feeling that though he had told him plenty, Stern had a lot more to tell.

Chapter Nine

A week later, Hildeborg made her first public appearance. Her imprisonment had been total. Her food was brought to her bedroom on a tray, and her visits to the bathroom were shadowed and timed by Moh, who first made sure of disconnecting the shower. As a warder he had untapped talents of which he had been hitherto unaware. He loved his job and hoped her sentence was for life. Yet in spite of the continuous privations, she remained obdurate. Von Henkel would visit her every day offering a chance to surrender. And every day she would repeat her love for Stanislav, and her determination that, one way or another, she would join him.

Then came the invitation from Mantoni. His wife was giving an afternoon tea to launch a memorial to Patricia Forrest. They had in mind a travel scholarship of sorts, open to students of the Third World. They would call it the Forrest Award to perpetuate her memory. Mr Mantoni felt that those who had known and worked with Patricia would feel privileged to associate themselves with the fund.

Von Henkel could have done without such a privilege. He could also have done without Louisa's lieder-launching. But it was an invitation difficult to refuse, lest it hint at meanness and lack of respect. Louisa herself had added a note to the invitation hoping that his wife would come as well, and that morning she had herself telephoned to ascertain that Hildeborg would be coming. It was so long since they had seen her. Ingrid too, she hoped. There'd be other children coming—natives, you know. The Forrest girl knew lots of children in the Djogja schools. 'It'll be a lovely party,' Louisa bubbled, for a moment forgetful of its purpose. 'I shall sing, of course. We should have a lot of fun.'

Von Henkel would have to take her. One or two people had already commented on her non-appearance, and he thought that people were whispering behind his back. He had to scotch any rumour that might be abroad regarding Hildeborg's present situation. But he would have to keep a firm watch on her the whole afternoon.

On the morning of the party he told her that he was taking her to the Mantonis for tea. He would allow her to take a shower. He noticed her excitement, her blissful anticipation of the cold jets on her sweating and itching skin, of a ride in a cool car, and tea in an air-conditioned room. It was all too tempting to refuse. He informed her of the purpose of the party, adding that if she made any attempt to escape, he would expose her in front of everybody. It did not occur to him that she might take the opportunity of a public appearance, to expose her arrogant spouse herself. It did not occur to Hildeborg either. Her husband was an influential man in the Organization. His colleagues and underlings would be obliged to take his side. So she had no thoughts of escape. She would be more than happy to settle for an afternoon of air-conditioning.

Ingrid refused to go with them. She preferred to spend the day at the club. Von Henkel tried to forbid her. He suspected that there was some male attraction at the swimming-pool. But he couldn't be warder to both his women, and Hildeborg, at present, was the more dangerous threat.

She devoted an hour to her toilette, most of which time was spent under the cold shower. Under the cooling jets, she itemised her valuables. A gold watch, a gold bracelet, her wedding ring, a diamond engagement ring, a ruby eternity ring. All portable. She would wear them innocently on her person—'I want to be a credit to you, Hermann'—and with them she might buy a loop-hole of escape. This afternoon might present an opportunity. She would go armed and fingered in currency.

Von Henkel gave her her shoes at the last moment, his hand already clamped on her arm. He guided her to the car. 'There is no reason at all why you shouldn't enjoy yourself,' he ordered her. 'They are all lovely people, of good standing. You should consider yourself lucky to have such friends, to live in a country of such beauty, to lead a life of luxury, servants and privilege. Your trouble is that you have been spoiled. You have never been deprived.'

As he droned on, Hildeborg wondered what term he had in

mind for her week's deprivation, and she clutched at her currency in fear that he might devise even more sophisticated methods of detaining her. She thought of Stanislav, and the smile of such thoughts she gave to Hermann, who took it as a sign that perhaps his stubborn mule of a wife was beginning to toe the line.

There was quite a crowd in the drawing-room when they arrived. Most of the UN personnel were there with a scattering of children. Some pupils from the local school were seated in a group around their teacher. Brownlow and Belinda were taking tea with the Mantonis. Emily and Burhan were handing out trays of cakes to the guests. Von Henkel pushed Hildeborg forward with a determined shove. 'Look, here she is,' he said to no one in particular, but as a proof that he was not trying to hide her.

'Hildeborg,' Louisa said, coming forward to greet her. 'He's been keeping you all to himself.' She smiled at Hermann.

'That's the truth,' Hildeborg said, in an attempt to put out a timid distress signal.

Hermann steered her away, and sat her down on one of the chairs arranged in rows for the recital. He took up his own position behind her, declaring their status as non-circulatory. Hildeborg fingered her currency. She looked around at the company and found nothing attractive in any of them. In her spasmodic sojourns in Java, she had never been able to make friends. For a small moment she considered the possibility of trying, of making a life for herself there. Then she shuddered at her own treachery.

Burhan came towards her with a tray of cakes. His was a friendly face, beaming with surprise and recognition, a face which said he hadn't seen her for ages and that it was nice to see her again.

In a rare moment of warmth, Hildeborg ruffled his hair. In Germany, whenever she'd given a thought to Djogja, it always included the ubiquitous Burhan. In the open market place, on the Sultan's square, shuffling on the Ambarrukmo driveway, hanging about the railway station. The railway station. My god, she thought, and slowly, ham-fistedly, with decisions and reversals, she formulated the skeleton of a plan.

The guests were taking their seats. Louisa went to the piano and checked on the scores. The pile was mercilessly thick, and the audience sighed in anticipation of a prolonged torture. Hildeborg turned to Hermann.

'I want to go to the lavatory,' she hissed. He glinted his eye.

'Honestly,' she said.

'You'll have to wait,' he ordered. He had not reckoned on such an eventuality. Surely she must have comforted herself before she left the house. He refused to believe her.

'I can't wait,' she whispered.

'You'll have to.'

'I shall disgrace you, Hermann,' a little louder this time. She was already on her feet. She had seen Burhan make his way to the back of the room, and she was timing her exit. Hermann couldn't stop her.

'I give you five minutes,' he said.

She moved to the back as quietly and as inconspicuously as her girth would allow. Then, seeing that all attention was on the hostess, she reached the back of the room, grabbed Burhan, who was standing by the door and yanked him behind her up the stairs. He was too astonished to cry out and he followed her with a curiosity that overrode his need to protest. She tested a few doors and finally found the bathroom. She dragged him in after her and locked the door. Burhan gaped at her as she sat on the lavatory seat and opened her handbag. The full nature of the expedition finally hit him. He backed to the door.

'Me no fuck lady,' he pleaded. 'Burhan no want fuck.'

She smiled at him, shaking her head. Neither did she, she managed to convey. She took a pencil from her bag and tore off a few sheets of lavatory paper. Then slipping off her shoe, she placed a stockinged foot on the tissue and drew its outline. This she handed to Burhan. Then she took off her rings and her watch, wrapped them in paper, and stuffed the packet into Burhan's shirt-pocket. He began to understand.

'Money?' he said.

She nodded. 'Me want shoes,' she said. Then tapping his pocket, 'Money for shoes.'

He shook his head. 'Too many money,' he said.

'Shoes and ticket,' she said. She imitated a train. 'Djogjakarta, Djakarta. Tonight. Three o'clock.'

He understood at once. He tapped his pocket. 'Shoes,' he said, pointing to the outline on the paper. 'Ticket. Train. Djakarta.' He cottoned on quickly, but the hardest was to come.

'Me,' Hildeborg thumped her chest, 'me, prisoner.'

He quizzed her. No connection had been made.

She tried again. She rattled the locked bathroom door. 'Mr von Henkel,' she said. 'Me,' she pointed, then she rattled the door again.

The rupiah dropped. Burhan giggled his understanding, and to make it known to her he clutched desperately at the bath rail, trying to get it off.

She smiled. She was pleased with him. 'You,' she said, pointing at him, 'to me. Tonight. Two o'clock. My house. 4 Maleboro. Ladder.' She affected a mime of climbing, and he nodded. '*Betchak*,' she went on, 'You, me, station. Train Djakarta. You bring shoes. Ticket. Change.'

'Change' was beyond him. So she took the currency from his pocket and indicated piece by piece that the watch was for the shoes and the ticket, and the rings were for change. 'Money,' she said, 'For me, for Burhan.'

He made flying movements with his hands. 'You, money Germany?' he said.

She nodded. He had understood perfectly. Once again she went over the procedure and then he repeated it to her.

'Me,' he said, 'sell silver. Then shoes,' he pointed to the drawing, 'and ticket. Djakarta. Money, flying. Two o'clock. Me, ladder, *betchak*, station.'

She threw her arms around him and kissed him. Then, putting her finger to her lips, she motioned him to say nothing to anybody.

Of course, he signalled. Silence was always part of a Burhan deal.

She went back to the drawing-room and waited at the back of the room until Madame Butterfly had, A-sharp-wise, declared her faith in her lover's return, and during the applause, she made her way back to her seat. And suddenly she badly wanted to relieve herself. But there was no second escape. She would have to sit it out till the recital's end.

Von Henkel breathed a sigh of relief as she took the chair in front of him, and he did not notice her ringless hands.

The recital was over and the business of fund-raising began. Burhan explained to Emily that he had a job to do, but that he would be at the hotel later to have supper with her. Lately, he had taken his evening meal with Emily, and they did a jigsaw together before Emily went to bed. He took her hand and kissed it. He didn't care that it was public, there was nothing in his love for Emily that called for concealment.

He scurried over to the market place. His favourite dealer had a covered stall in the batik section. Occasionally he would sell a roll of material, but by upping his prices, he discouraged batik sales. His business was chiefly as a fence for dope and stolen goods. The bolts of batik were his cover.

Burhan squatted beside him, and under cover of a piece of cloth, he displayed his loot. Their bargaining was solemn, slow, and much pause-punctuated. At one point, Burhan stuffed the jewellery back into his pocket, shrugged, and made to move away. It was a manoeuvre he'd learned with profit from the tourists. The dealer caught his ankle. Burhan sat down, and the bargaining continued. At last, money and goods were exchanged, and Burhan beetled down the aisles between the stalls, and made for the railway station.

Burhan on principle would never pay the asking price for anything. That was too legitimate. It was normal to beat the price down on everything, including a railway ticket. He leaned over the grille, and the bargaining began. He knew that whatever he paid for the ticket would represent a hundred per cent profit for the ticket-collector, since he would never dream of putting it through the books. Burhan put in his first bid. The ticket-officer upped it. Pause. Burhan offered a little more. The officer would not budge. Another pause. Burhan repeated his last offer with a tone of finality. The ticket-officer shook his head. Deadlock. Over to Burhan. The tourist-moving gambit. When he reached the barrier, the officer called him back. In a whisper, he lowered his previous price. His tone was final too. Burhan passed the money over. He'd negotiated a first-class sleeper for the price of a piece of freight in the goods van. It was a fair deal.

His pockets were bulging with money. 'Change,' he said to himself, practising his new word. 'Change. For Mrs von Henkel and me.'

It did not occur to him to *buy* shoes. You bought nothing if you could steal it. And shoes were easy pickings. He made his way to the Ambarrukmo.

Von Henkel took his wife home, requisitioned her shoes, and re-locked her in the bedroom. He was not surprised at her submissiveness. From his own experience as a prisoner the initial period of stubbornness and resistance was always followed by one of passive acceptance. This stage would be of short duration. Then would come a period of desperate defiance, a last and usually violent bid for freedom. And it was usually a prelude to complete surrender. It was all going according to plan. Another week, he thought, and she would be on her knees begging forgiveness. He stationed Moh outside her door and went to the club.

In her bedroom, Hildeborg closed up her cases. She was ready to leave. Though she had no watch, she knew that there were some hours to go before two o'clock in the morning. As long as it was light, she could still see the clock on the market tower. It was a full moon, and she was able to check on the time by its luminous dial. She lay on her bed and waited.

Burhan waited too, crouching in the corridor on the fifth floor of the Ambarrukmo Hotel. He had been there since leaving Emily, waiting for the hotel guests to retire and put out their shoes. There were a couple of early-to-bedders, but from where he crouched, Burhan could judge that the lady's pair was smaller and narrower than the outline on the paper. He waited. He had time. All he had to do was to pick up a *betchak* and steal a ladder. The latter was as easy as the former. Almost every house in the von Henkel quarter boasted a ladder that hadn't been put away. He hoped she'd have the sense to leave a light on, so that he could find the right window.

A couple came out of the lift. The woman had Hildeborg's build, though she was younger. Burhan eyed her extremities with optimism. They went into their room and shut the door. He waited. Within moments their footwear appeared, neatly placed, side by side, not in pairs, but one of each, snuggled to the other. The design was a declaration of their togetherness, and Burhan was wary of dissolving such a partnership. But he could not wait indefinitely. He crept along to the door and measured the shoe on his piece of paper. It fitted. The heel was extraordinarily high, but it was supposed to be fashionable. Mrs von Henkel

should be very pleased. He pushed the shoes under his jacket
and sadly placed the man's pair side by side. If he'd had time
and equipment, he would have polished them with extra-loving
care. He darted down the stairs at the back of the lifts and found
himself at the side-entrance of the hotel. No one saw him as he
ran off down the driveway.

He knew most of the *betchak* drivers in Djogja, and he waited
around until he saw someone familiar. Kayam was waiting on the
corner. He knew it was Kayam by his *betchak*. All *betchaks* in
Djogja were painted with colourful designs, but Kayam's taxi
was outstanding. Unlike the others, it was a geometrical pattern
in browns and yellows. It had a kinetic quality, almost three-
dimensional, and as you looked at it, and walked around it, it
assumed new perspectives. People in Djogja would wait until
Kayam appeared, though he was rarely without a passenger,
and they would drive with him anywhere, just for the pleasure
of being stared at by passers-by.

It was late and there were few people around, so Kayam was
empty. Burhan went over to him. He told him as much of the
story as Kayam needed to know. He was to drive to von Henkel's
address and wait on the corner of the block out of sight of the
house. Burhan did not want him to see the ladder, or the sight
of Mrs von Henkel being sprung. He was then to drive them to
the station, and forever to hold his mouth firmly shut regarding
his traveller. Burhan indicated that there would be more in it
for him than the normal *betchak* fare. He reckoned that what he
had saved on the shoes, he would give to Kayam.

They set off in the direction of Maleboro, the exclusive European reserve. It was one-thirty in the morning. They were in
good time. Kayam stopped at the end of the street, and Burhan
walked to number four. The house was in darkness, but for a
single light in a window on the first floor. Along the side wall,
roped between its rungs, as some half-hearted security measure,
stretched a ladder. Burhan was not surprised but he was relieved
that it was so close to hand. Quickly and deftly he untied the
ropes and leaned the ladder against the wall. It was just high
enough, touching the sill of the lighted window. He climbed to
the top and knocked lightly on the pane. She came at once,
blushing like an eloper. Quietly she opened it, and he passed the
shoes through, together with the ticket and the money. 'Change,'

he whispered, beaming, conscious that he was a good pupil. She kissed him in gratitude. But for her shoelessness, she was absolutely ready to go. She handed him her cases, then returned to the bed to put on the shoes. She noticed that they were second-hand, but now was no time to question. They fitted her in every particular and would have been perfect had she been able to walk in them. But the heels were too high. She could only totter. Still, ownership of shoes spelt the difference between solvency and destitution. Until she reached Djakarta, she would have to spend most of her time sitting.

She turned off the bedroom light, and smiled as she heard Moh snoring outside her door. Hermann would give him short shrift for his negligence. Gingerly she stepped down the ladder. Burhan watched her as she tottered towards the *betchak*, and he wondered whether the shoes could hang on to her till Djakarta. He pointed to his own bare feet, then to her stilettoes, shrugging his shoulders and beaming. And what he meant by it all, and with which Hildeborg painfully agreed, was that half a loaf was better than you know what.

They clambered into the *betchak*. Kayam took to the back streets where no one was about. As they reached the vicinity of the station, it was more difficult to avoid the occasional passer-by, and Hildeborg crouched down on the seat, hidden by Burhan's jacket. They waited in the station driveway until they heard the train draw in from Surabaya. Then Burhan ran to the platform with her luggage. Hildeborg tottered behind him. He helped her into the first-class sleeper. And immediately she took off the shoes. Then reaching in her bag, she gave him a handful of notes. Her gold and portable currency had bought her her freedom and a ticket back to Stanislav, and enough grease for travelling papers. Burhan crumpled the notes in his hand. He knew by the thickness of them that he was a very rich man indeed, and he regretted that he hadn't gone into a proper shop and bargained for a proper pair of shoes. He flung his arms round her ample waist which was parallel to his eye-line, and he disentangled himself just as the train was pulling out of the station. He waved to her as he fingered his new-found wealth. As the train wound itself out of the platform, he wondered what present he could buy for Emily.

* * *

Von Henkel and Ingrid did not get back till four in the morning. There had been an impromptu party at the club. One of the field-workers, John Marsh from England, had come to the end of his five-year contract, and he was leaving Java for good. He was upset, for he had come to love the country, and the farmers and their families with whom he lived. And in order to offset his melancholy, he had decided to spend his last evening in the company of those people he disliked, whose social round he had, for five years, strenuously avoided. Returning to England, he would be deprived of that too, but that was the only advantage he could reap from leaving the country. Everybody had got very drunk and sworn eternal love for each other. Even Stern had managed a smile to von Henkel. Ingrid had danced with John Marsh for the first and last time, and regretted that she had not cultivated him earlier. He, for his part, clasped her with feigned passion, bolstered by the knowledge that he would never have to see her again.

They entered the house noisily. 'Sh,' von Henkel said, 'you'll wake your mother.' Normally, before he went to bed he would go to her room and offer her her nightly chance of surrender. A signed oath of fidelity would have been enough to throw the air-conditioning switch. Now, he reckoned, she would be fast asleep, so he would lay into her firmly and doubly in the morning. He tip-toed past Moh on the landing, snoring on his rush-matting outside Hildeborg's door. Von Henkel was tired and content. Tomorrow he would send his driver to the river for carp.

After a drunk-sodden and restless night, von Henkel overslept. As he went to the bathroom, he was surprised to find Moh still standing outside Hildeborg's door. The boy looked bewildered. 'It's ten o'clock, Master,' he said. 'The lady has not yet called for the bathroom.'

'Then open the door,' von Henkel said. 'Wake her up. It's late.' He himself went to the bathroom and hurried over his ablutions. When he came out, Moh was trembling at the door. 'Madame not there,' he said. 'Madame gone.'

Von Henkel brushed past him and dashed into her bedroom. All trace of her had disappeared. The bed was made and the counterpane smooth. A slight film of face powder coated the dressing-table glass, her only spoor. He turned on Moh. 'Where is she?' he screamed. Then he saw the ladder, left nuzzling the sill outside. She must have had an accomplice. Did she flee bare-footed? And what was she using for money? He decided that she couldn't have gone very far. Most likely she would return during the day, her tail between her shoe-less legs, begging for shelter. Though it comforted him to think in these terms, he had little confidence in her return. Hildeborg was thorough. She took no half-measures. He regretted that he hadn't killed her in the first place. He didn't know what move to make, or whether he should make a move at all. If he investigated her disappearance through official channels, he would have to offer all the information. The breakdown of his marriage, and its rotten red cause would be known all over the town, bruited about the drawing-rooms, and drooled over with glee by his enemies. Alternatively he could say nothing and if, after a few days, she did not return, he could explain that she had left for home on finding once again that the humidity was too much for her constitution. An eminently buyable story since Hildeborg had quit once or twice before. It niggled him though, that he'd been worsted, that somehow or other, against all the odds, she had got the better of him. And he was curious as to how she'd pulled it off. Knowing his thorough wife, she was probably by now negotiating a passport in Djakarta. She would be on the next plane to Berlin. He could of course ring the airlines and check the passenger-lists, but somehow he couldn't be bothered. Suddenly he didn't care where she was, or with whom. The only thing that mattered was that in the public eye, no one had taken him for a ride.

At breakfast, he told Ingrid that her mother had gone. And though she appeared as indifferent to Hildeborg's flight as she had been to her sudden appearance a week before, von Henkel felt the need to tell her the whole story. He spoke with his mouth full of egg and toast, and he never stopped chewing during the recital. On the name of Stanislav, he practically choked, and Ingrid stretched across the table to thump him on the back. 'You're well rid of her,' she said.

Through his coughing, he smiled at her.

'We two don't need her,' Ingrid said.

And all his pain and humiliation evaporated.

Chapter Ten

It had taken a long time to complete the formalities concerning the death of Patricia Forrest, and it was almost three weeks later that clearance was given to transport her body back to England. A small delegation of UN personnel followed the funeral car to the airfield. Isani and Brownlow were in the first car, sitting in the front, staring fixedly at the brass trimmings on the long box ahead. Behind sat Veronica Tidmarsh, weeping, and bodily wedged, but with no logical connection, between Stern and von Henkel. Occasionally von Henkel would mutter, 'Terrible, terrible', and he might well have been referring to the condition of the road, which became progressively more and more bumpy as they approached the field. A few villagers on the roadside put down their bundles and stopped and stared, not necessarily out of respect but out of curiosity as to the manner of the ceremony. When someone in the village died, his corpse was bound in a sheet and carried on a stretcher through the streets. The mourners would follow on foot, and there might be a small gamelan band bringing up the rear. Death was open and familiar, unhidden in boxes and black cars, and they wondered why the white man was so afraid.

When the cars reached the airfield gate, Brownlow caught sight of Weiner, standing to attention by the hut. Though he wore khaki shorts and an open-necked shirt, his stance was one of a man in full-dress uniform. Brownlow suddenly recalled the story of the felled trees. He hadn't mentioned it to Isani, because he was loath to involve himself in the investigations. Besides, he liked Weiner, and despite the inconsistencies in his story, he could not believe that Weiner was a dishonest man. His lover had been killed. He could hardly have had a hand in his disposal. Nevertheless, he thought he might have a quiet word with

Weiner on the side, and at the same time repeat his invitation to the Ambarrukmo.

The official mourners stepped out of the cars and lined themselves alongside the small aircraft. The hearse-driver and his assistant carried the coffin between them, not shoulder-high, for they were ignorant of the pall-bearing role, but like a chest, each one gripping a brass handle, so that the coffin rocked like a cradle between them. The aeroplane crew gave them a hand as they lifted the box into the open side door. Someone inside the plane pulled it through and it disappeared from sight as if into the fire. It was handled with no more respect than an ordinary piece of freight, and Brownlow was saddened by its pedestrian dispatch.

They turned away from the plane and walked back towards the cars. Weiner was talking to the pilot and when he saw Brownlow move off, he walked quickly towards him. Brownlow was glad that the approach had come from Weiner. It would make less of an issue of what he had to say to him.

Weiner touched his arm. 'Has there been any news?' he said, 'about the sabotage?'

'It's in Isani's hands,' Brownlow said. 'As far as I know, there's nothing. I think the Germans are sending over one of their top men.' He thought he saw Weiner tremble, and he tried hard to attribute it to the recall of his lost love. 'How are you?' Brownlow said quickly.

'I work,' Weiner said, 'and while I work, I forget.'

'Don't forget my invitation,' Brownlow said.

Weiner clicked his heels. 'Thank you,' he said, and he made to walk back to the plane, leaving Brownlow standing, his fears unspoken. He hesitated, then called after him. 'Those trees,' he said, 'the farmers say they haven't felled in the village for three months.' If he said no more than that, it would simply convey to Weiner his uneasy suspicion. But he had to add a rider that would offset such an interpretation. 'Maybe they were lying,' he said. 'They're not supposed to fell without giving notice to the Forestry Commission.' From where Brownlow stood, and it was a distance of some ten yards from Weiner, he noticed how the man faltered in his stance. 'Don't forget to come and see us,' he shouted, as if apologising for any disturbance he had caused, but as he walked towards the car, he began to regret he'd men-

tioned the incident at all. From the inside of the car, he kept his
eye on Weiner. He stood where he had left him, as if rooted.
He was staring in the direction of the car, but it was clear from
his vacant and panicked expression, that he was seeing nothing.

Occasionally on the journey back to Djogja, Brownlow opened
his mouth to pass the tree information to Isani, but each time
he thought better of it. What did it matter, he thought, who had
killed Patricia Forrest, or who had sabotaged Klaus's plane.
Knowing the murderers could not bring either of them back.
Besides, it was none of his business. It was Isani's province, and
Isani might resent his interference. He was happy thus to ration-
alise his silence. In any case, he had a great deal of work to do
on his own account. In a week's time, one of the FAO executive
was coming to Djogja in the course of a Third World tour.
There were certain projects in which the visitor, an economist
by training, had a special interest, and there was much still to be
prepared for his visit. As he thought of it, he experienced once
again what was now occurring with regular monotony, that sudden intake of fear that could find no cause. He felt that something quite dreadful was going to happen, and that it might
almost be a relief when it did. He wished the car would go faster.
He would drop off at the hotel to see Belinda before going on to
the office.

'It's terrible, terrible,' von Henkel still muttered from behind,
and the car was filled with a sudden need to talk. All started at
once, and they laughed to break their embarrassment. Brownlow
wanted to avoid any discussion of the purpose of their present
journey and any speculation as to the meaning of the twin deaths.
He turned to von Henkel and Stern. 'I've scheduled Boxham's
visit to the school feeding programme for the Wednesday afternoon. Will that be all right?'

'It's already arranged,' Stern said. 'Not specifically for the
Wednesday but they'll be ready to receive us any day.'

'Don't lay on anything special,' Brownlow said. 'I want him to
see it as it is.' He turned to Isani. 'You got my invitation to the
reception?' he said. 'You'll be coming I hope, with your wife.'

'Friday, isn't it?' Isani said. 'I hope so. Usual security
measures?'

'Who would want to harm old Boxham?' von Henkel said.

Brownlow would have been happy to ignore von Henkel's

naïveté, but Isani was intent on clarifying the nature and the extent of possible hostility to any official UN visit. 'In the first place,' he said, 'there's the PKI. They're always a threat, whatever the occasion, and they don't need any excuses.'

'Who are they?' Veronica said, anxious to be included in the post-funeral relief.

'They're the Communists,' Isani explained. 'You'd think after the 300,000 we killed in '65 there'd be none left, but they're in the hills. Mostly these parts, and the east of the island. Plenty of them.' Isani's voice had risen, and Brownlow noted how his friend suddenly sweated, as if he had a personal vendetta against the whole PKI movement. It was known that his youngest and favourite son, Oyung, had disappeared some months ago and it was rumoured that he had joined a PKI cell. And if such a rumour were ever to find justification in fact, Isani's job would be severely in jeopardy. So he was far more vociferously anti-communist than he might have been had his job been a non-official one. Privately he was following every known thread to discover where Oyung was hiding, so at least, in his official capacity, he could call off any investigation of that district. He hoped that the boy had stayed within his own area of control and not gone off east to Surabaya, where his opposite number was ruthlessly corrupt and right-wing and would take inordinate pleasure in landing a police chief's son amongst his regular and ruthless catch. Isani paled as he thought of the lawful punishment. Questioning under torture until just enough life was left in the prisoner for the firing squad to consume. Isani himself had sometimes had to carry out such orders, and he tried not to see Oyung in each young and bullet-riddled body. Isani wiped the sweat from his forehead.

'But how could they disrupt the visit?' von Henkel insisted.

'They could arrange strikes on the farms, fell trees on the village roads'—Brownlow caught his breath—'all kinds of obstruction. And they're armed too.'

'But they've been pretty quiet for the last few months,' Stern said.

'The lull before the storm,' von Henkel offered, looking round for acknowledgement of his English proverbial flair.

'How are the investigations?' Stern asked, moving from one precarious subject to another.

'Everything is under control,' Isani said. In other words, he had nothing to report. No leads, no clues. Somewhere on the island, or maybe by now well off it, were two people with sabotage and murder on their hands, and Isani was no nearer to their capture now than he had been almost a month ago.

They were reaching the outskirts of Djogja. 'Drop me off at the Ambarrukmo,' Brownlow said to the driver, and to those at the back, 'I'll be with you later.'

Brownlow hurried through the foyer and took the lift to his suite. During the drive from the airfield, he'd had thoughts of resigning from the Ponsonby Post. The manifold duties of liaison officer had been side-tracked ever since his arrival. The rigidity of UN bureaucracy did not allow for such a flexible pursuit, and every effort he made was met with a sulking and grudging co-operation. And on top of everything, the Forrest murder and the crashed Piper.

Belinda was sitting on the balcony. 'Did it go off all right?' she asked.

He took a deckchair next to her. 'Belinda,' he said. 'D'you want to stay here? In Java, I mean.'

She looked at him, astonished. 'I could stay here for ever,' she said. 'What's wrong?'

'Nothing,' he said. 'Not as long as you want it.'

'You're upset about Patricia,' she said, 'but it's not going to be like that all the time. After Boxham's visit, perhaps you can take a few days off, and the three of us can go to Bali. You've been working all out since we arrived.'

He got up and kissed her on the cheek. 'Maybe you're right. They say Bali is beautiful. I'll try,' he said, cheering up, but even as he thought of the idyllic Bali beaches, the music, the dancing and the lotus-living, he knew that the fear would pursue him there too, and once more he wished to God that whatever there was in store for him would come about and be done with.

Though he was late for the office, he ignored the *betchak* drivers outside the hotel. He wanted to walk to the office. He wanted to forget all the reasons he'd been sent out to Java, all the purposes of the Ponsonby Post. He wanted to walk down the main street like a tourist. He wanted to wander through the market, bargain for batiks, watch the dancing troupe from Solo dancing on the square. He wanted to sit alone and quiet in a

cafe and sip the king-coconut juice through a bamboo straw.
And he would have done just that had he not seen Richard
approach him. Brownlow hesitated. There were a number of
hovering questions in his mind, and only Richard knew the
answers. Richard, who was the son of Patricia's lover, and the
friend, a close friend, people said, of the dead pilot. He was
central to the whole sorry story. He wondered why Isani had not
yet brought the boy in for questioning. Was it possible that he
saw no link, or was he perhaps keeping him on ice till he had
more evidence?

'Hello,' Richard called out, when almost alongside him. He
walked with a jaunty swing, almost too jaunty, Brownlow
thought, with an over-protesting nonchalance.

'Hello,' Brownlow said.

Richard slowed down as if ready for conversation, but Brownlow suddenly decided that he wanted no more part of it. It was
Isani's job, and he owed it to Belinda and to Emily and to his
own peace of mind to stay well clear of it. 'Must hurry,' he said.
'I'm late already.' He walked quickly on, down to the square of
the Sultan's Palace, anxious to see Burhan, not for any specific
reason, but because the boy's presence was a reassurance, as much
as his absence was a threat.

Burhan was busy at his stand. Not only with one client. He
actually had a small queue. Even though the other shoe-shiners
were idle, they accepted the fact that a client could assume pro-
priety rights on a shiner as they might equally on a tailor or
other private service. The men were queueing for the distinctive
Burhan style. Brownlow waited on the corner, watching him. He
worked deftly and with quicksilver energy. He exchanged no
words with his client, nor looked at him. His mode of recognition was through people's shoes. Only when the man paid him
did Burhan look up and flash a smile. Then his face lowered
again for the next customer. There were two more in the queue.
It was the turn of a soldier. Burhan looked at the large army
boot, then up to the man's face. Then Brownlow noticed that the
soldier stepped aside, allowing the man behind him to take his
turn. It was obvious that the soldier had private business with
Burhan. Brownlow waited until it was the soldier's turn, then he
started to walk across the Square. He reached Burhan's stand
and hovered alongside the soldier. The man was bent, whisper-

ing in Burhan's ear. Burhan continued polishing, or rather, rubbing the boot as a mere formality. The soldier had obviously stopped by for less trivial purposes. Brownlow waited, standing to one side. When the boot was finished, the soldier gave Burhan a piece of paper, and it was clearly not money. Burhan nodded again, and the soldier, with one shoe unrubbed, left the stand.

Brownlow lifted his foot, and Burhan recognised it immediately. He looked up quickly, and reddened as he stuffed the paper into his pocket. Then he smiled. 'Emily?' he asked.

'School,' Brownlow said, pointing to his watch. 'This morning she went by car.'

Burhan smiled with relief.

'You can see her at supper,' Brownlow said, and he was not surprised when Burhan shook his head.

'Tonight, no possible,' Burhan said. 'Maybe tomorrow. Business,' he added shrugging.

'Emily will be sad,' Brownlow said.

'Burhan sad too,' and he started to polish the shoe. With such energy, Brownlow thought, as if the shine was going to have to last a long time. When they were finished, Brownlow made his customary over-payment. 'Tomorrow?' he said.

Burhan shrugged. 'Maybe,' he said sadly.

When Brownlow reached the end of the Square, he looked around in time to see Burhan scuttling off, his little box of camouflage bouncing beside him. He would miss Burhan at supper, almost as much as Emily. The boy had become part of the family. He was becoming a palpable reason why they would remain in Java. But that meant too the Ponsonby Post, and once again, Brownlow was reluctant to reach his office.

The dancers from Solo were setting up on the Square. Why not? he thought, and he took his stand, along with others who were gathering beneath the giant banyan tree. In its branches hung a bird in a cage. Such a sight was common on the island. For Brownlow it symbolised a colonial hangover, a token, as it were, of semi-prison, with freedom tangible, but out of reach.

The dancers were arranging their props, while the small gamelan band positioned themselves on one side. They were going to perform the horse dance, for which the Solo group were famous. The dancers formed a circle, and one of their number began to sing. Or rather, she threw out a note and seemed to follow it where it took her, and though it appeared not to her making, and certainly not within her control, it was nevertheless melodious and full of grace. The band took up the note, and followed it, as if stalking a bird of prey, echoing it for a while, then holding it, before teasing it into further flight. Meanwhile the other dancers joined in, moving slowly in a circle to a step dictated by the unpredictable flight of song. Slowly the music simmered, and one amongst the dancers, a young man, faltered in his steps, and sank down on all fours. Slowly he moved within the circle in a gentle pattern of a trot. Gradually the song grew more frenzied, as if goading him to gallop, and one of their number, a man with a huge whip, stood outside the circle, and urged the trotter gently into his horse trance. Brownlow knew it was genuine. He had seen the dance before. Sometimes two, or even three dancers were transported through the music and song into some manner of metamorphosis. So he too, with the rest of the audience, shouted encouraging words to the quadruped figure, and one child amongst the crowd, so convinced, rushed into the ring and stroked the dancer's nose and back. Then the whip-man goaded the horse with his rope until he was circling the Square in a gallop, and the froth dribbled from his lips. Then suddenly he stopped, exhausted. One of the dancers fed him a handful of hay, while another took a glass light bulb from the prop bag and shattered it into small fragments in the palm of his hand. Then, approaching the man-horse, he gave it to him for feed. The man licked it off his palm, relishing each sliver of glass, and when the palm was licked clean, he took off again in a frenzied gallop. Just one wild circling, then he sank slowly on to his back, his limbs kicking, his eyes ablaze, while the troop stood about him, singing a dirge to accompany the horse-soul out of the man's body. Gradually he became still, and the whip-man lifted him gently, and propped him against the banyan tree, and a dancer came round with the hat. The crowd were generous. It was a show of courage and faith and it served to cast away their earth-bound doubts and uncertainties.

As Brownlow threaded his way through the crowd, he saw Richard again, and again he made to avoid him. He walked quickly to the other side of the Square.

'Thought you were in a hurry,' he heard Richard's voice behind him. It was as if the boy were seeking him out, as if he too wanted some information only Brownlow could provide. 'I'll walk along with you,' Richard said. For a while, they walked in silence. Then 'Any news?' Richard said.

'Of what?'

'The murder. The plane. Any old thing,' he said with a forced light-heartedness.

'Isani's dealing with all that,' Brownlow said.

'Oh.'

There was a further silence. Then Brownlow took the plunge. 'You knew Klaus Schmidt very well, didn't you?'

'I know lots of people very well,' Richard gave a nervous laugh.

'But you were especially friendly with Klaus,' Brownlow pressed on, against his own stubborn reasoning.

'What's that got to do with anything?' Richard almost shouted. 'How did you know we were friendly?'

So Brownlow thought he'd give it a try, and take the consequences of Richard's reaction. 'Weiner told me,' he said quietly.

Richard stood still, and Brownlow looked at him. He had paled, undeniably. His voice came out in a squeak. 'And you believe that rotten German fairy?' he screamed. A few passers-by stared at him, and Brownlow put his hand on Richard's shoulder to get him moving again. And suddenly his hand was mid-air and he turned and watched Richard race in a panic across the Square as if he were being pursued. Brownlow walked on. He should never have asked. He should never have thrown out the Weiner bait, but he'd never dreamed that Richard would react so violently. It's Isani's business, he kept telling himself on his way to the office, and mine, for what it is worth, is the Ponsonby Post. He strode into his office, determined to get on with it.

Chapter Eleven

Richard raced down the main street, sweating, and stole the first car he found unlocked. He always carried a ready bunch of keys, and with little ado found one to fit the ignition. And like a madman, he drove out to the airfield. He skidded the car to an abrupt stop at the gate, and rushed over to the hut. The door was shut but unlocked. He burst inside. It was empty. He opened the window that looked out on to the field. 'Peter,' he shouted. Then he felt a pair of hands on his shoulders, and heard a voice whose gentleness he'd not bargained for.

'Liebchen,' Peter said, turning him round to face him. 'You've come back. You've come back to your Peter.' He buried his head on Richard's shoulder. 'I knew you would,' he said. 'I prayed for it.' He was kissing Richard's neck, and as gently as he could, for this was no time to fight the man, Richard pushed him from him.

'I've not come back,' he said slowly. 'It's all over between us. It has been for a long time.'

'Ever since Klaus,' Peter muttered. 'But he's dead now, don't you see,' Peter said, bewildered by Richard's lack of logic. 'We can be together again. I'm sorry he's dead,' he went on hastily, 'but he's . . . he's just not here any more.'

'I loved him, Peter,' Richard said. 'I loved him more than my life.'

'As I love you,' Peter said, and he began to sob aloud.

'Stop it,' Richard screamed at him. 'I didn't come here to talk about Klaus.'

'Then why have you come? To torment me?'

Richard went towards him. He needed the man's friendship. He needed his confidence. 'No,' he said. 'I'm still your friend, you know that.'

Peter took his hand, and Richard let him hold it, as he would

76

let him hold it, he thought, just as long as he could be of service.

'Why have you come then?' Peter asked.

'I was talking to Brownlow.'

'Brownlow who?'

Richard stared at him, incredulous. 'You know Brownlow,' he said. 'The Ponsonby man.'

'Oh *him*,' Peter said quickly, feeling he might have perhaps overdone the outsider role. 'Of course I know him. I saw him this morning.'

'Why did you tell him?' Richard said.

'Tell him what?'

'Come on, Peter. You know.'

'I know nothing. I don't know what you're talking about.'

'You told him I was friendly with Klaus.' He did not take his eyes off Peter's face. Then he shouted at him, 'You told him I was *very* friendly with Klaus.'

'I didn't,' Peter said, with utter simplicity. 'I didn't. Honestly I didn't.'

'Then it was a trap,' Richard said, almost to himself, and he felt suddenly sick inside. 'He must know something.'

Peter walked over to the table, sat on it, his one leg dangling. He was smiling ever so slightly. 'Why are you so frightened, Richard?' he said.

'I've nothing to be afraid of,' Richard said quickly. 'Nothing at all.'

'I think you have,' Peter said, his leg swinging.

'What d'you mean?' Richard asked tentatively. Then he saw Peter's smile, and suddenly he knew that Peter knew everything. 'I've nothing to be afraid of. Absolutely nothing.'

'Klaus told me everything,' Peter said, and his foot stopped swinging.

'There was nothing to tell.'

'He told me plenty,' Peter said.

'For instance?'

'Well, the morning he crashed he was on his way to meet you. He was going to pick you up in Simpang field behind the barracks. He was going to take you to Bali.'

'That's right,' Richard said. He saw no point in denying it. 'We'd arranged to go for a holiday.'

'So he told me. But why Bali? Why not another island. There are plenty of beauty spots here in Java.'

'I just like Bali, that's all.'

Peter was silent. He needed a pause to give extra weight to his next question. 'But what was the desperate hurry?'

How much did Peter know, Richard wondered. The leg had begun swinging again with mounting confidence. 'There was no hurry,' Richard said. 'Klaus wanted to get away too. He said he was going to tell you. He thought it would be less painful if we did it quickly.'

'I don't think you were too worried about my pain,' Peter said with a sneer. 'I think you had reason to run. Klaus told me everything.'

Richard was silent. Until Peter revealed that he knew all that had happened, he would give him no clues. 'What did he tell you?' he said.

'He told me how you both went to your father's house.'

Richard's stomach heaved, but he choked it back. Why in God's name had Klaus told him?

'It was quiet,' Peter was saying, 'and you thought no one was at home. You sat side by side on the sofa. His hand was on your knee.'

'What does it matter where his hand was?' Richard sobbed, as much in fear of further disclosures as the reminder of his lost love.

'You lay on the couch together, and all was silent,' Peter went on, relentlessly punishing himself. 'Then you heard a noise, a giggle, coming from your parents' bedroom. You rushed to your father's door. Klaus followed you. Your father lay naked on the bed. Straddling him, and naked too, was Patricia Forrest. She didn't see you for her back was towards the door. But through her open thighs your father saw you, wild in the doorway. Klaus told me he thought your father smiled at you, as if he was proud to be caught by his son in an act of youth and virility. That's why Klaus thought you lost your cool.'

'I don't want to hear any more,' Richard said.

'Nevertheless, you're going to hear it. Klaus told me everything.'

He didn't doubt it now. Peter knew the whole story.

'You crossed over to the bed,' Peter went on. 'You stood

behind her as she pumped away. Then you struck a karate blow on the back of her neck. She fell across your father's body. Klaus said she must have died immediately. You and he lifted her body on to the floor, and between you, you dressed her. Your father stared from the bed, and didn't say a word. Then you bundled her into Klaus's car, and drove her to the thicket where you dumped her.'

Richard shivered. Klaus's report had been exact. But why had he spoken of things that no one on earth should be told? 'Why did he tell you?' Richard pleaded.

'He had to, I suppose,' Peter said. 'He told me he was going to run away with you to Bali. He told me he'd never bring you back. I said I would stop him. By force if necessary. Then he told me you had to get away. And finally he had to tell me why.'

'And you still let him go?'

'I love you too,' Peter reminded him. 'I wanted to save you. I wanted you to live, even if it had to be with someone else.'

Then Richard sobbed aloud. He sobbed because he understood why Klaus had had to share their secret, and he forgave him. He sobbed because he knew that his father, whatever happened, would never betray him. And he sobbed for the love that Peter still bore him, a love that for the sake of his own survival he would have to nurture. But he sobbed most of all for Klaus. 'How did he die?' he whispered. He noticed that Peter's leg was swinging again.

'Someone from the village, I imagine. There's a lot of hostility to us there. And there's plenty of PKI sympathisers in the village. Who knows?' Peter shouted, his leg slicing the air with fury. Then he slouched off the table and walked towards Richard. He clasped Richard's head, and pressed it to his thighs.

Richard's stomach heaved with revulsion. Peter's gesture, he knew, was a down payment claim, the first of God knows how many, and he would be paying them forever. He tried to free his head, but Peter held it in a gentle vice.

'What d'you want me to do?' Peter said. He lifted Richard's head so that he had to look at him.

'Brownlow knows,' Richard said. 'I'm sure he knows. And if he doesn't know, he suspects. And his daughter's friendly with Burhan.'

'What's Burhan got to do with it?' Richard noted the alarm in Peter's voice.

'When Klaus didn't show up, I asked Burhan to take me to the mountains. We were half way there and I saw the plane.'

'Burhan won't say anything,' Peter said.

'But he's almost part of the Brownlow family,' Richard panicked. He drew away from Peter's grasp and Peter made no move to stop him. Richard walked over to the window, and looking out over the airfield, he said, 'We've got to get rid of Brownlow. And quickly.'

It was a suggestion that had crossed Peter's mind too. He himself would be happily shot of Brownlow, and for his own personal reasons. The man was too curious, too honest, and he asked too many questions. He was an interferer. Yes, Peter would gladly assist at his dispatch, but he dared not reveal to Richard his personal enthusiasm for the scheme. So he tried gently to talk him out of it. 'I shouldn't let Brownlow worry you,' he said. 'He's leaving all the investigations to Isani. He's very loathe to interfere with police work. He told me so. Anyway, we can't just get rid of him. There would be an international scandal.'

'He can die, can't he?' Richard said. 'We could fake an accident. We've got to do something, and quickly.'

'Maybe you're right,' Peter said. 'Now I remember, he did say this morning . . .'

'Say what?' Richard hung on his words.

'Well, he was joking really. He wanted to go climbing. He wanted to get as close to Merapi as possible. Close enough, he said, to see the crater. He suggested that I help make up a climbing party.'

'What's that got to do with anything?' Richard shouted.

'Nothing,' Peter said, 'except that he said, "Don't bring that Stern boy". That's exactly what he called you,' Peter said, warming to his cunning fabrication. ' "Don't bring that Stern boy. Burhan tells me he's a rotten climber." '

Richard crumpled. 'Then Burhan talked,' he said. 'Brownlow knows,' he panicked. 'We've got to get him out of the way. Help me, Peter,' he pleaded.

'If you're set on it,' Peter said happily. 'But how?'

'There's a reception for Dr Boxham on Friday. Everybody will be there.'

'I'm not invited,' Peter said, 'but I could go, I suppose. He's always asking me to come over. But then what? Poison him?' he laughed.

'I don't know,' Richard said. 'I don't know. We could take him off his guard. Anything, anything,' he shouted helplessly, 'just so's we get rid of him. Help me, Peter.'

Peter took him in his arms. 'Of course,' he said. 'I'll think of something. My Richard's come home, hasn't he, *liebchen*?'

Richard put up no defence. 'I'm broken, Peter,' he said.

'I'm here, *liebe*. I'm with you always.'

It was what Richard most feared. 'But I loved him. I loved him more than my life.'

Peter stiffened, but he tightened his embrace.

'He was so gentle,' Richard was saying, 'he would open me like a rose.'

'D'you want my help?' Peter said steadily.

'He was so tender,' Richard went on, as if ignorant of Peter's presence. 'We would lay on a bed of tobacco leaves. That was our favourite place, you know, the tobacco go-down near Djogja. And the smell of the leaves, and the . . .'

A vicious blow from Peter stopped his love-making mouth. Richard lay sprawled on the floor. He licked the blood dropping on his chin and swallowed it. Then, staring fixedly at the straw-matting covering on the floor, he said, 'If you want me, you have to take Klaus too.'

Peter kicked Richard's legs apart. He began to hum, loudly and firmly, to drown the sweet nothings that Richard still mumbled to his love. The hum rose almost to a scream, and Richard had to compete, so his endearments swelled with sad and loud passion. Then Peter broke into song, 'O Tannenbaum', relishing every single whiter-than-white Aryan syllable, wallowing in a true Teutonic mish-mash of sentimentality and cruelty. And to the accompaniment of this cacophonous trio, for Richard insisted on that form of ensemble, Peter threw himself on the sobbing hulk, and with a raging and punitive love, he buggered him.

Chapter Twelve

It was almost dark when Burhan reached the top of the
mountain. He had been climbing most of the day, stopping only
occasionally to drink water from a stream. He was hungry but
he was sure of food once he got to the hide-out. Whenever he
went there, they made a little feast for him out of their meagre
rations. He liked going there, but tonight he would have preferred
to be with Emily, as on every other night and day since he had
met her. He would stay the night at the hide-out. With luck, if
they didn't need him for more running, he could get back to
Djogja in time to meet Emily from school the following day.
He peered round in the falling darkness for his landmark.
Without the signposts, the caves were impossible to find.
Somewhere along the mountain side was a huge rock-boulder,
fallen from Merapi in a long-ago eruption, balanced snugly in a
dip on the mountain ridge. He had to find it before darkness fell.
He ran quickly up the slope, then to his left. He heard a stream.
Unfamiliar. He turned back down the slope and ran the other
way. Nothing. He had a torch in his pocket, but he dared not
use it. He had promised his friends never, on pain of death, to
show a light within a mile of their hide-out, and he must be that
close, he thought, for once past the boulder-landmark, it was
only a few minutes to the cave. He was tempted to shout, so that
he could pick up the direction of the echo that the boulder
would throw back at him, but shouting was forbidden too. He
stood very still and listened to the piercing silence about him.
He was a little afraid. But there was no time to lose. The moon
was coming up, but it was only a quarter, and not light enough
to pick out his signpost. He ran back to the top of the ridge and
looked about him. All he saw was a huge range of mountain-
tops to his left and right. He had no notion of where he was.
He sat down and tried not to cry. He knew he would have to

stay on the mountain that night, and look for the boulder once
it was light again, so he turned back to find a resting-place.
And there, only a few feet behind him, loomed the boulder.
He was about to cry out with joy, then, remembering the rules,
he clapped his hand on his mouth, and ran to the rock to
embrace it. He must have skirted it as he came up from the
stream, and thereafter he'd kept it always behind him. He
reached up, fingering the outline. It was shaped like two
soldered triangles, one higher than the other. His clue was to
follow with his finger the left side of the lower peak until it
reached the ground, and from there to follow a tortuous path
that led to the cave. Once located, he scrambled down its slope.
There was still just enough light for him to see the curtain of
rush matting that covered the entrance. He crawled underneath.
Then, taking a deep breath, he whistled his shibboleth, and
listened to its echo through the cave. He waited until he heard
footsteps. Then a man, but on closer examination, little more
than a boy appeared at the end of a stone passageway. 'Burhan,'
he shouted with delight. They ran towards each other and
embraced. Oyung was sixteen, and amongst the group of men,
he was Burhan's special friend. It was he who had first started
using Burhan as a runner. It was Burhan who had carried
Oyung's written wish to the guerrilla leader that he be allowed
to join their band. Burhan had come hotfoot from the
mountains, a crumpled sweaty letter in his hand. The leader's
reply had stated that Oyung, as the Police Inspector's son, was
in a much better position to help the cause if he stayed and
reported police movements from Djogja. For a while, Oyung
complied, but he was restless, and every week he sent another
begging missive to the partisans. Finally, almost a year ago,
Burhan had brought his summons, and the following day, he
had led him over the mountains to the hide-out. Oyung trusted
Burhan implicitly, and Burhan would have died sooner than
betray him.

He followed him through the cave. There were about forty
partisans in the hide-out. Burhan knew the number, because
sometimes they played team games with him, and he was
allowed to pick his own side, which was twenty, and though
Burhan knew few of their names, he knew every face by heart.
Not that they withheld their names, for Burhan was trusted by

everybody. But Burhan never asked. Somehow he felt safer not knowing.

Along the passageway, at intervals, stood a few armed men. Some sat on rock shelves that looked out over the mountain range. The main living, sleeping and cooking space spread over a large area, occasionally open to the sky. Most of the men were lying on bunks and reading. Burhan could smell food but no one was cooking. He concluded that they had already eaten.

'Are you hungry?' Oyung asked.

Burhan nodded, his mouth watering.

'We have rice cooked. It's still hot,' one of the men said, 'and we kept some dog for you.' He went to the shelf for a bowl.

But first things first. He took the note the soldier had given him and thrust it into Roschun's hand. Roschun was the leader of the men. He wore an invisible authority which Burhan had sensed the first time he'd come to the cave. The man spread the note on his lap. As he read it, Burhan watched him, as did the other men standing around. A slow smile spread across his features, then he broke into loud and gleeful laughter. 'It's all arranged,' he said. 'Friday next. Zein has arranged everything. Now eat, boy,' he clapped Burhan on the shoulder, and the bowl of food was brought to him. As he ate, he wondered what sort of arrangements Roschun was speaking of, but he knew better than to ask. It was none of his business, but he was curious about the disparate nature of the connections he was making. His soldier friend Zein belonged to the army. He worked for the government. That was respectable. Yet he was sending messages to people who, Burhan knew, were not considered respectable at all. He couldn't make it out. For over a year, he'd been up and down the mountain with little bits of paper. He'd noticed how, a few days after every mission, some event of importance happened on the island. He couldn't read about it in the papers, but he heard from his friends about student riots, strikes at the docks in Djakarta, and peasant revolt against the landlords. He knew that somehow he had helped to arrange these events, and he felt very proud, for though he had little political understanding, he knew that his mountain friends must be in the right. 'What day is it today?' he asked the men.

'It's nearly Wednesday.'

He went on eating his rice. That meant two more days to a happening.

Siswamarto came and crouched beside him. He was the oldest of the men and their counsellor. He was a peasant, and had been in the movement since his youth. He'd farmed a few acres of the *Lurah's* land in the village of Harbobingangun, he, his wife and only son, Wan. The boy worshipped his father, and when the coup was attempted five years ago, he'd gone with his father's fearful blessing to join the partisans in Djakarta. He was then only sixteen. For a long year no word had been heard of him. Then a young convict, a petty thief, escaped from the prison in Djogja. He made his way to the village and Siswamarto's hut, and there he begged for hiding. 'Wan said you would help me,' the man said.

Siswamarto embraced him. 'Where is he?' he swallowed the words in his joy.

The convict gave him Wan's medallion. 'He sent this to you,' he said. 'He was taken prisoner in the battle of Merdeka Square,' he said. 'He's in Djogja.'

That same day, Siswamarto hung the chain around his neck and made his way into the mountains, swearing to devote his life to freeing his son.

Although their ambitions were less private, the other men had great respect for Siswamarto. He was one of the few of them who could read and write, and it was his job to read them the newspapers that were smuggled up from the surrounding villages, and to keep a diary of sorties from the hide-out and to take stock of their food and ammunition. He had a special feeling for Burhan. Of them all, Burhan was the only one who had never known Wan. Most of them knew him from the same village school, or even from the Djakarta siege from which they'd escaped. So there was nothing new that he could tell them about his son. But Burhan's was an untapped ear, and each time he came up to the hide-out, he would tell him another story of Wan's childhood. 'One day I shall free him,' he said to Burhan, 'and we'll go back to the village together.'

In the corner of the cave, Mohammed took out his bamboo flute and started to play. Mohammed was the minstrel of the group, and the story-teller. But he was a proven fighter too. His father and elder brother had been killed in the Djakarta siege, and he was in the mountains to seek vengeance. He was no political thinker, but as a devout Muslim, it was incumbent on him to avenge the blood of his kin. Now he sang the story of the minstrel boy who went to war, his only weapon, the *Anklung* harp. And the enemy, on hearing his song, came over one by one to his side, until one of their group shot the harp from the boy's hands, and in his unarmed silence, they slew him.

The men in the cave joined in the song. Seldom they sang in a group, for fear of echo across mountains, but whenever Burhan came, as part of his treat, Mohammed would bring out his flute, and the men kept their voices low.

Oyung came to Burhan's side. The ritual was always the same whenever he visited the hide-out. He would hand over his message, eat his supper, and Oyung would come and crouch by his side. Burhan would then give him news of Djogja.

'I saw him yesterday,' Burhan said. 'Talking to an Englishman, and they were laughing. But he's very busy.' Then he told Oyung as much as he knew about the Patricia Forrest murder and the crashed plane. Oyung was less interested in the stories than he was in the fact that his father was still in his job, that nothing had leaked, that his own defection had jeopardised nobody. He needed this reassurance at every visit. His family welfare settled, he wanted news of his great passion, kite-fighting. In his civilian days, Oyung had been a champion kite-fighter. He had patented a special mixture of crushed glass and glue, which when rubbed on a kite string, gave it a lethal cutting edge. All competitors used their own home-grown methods, but Oyung's was the finest of them all. He'd taken the secret of his formula into the mountains with him, and it was Burhan's cherished hope that one day he would share it. Every Sunday Burhan went to the kite-game. He had his own stand, and his own book, and he took bets and gave the odds as if he'd spent a life-time on the course. He described to Oyung every fight manoeuvre, who had a new kite, and the nature of its design. Everyone in Djogja was preparing for the annual inter-island kite championships, but Burhan didn't want to mention it, for he sensed that if Oyung had any doubts about his present pursuit, they would be on account of his kite-flying talents. He had been champion of Djogja for as long as Burhan could remember, and it would have been painful to him to hear how

he had been superseded. Then Burhan told him that the dancers
from Solo had come to Djogja, omitting to mention that they had
come as part of the games celebrations, and that he'd seen his
brother amongst the crowd.

'Well?' Oyung said.

'Laughing. He's always laughing. On that bike that's much
too big for him.'

'My old bike,' Oyung said.

They were silent. Burhan had told him everything. Except
about Emily. He had never spoken to anybody about their
friendship. Somehow it was too private to share. But now, away
from her, in the secrecy of the mountains, he wanted to tell
Oyung, for he knew that his friend would hold his secret.

'What else?' Oyung said, for he sensed that there was
something.

Burhan looked into his rice bowl, and Oyung saw that he
was blushing. He whispered in his ear. 'You're in love.'

Burhan giggled and nodded.

'Tell me,' Oyung said.

Then Burhan spilt it out, each event of his love-growth, with
no respect to chronology, for Burhan didn't know how it began,
or even when. He couldn't imagine that there was any time in his
life in which Emily had not played a major role. He began to
describe her.

'Wait,' Oyung said, and he ran to the table to fetch a pad of
paper. 'Start with her hair,' he said. And as Burhan spoke,
Oyung drew, but when Burhan had finished with each blonde
curl, he stopped. He frowned. 'What about her eyes?' Oyung
said.

Burhan shook his head. He couldn't remember what she
looked like. He couldn't recall a single feature. He turned her
round, her back to him, a familiar position when she stood on
the balcony. Nothing. Not even her height. 'She's got a pink
dress,' he said suddenly, 'with a big skirt.' But that was all. He
turned her round again, watching him shine her father's shoes,
but she was a blurred shadow. 'I've got to go back,' he said.
He was frightened. If he could forget what Emily looked like,
it was logical that she would forget him too. He had to be there
in the morning to shine her father's shoes. He stood up. 'I'm
going,' he said. But even as he stood, his legs weakened. He was

overwhelmingly tired. He knew he couldn't manage the mountain, and in the dark, it was likely too that he would lose his way. He needed little dissuasion. Oyung put his arms around him and lifted him on to a bunk. 'We'll finish the drawing in the morning,' he said. He covered Burhan with a blanket. He noticed that the boy's eyes were already closed. As Burhan sank into sleep, he saw Emily loud and clear, with every single detail of her face in sharp focus. Roschun came over to the bunk and stroked Burhan's cheek. 'Our little guerrilla,' he said. 'One day, he'll be President.'

In the morning, Burhan left the hide-out, clutching another piece of paper. He was to take it to the village of Harbo-bingangun, and give it to the medicine-man there. Roschun had told him that it was urgent and that he must hurrry. But Burhan needed no bidding. Harbobingangun meant a slight detour on his way back to Djogja, but he knew of a short-cut of a path, beaten out a few years ago by the falling lava, and that would take him to within a few yards of the medicine-man's house. At the same time when the lava fell, the villagers had gathered in the clearing around the witch-doctor's hut, taking up a position that they knew with an absolute faith, was one of safety. For the lava would stop short of the clearing. And it did, and they did not even rejoice, because it was in the natural order of things that the medicine-man and all his goods and chattels would be spared.

Burhan reached the twin-triangle rock and took his direction from its contours. It was downhill most of the way, so he was able to run, all the time thinking of Emily, whose image had once again slipped from his mind. Half way down, before a steep slope began, he sat down and rested. He thought that with luck, he'd reach Djogja by the time Emily came out of school, provided that the medicine-man didn't need another errand. It was rarely that he had to run twice during a mission. He supposed it all had to do with something that was going to happen on Friday, and that that event was going to be important to the cause of his mountain friends. He tried once again to recall Emily's features, but with little success. In his pocket he had the sheet of paper on which Oyung had drawn her hair. Oyung had told him to fill it in as soon as he saw her, then he could just look at her image whenever he wanted to. But he

couldn't draw, and somehow he'd grown to like the shock of
curled hair on the paper framing a blank face. It was a token of
how often he thought about her, so often, and with such inten-
sity, that his memory had overreached itself into oblivion.

He reached the lava track at about noon. Although it was
downhill, it could be rough on bare feet, even when the sole-
skin was as hard and tough as Burhan's. He had never in his
life worn shoes. When he'd first entered the Ambarrukmo, a few
eyebrows were raised, but quickly lowered on observing the
company he kept. He always admired a good shoe, especially
when the leather was soft and old enough to have affectionately
accommodated the foot, but he never envied the shod. He
recalled how imprisoned and helpless Hildeborg had felt, bereft
of shoes. He smiled as he remembered that mission. It had been
a profitable one. *Her* fat dumpling of a face he could recall in
minute detail, and he supposed therefore that he couldn't have
liked her very much.

He stepped gingerly on to the lava track, picking out the
blunt stones as footholds. He zig-zagged most of the way,
keeping his eyes firmly on the track. He knew when he was close
to the end, for there were noises coming from the clearing. The
space in front of the medicine-man's house was used for his
daily surgery. All patients were treated in the open air under the
shade of coconut trees. There was always an audience, mostly
of women and children, though only a few of them had come
for the doctor's services. Burhan joined the circle of onlookers.
The patient under treatment was an old man. He lay on his
back on a piece of rush-matting. There were bunches of herbs
tied round the man's neck, and the doctor was massaging his
feet. Burhan knew enough about village medicine to know that
if a doctor was working on a patient's feet, that patient was
having trouble with his neck. Herbs and infusions were placed
on the site of the pain, but the actual treatment took place in
the area of energy congestion. The reverse was also true, so
Burhan decided that he would tell the doctor that he had pains
in his feet, since he had no shoes as a hiding-place. Quickly and
unobserved, he stuffed Roschun's note into the back of his shirt-
collar, for message carrying was not just a simple deliver-and-run
affair. Respect had to be paid to the addressee, and since he was
usually at his work, due acknowledgement of his profession had

to be accorded. In the same way as Zein had handed Burhan the note in the course of a shoe-shine, so Burhan would deliver while under the medicine-man's healing.

The old man had been dealt with, and since no one else came forward, Burhan limped into the clearing. He lifted his foot to the medicine man, then lay down on the mat. The doctor poured an infusion between Burhan's toes and around the ankles. Then he started to gently massage his neck. His fingers quickly caught the piece of paper. He began to hum, by way of a receipt. He went on massaging, though now he knew it only for a formality. Then he stood up, and turning his back to the audience, read the note. From where he lay, Burhan could see his face. A huge smile re-wrinkled the skin around his eyes and mouth. Something really good must be happening on Friday, Burhan thought. Then the doctor nodded to Burhan as a sign of dismissal.

Forgetting his limp, Burhan rushed out of the clearing, through the village and past the headman's house, where Sastro sat on the steps drinking mint-tea. Then out into the road, just in time to stop the fruit and vegetable lorry on its way to Djogja market. He climbed on to the back and burrowed a small nest amongst the coconuts. From the position of the sun, it must be three o'clock. He would be well in time for Emily.

Chapter Thirteen

Between quarrelling, guarded reconciliations, and bitter coupling, Peter Weiner and Richard had drawn up a plan, the final move of which was open-ended, and was still unresolved as they made their way that Friday to the Ambarrukmo Hotel.

They had decided to arrive at the party early. They wanted to draw attention to the nature of their arrival, the attention, that is, of the hotel receptionist and desk staff, but at the same time they did not want to be too conspicuous to other guests.

The party was to begin at nine o'clock, and on the stroke of the hour, Peter and Richard entered the hotel foyer. Peter was in an invalid chair. He wore a tuxedo which would be the uniform of all the male guests, and a silk scarf was wound about his neck. It casually covered the lower part of his face, and he kept his head down. Richard wheeled him into the hall, taking a wide swing towards the reception desk, hovered long enough to leave the impression of a wheel-chair plus handler ensemble, and made for the lift. Once inside, Peter threw off the scarf and folded the chair, and once on Brownlow's floor, they stashed the chair into the linen cupboard. Then they made their way to the Brownlow suite.

Despite the earliness of the hour, there were already a few guests in the room, notably von Henkel and Ingrid, who had never been known to miss out on eating time. Both were handling some chicken. A great deal of food was laid out on a long table, and a side-table held glasses and two gigantic punch bowls. The Ambarrukmo was famous for its punch, and its recipe was called for at every civic reception on the island. Its inventor was head barman at the hotel, and he had culled the recipe from a book of ancient love-potions. He had chemically researched the modern equivalent of each and every ingredient; apart from its alcoholic content, it was laced liberally with herbs and essences, and its aphrodisiac effect was due, so people said, to the addition of toad's urine. The whole concoction was known as Herawati, the name of the barman's mother, to whom he was devoted.

A waiter was ladling drinks from the bowl, and handed one each to Peter and Richard as they arrived. Formal greetings followed together with an introduction to Dr Boxham. The punch waiter was not busy since there were only a few guests, and each one had been served, so he idled away at the table. It was a good time to draw him away from his stand and to engage him in conversation. Peter walked casually over to the table, while Richard tried to catch the waiter's eye. Finally succeeding, he insolently crooked his finger towards him. The waiter, born and bred to obey, answered the summons.

'Waiter,' Richard said in friendly tones, 'now you must know the secret of this punch. What's it worth to you to tell me?'

The waiter pleaded his innocence, and Richard kept up the badinage long enough to allow Peter to get going, and out of the corner of his eye, he supervised Peter's actions. Peter's hand was in his pocket, making an unscrewing motion. Then, turning his back to the room, he took out a bottle and poured its contents of highly charged hash-oil into the punch bowls. The whole manoeuvre had taken a few seconds. Richard dismissed the waiter, and finished his glass of punch. It would be his first and last drink of the evening. Likewise for Peter, who now was inspecting the bunch bowl like a tourist, and mixing it with the ladle, in the feigned attempt, so he explained to the waiter, of discovering its secrets.

More and more guests began to arrive, and Brownlow greeted each one personally. Isani came with his reluctant and rather beautiful wife in tow. Since Oyung's defection, she rarely made public appearances. She was fearful of two things; one that people would comment on her son's disappearance, and the other that they wouldn't. Both would have caused her pain, and she couldn't have dealt with either. Isani, on the other hand, was in jovial mood, and Richard watched him warily, for his light-heartedness might have been due to a recent clue discovery. But as Isani was quick to point out, for that was one of the first questions levelled at him, there was nothing new to report. Murders and sabotage, he added, were so rife on this politically torn island, that either tragedy could have been caused by anybody mad enough to see it as furthering their cause. Like all the other murders, he added, day-to-day investigation had been abandoned. 'Though the files are kept well open,' he insisted, 'even if their papers were gathering dust.' His contentment was probably due to the fact that enough time had now elapsed to pass the verdicts on both mishaps as 'by person or persons unknown', and leave it at that. 'This is a party,' he was saying, 'a time to make ourselves comfortable.' And that he certainly was doing, as he offered the waiter his empty glass for a second filling.

Richard's father came alone. Since the Forrest affair, and by now, his publicly known involvement, he had been much befriended. He'd always been liked amongst his colleagues, mainly because of his hostility towards von Henkel, whom nobody had much time for. But now he was liked for his own sake. His love of the Forrest girl, and it was clear that he had loved her deeply, pin-pointed his loneliness. His dignity during official and unofficial cross-examination, had impressed everybody, and when he came into the room, quietly composed, there were many who came forward to greet him. Richard was amongst them. His public *persona*, despite the rumours, was of a good and loving son, and he called the waiter to give his father a glass of punch.

'Where's yours, Richard?' Stern said.

'I've already had quite a bit,' Richard laughed. Then back in the far corner of the room, he caught sight of Peter talking to Brownlow, and he went quickly to join them, eager to miss out on nothing. Belinda was pressing a regular invitation on Peter, and Richard was anxious to break up their *bonhomie*, for fear that Peter would lose appetite for their evening's mission. But Belinda was then taken away by another guest, leaving Peter and Richard to assess the progress of their conspiracy.

The punch was having its effect, and it was universal. Isani was so high that he was on the point of blowing. But there was no fear of violence, or even sickness. The most that could result was stupor, and that would harm nobody. Richard was watching Ingrid. She was doing the most extraordinary things with her hands. She was handling her body as a love object, as if it belonged to somebody else, a lover perhaps. He wondered whether anybody else had noticed it, but looking round the company, he had to conclude that even if they had, they would have found nothing amiss in her behaviour. He turned back to look at her, and to his sober horror, she was making a slow but sure bee-line towards him, intent all the while on her fingered excursions. Quickly he ran through his defences. 'I'm sorry, but I'm waiting for my girl-friend.' It was unlikely that Ingrid would buy that one. Her condition disallowed concern with sexual poaching. 'I've got the pox', was a last resort, but it was possible that in Ingrid's present state of euphoria, pox was beautiful, and moreover it was good for you. He could have come out with the simple and absolute truth, 'I'm a homosexual', but in the light of Brownlow's present suspicions, it was inopportune to advertise his sexual proclivities. He moved deftly sideways, only to bump into Pijoux, who was idly leafing through Brownlow's record collection, and with intense concentration, was putting to one side anything that could be danced to. He had stacked a pile of about twenty records. He intended the evening to last for ever.

When the first chord sounded, some guests gave cries of approval and delight. This was unlike any official reception they had known. It looked like a licence for total diplomatic immunity.

Richard crossed the room to join Peter, who once more was entangled with Belinda, whose gestures were becoming not unlike Ingrid's, but with an added touch of class and camouflage. He drew Peter aside, and together they viewed the progress of their plan.

All was going well. The punch bowls had been refilled, and Peter had donated his hash contribution. In another hour, close on midnight, they would all have drunk their way into their other and true selves. And so it was interesting to watch the nature of that hidden self, as slowly it was shed of all pretences and social requirements. Stern, for instance, was threading a slow and benign path to von Henkel. Richard watched him. When von Henkel saw Stern, he bowed, and Stern did likewise. They held hands out to each other, and without a word, embraced into a dance, which tune happened at the time to be an old Vienna waltz, and the two men skirted the floor to the melody of their mutual birthright. Stern's hatred of von Henkel had been based solely on a rational principle. Now, stripped of his compulsive scruple, he was able to view their common past in historical perspective. Tomorrow no doubt, in his social strait-jacket, he would spit on von Henkel, as he had always done, and the *status quo* of battlefield would be restored. Meanwhile they lilted to the waltz, and Stern, who, for the past twenty or so years had never soiled his lips with one German word, now joined with von Henkel in the passionate love lyric of the song. Their union was one out of time and out of place, but against the general background of unguarded defences, it was splendidly in season.

Ingrid had settled on Pijoux. They stood together in the corner of the room, and very publicly, and to everyone else's total indifference, they explored each other's bodies. Belinda, on the couch, was folded into a waiter, who had long ago abandoned his silver tray of pretty little things on toast, and they too were bridging the gaps, which was, after all, the core of her husband's calling. Mantoni squatted alone on the floor. His miniature roulette felt and wooden wheel was spread before him, and he was placing his bets against nobody. It was a sad revelation of a man's honest centre. His wife Louisa was dancing with Henderson, and they sailed past where Richard stood.

'You really do sing like a pig, my dear,' Henderson was saying.

'Yes,' she laughed, kissing his cheeks, 'simply because pigs are my audience.' And so they opened their joint and honest account.

Most surprising of all was Isani, lolling on a couch like Bacchus. 'I've got friends in the PKI,' he was telling all dancers-by. 'Good friends,' and his wife, kneeling by his side, nodded in beatific agreement. Brownlow sailed by with Threes. He was talking to her about his days at Eton. Under hash, the man will out, even if he has not become a man at all.

And threading his lone way through this gentle confessional, was the bewitched Boxham, guest of honour, plucking at the occasional sleeve like some ancient mariner.

It was almost midnight. The party had found its level, which according to Richard's vast knowledge of dope-culture, would maintain itself until morning. He tugged at Peter's sleeve. As they were walking towards Brownlow, Katoppo, Isani's deputy, wide-eyed and fearful, crept in at the door. He looked around for his boss, swallowed hard and long when he saw him, but nevertheless, pressed on to do his duty. Richard followed him and eavesdropped on the news.

'Isani,' Katoppo shouted in his boss's ear, 'the barracks have been raided. All the ammunition has gone.'

Isani's response, and he had heard well enough, was a great guffaw of laughter. He staggered to his feet. 'My friends,' he shouted, though few were listening. 'Peace has come,' and with a flickering recall from an old school text-book, 'Mafeking has been relieved.' Whereupon he embraced his wife, and they settled on the couch to celebrate the armistice together.

Katoppo gave one quick look round the room, decided that little assistance would come from this quarter, and that he must duly report such disgusting goings-on to higher authorities. 'All is confusion,' he said helplessly, and it crossed Richard's mind to slip him a glass of time-honoured Herawati, but Peter was ably there before him.

'Wait a few minutes, Katoppo,' he said, pressing the glass into his hand. 'He'll be all right shortly.'

Katoppo hesitated, then seeing no alternative, and loath to deal with the barracks affair on his own, he drank the punch at one gulp, and slumped like a faithful dog at his master's side, waiting for orders.

Peter and Richard went over to Brownlow and gently taking his arm they manoeuvred him towards the door. 'There's a full moon tonight,' Peter was saying. 'Let's go down to the pool for a swim.'

'Wonderful idea,' Brownlow said. 'We used to do that at Eton you know, in the summers. Halcyon days,' he murmured.

By now, Peter had him in the corridor, and Richard was waiting with the chair. They sat the unprotesting Brownlow inside, and wound the scarf about his neck. Richard wheeled him to the lift, and down to the ground floor. The foyer was obligingly empty, and the same hotel receptionist was bleary-eyed at his desk. He nodded a goodnight to Richard as he swung past him with the chair, and another goodnight to Peter who had come down alone in the following lift.

Richard waited for Peter at the car parked in the drive. Together they helped Brownlow into the car, and parked the chair in the boot. One or two *betchak* drivers might have noticed them, but there was nothing remarkable in the sight of three men leaving a party. There was no hurry. All had gone according to plan.

They drove out to the airfield. Finding himself in the car, it was possible that Brownlow thought that the pool had moved, or that they were indeed going back to Eton. Richard, sitting with him at the back of the car, put his arm around his shoulder. 'What song did they sing at Eton?' he said.

A liquid joy spread over Brownlow's face as he picked delicately at the joy-strings of his boyhood. He began to hum, while Richard poured some brandy from a flask. One glass for each of them, but into Brownlow's he dissolved two sleeping pills. 'One for the road,' he said, and he stretched over to Peter at the wheel. They drank to each other's boyhood, and while Brownlow hummed his way through the nursery corridors of his Alma Mater, Richard's and Peter's thoughts were on other matters. And both were the same. The dénouement of their plan. All had gone well so far, and during the course of the whole evening, neither of them had spoken of what they would finally do. Perhaps neither thought that things would go so smoothly, that some hitch during the evening would have obviated the need for a final decision. Now that they were faced with it, both hid their fears from each other.

Brownlow had by now fully trapped the words and melody of his school song, and he sang it out in tones of pride and glory. He looked at his most vulnerable, and Richard turned way from him, fearful of being diverted from his purpose, whatever form that should take. He wished that Peter would hurry.

'Where's the full moon?' Brownlow was saying.

'It's coming,' Richard said, staring at the shameless quarter in the sky.

'It will meet us at the pool,' Brownlow said.

The airport was in sight, and Peter took the dirt-track that led straight on to the field. 'We'll do what we have to do,' he said with some authority, and was thereafter silent until the small plane came in sight. He pulled up alongside, switched off the engine and turned to Richard. 'O.K?' he said.

Richard nodded, unaware of what specifics he was sanctioning. He opened the car door on Brownlow's side, and together with Peter, helped him out of the car.

Chapter Fourteen

If Brownlow thought he was flying, he was. He was still singing his school song as the plane soared above Djogja, but he was only humming now, the words beyond his labial strength. He would soon be asleep and totally at their mercy. Richard was quietly sick in the corner.

Peter flew on. He seemed to have a destination in mind, but he hadn't shared it with Richard. Richard didn't want to know. He was on Brownlow's side now, he decided, whatever the consequences, and Peter would have to deal with both of them. He heard Brownlow's gentle snoring and still he could not look at him. He looked at the dashboard. Gauging Peter's compass, they were flying east. 'Where are we going?' he said.

'Don't worry,' Peter said. 'I know a place. Is he asleep?'

'Yes.'

'Then come and sit beside me.'

Richard obliged. Now was no time for a falling-out. He moved alongside him, and allowed Peter's hand on his knee. They flew in silence broken only by Brownlow's now heavy snoring and the dark hum of the plane. Peter took Richard's head, and placed it on his own thigh. It was a silent order for it to get to work. Richard let his head lie there. He was prepared to be a passive partner on this enforced two-some. He certainly had no appetite for an active role. Peter grabbed the head, and placed it firmly between his legs. 'Get going, Stern,' he said.

'No.'

Peter gripped the head. 'I'm going to land,' he said. 'You've got five minutes.'

Richard was practically suffocating, but he made no move.

'I'm doing you a favour, don't forget,' he heard Peter say. 'I can call this off any time.'

'Then do it,' Richard's voice was muffled because Peter's hand still clamped his head. 'Let's go back.'

'You run the risk, I'll tell Brownlow everything.'

'Then tell him,' Richard said in despair.

The plane did not veer from its landing course. Richard tugged himself free, and sitting up, he said, 'I'm sick of the whole business.'

They were silent for a while. 'Where are we?' Richard said.

'Close to Merapi. There's a field I know. I landed there once.' He seemed to have collected himself and Richard felt it was possible to talk to him rationally. 'What are we going to do?' he said.

Peter opened a leather pocket on the flight deck and pulled out a revolver. He handed it to Richard. 'We're going to land,' Peter said, 'take him out of the plane, and you're going to kill him. The vultures will do the rest.'

'No.'

'And what do you expect, my dear boy?' Peter laughed. 'D'you want *me* to kill him?'

'Why not? We're in it together, aren't we?'

'Wait a minute,' Peter said, very precisely. 'Brownlow has nothing on me. I'm innocent. As far as I'm concerned, he can plod on the Ponsonby beat for as long as he lives.'

'I can't kill him,' Richard said.

'Well, you're just going to have to try.'

'I can't,' Richard shouted, 'not in cold blood.'

'It won't be the first time,' Peter sneered.

'That was different. I didn't stop to think. If you'd been in my position, you would have done the same.'

'I doubt it,' Peter said. 'Anyway, we'll be landing soon. You'd better pull yourself together.'

'No,' Richard said softly. 'Never.'

'Put your head in my lap,' Peter said gently. 'It will calm you.'

'No,' Richard shouted. 'Not that either.' His voice rattled with revulsion and hate, and Peter grabbed his neck and forced him down.

'I hate you,' Richard said, His voice, though muffled, was raddled with despair. 'I never loved you. Ever, ever. It's Klaus I loved. I loved him from the beginning.'

'That punk?' Peter shouted, relaxing his hold. 'That toad?'

'I loved him,' Richard insisted. 'D'you hear that?' He leaned over to Peter's ear and yelled at him. 'I loved him, and I always will.'

'Then I'm bloody glad I killed him,' Peter said. He clapped his hand over his raging mouth, but the words were out and he simmered with his own stupidity.

'You . . . what?' Richard said, incredulous.

And then the plane touched down. It jerked some distance across a bumpy field, then shuddered to a stop.

Peter steadied himself. 'I couldn't take it,' he said, 'him taking you away. So I got to the airfield before him, and I screwed up the plane.' He sighed. 'I'm sorry,' he said. 'We're both of us in an awful mess.'

'Does Brownlow know?' Richard could hardly speak.

'I don't know, he's certainly suspicious. He found a loop-hole in my story.'

'We'll kill him together,' Richard said with determination. 'And when it's all over, I never, but never in my life, want to see you again.' He turned round and looked at Brownlow. He was in a deep sleep. 'Come on,' Richard said. 'Let's get it over with.'

Together they bundled Brownlow out of the plane, and laid him on the field. Peter shone a torch on to his face. He looked unbearably innocent.

'Well?' Richard said, weighing the gun in his hand.

'I can't,' Peter said.

Richard walked back to the plane. 'Neither can I.'

They took off without either of them looking back. They were leaving an open wilderness with no form of habitation in sight. A parched land whose thirst for the rainy season would shortly be assuaged. He would be a man of inordinate fitness and courage who would survive such a mean unyielding terrain. But for Richard and Peter, the alternative was unspeakable.

The flight back to the airfield took almost an hour, during which time not a word passed between them. Both knew that though they might never see each other again, their mutual distrust and fear would bind them for a lifetime. In the car back to Djogja, they were silent too. Neither did they look at one another. Peter pulled up a few yards from Richard's house, leaving the engine running. Richard jumped out, and as his foot touched the ground, Peter was already into a U-turn, and bound for home.

Richard walked slowly to his house. He tried not to think of that gentle human bundle lying in that godforsaken field, millions of miles from nowhere. Brownlow had been disposed of, but for some reason he felt no relief, and he wished with all his heart that he could have the evening all over again. He wanted to run back to that field and bring Brownlow home, or at least to report it all to Isani, and in its wake, the whole sorry story. He wondered whether that would be easier than to carry for the rest of his natural life the perilous knowledge that so burdened him.

He opened the front door. There was no sign that his father was home, though it was well past three o'clock. He shuffled into his bedroom. From under his pillow, he pulled out a picture of Klaus. And all his pent-up fear, anger and remorse, now crystallised into a titanic hatred for Peter Weiner, and for the first time of what would be many many times in his life, he thought of shopping him.

A few miles away, in a small bunk in a thatched village hut, the same thought crossed Peter's mind, but the obvious consequences of such an act was mutually unthinkable.

So, across time and space, they would be soldered together, and all that was left for each of them, was a prayer for the other's early and natural grave.

Chapter Fifteen

Poor Isani. He sat crouched behind his desk. He'd taken the phone off the hook, and locked his door. To make doubly sure of non-interruption, he told his staff that he was not to be disturbed. He had a mountain of work to do, but that was not the reason he'd barricaded himself behind his desk. His plea of 'do not disturb' referred to his total paralysis, his utter inability to cope with the case-load that day by day grew heavier.

The Forrest murder was at the bottom of the pile; next to it though not necessarily connected, was the sabotaged Piper. The single-page file on the pair of ladies' shoes stolen from the Ambarrukmo hotel, was small fry, but he couldn't even deal with that. In front of him lay details of the latest calamity. The whole barracks ransacked the night before, and every single piece of portable ammunition, together with an army truck to carry off the spoils. It was not just the theft that worried him. It was the purpose of it all. It must have been an inside job. It was known that PKI sympathisers had infiltrated the army, and the movement didn't want the haul for party games. Some big mission was being planned, and with last night's theft they had already won half their battle. But what worried him most of all was his part, or more accurately, his non-part, in the investigation. The whole operation had been handled, or rather, mis-handled by a handful of beat coppers. Taken unawares, and totally disorganised, the raid was practically over before they'd even reached the scene, and the only shred of evidence he was able to get out of them was that the lorry had taken off in the direction of Mount Merapi.

It was a useless clue. Between Djogja and Merapi alone were at least twenty villages, all riddled with PKI sympathisers, and a fine-toothed comb through all of them, Isani knew from weary experience, would yield nothing. But how in God's name, he tortured himself, had he managed not to be there, And who had laced his drink and that of his deputy, in order to keep them out of the way. Once more and for the hundredth time, he itemised a post-mortem on the Brownlow party. He remembered it with a great sense of enjoyment, but not one detail could he recall. He couldn't even manage a guest list. All he knew was that he had loved everybody.

He thought of Oyung. If his own indisposition of last night was ever investigated by higher authorities, it would be linked undoubtedly with his parental dilemma. He decided to start work on a cover-up. He unlocked his door, and called for Kapotto.

Kapotto had barricaded himself in his office with exactly the same thoughts. He was relieved when Isani called for him. He too was concerned for his cover-up, and it had to be worked out jointly. Their two stories had to tally. He sat down opposite Isani.

'I don't know,' Kapotto said, before Isani had a chance to say anything. 'I don't remember a single thing. I know that I came to the hotel to tell you about the raid. I thought you were drunk. Somebody gave me a glass.'

'Who?' Isani pleaded.

'I don't know. I don't even remember if it was a man or a woman. Everything else is a blur after that. Perhaps I may have danced with your wife. But perhaps I only dreamed it. I woke up at five o'clock. There were a few people still asleep on the floor, including a waiter. But I didn't know any of them. I came straight to the office. You had just arrived.'

'You remember more than I,' Isani said. 'My wife woke me up and took me home. I remember seeing some bodies on the floor, but I thought I was ill and imagining things. At home I had a cold shower. I tried to remember, but I had forgotten everything.'

They were silent. Then Kapotto said, 'Djakarta will want an explanation.'

'We must tell them the truth,' Isani decided. 'It was not our fault. We were at an official reception. We are obliged to be represented at such functions. There was a conspiracy. It had all been planned in advance. The raid was to coincide with the reception, and the drinks were tampered with. Our first job,' he said, a little more perky now, with the relief of having someone to share his problems with, 'is to get hold of a complete guest list.'

His telephone rang. He was loathe to answer it. He feared it might be from Djakarta and he wanted at least a few hours to himself to investigate. They would lay less blame on his non-appearance at the scene of the crime if he was able to offer some concrete clues to an arrest. 'You answer it, Kapotto,' he said.

Gingerly his deputy picked up the receiver and listened. 'It's your secretary,' he said. 'Mrs Brownlow's outside. She must see you urgently.'

'And I'll be very pleased to see her,' Isani said. He ordered Kapotto to remain. She was no doubt coming to him with information, and he wanted his deputy to be witness.

He was astonished at her appearance. A striking pallor seemed to add to her beauty. Her one hand seemed almost glued to the side of her face, keeping her head upright, as if fighting an overwhelming desire to sleep. Kapotto drew up a chair.

'Make yourself comfortable,' Isani said, and seeing her distress, 'can I get you something?' He spoke into the desk phone. 'Bring Mrs Brownlow a mint-tea,' he said. He looked at her, wondering what was so disturbing her.

'He's gone,' he heard her say.

Isani looked at Kapotto. 'Who's gone?' he asked her.

'My husband.'

Isani was slightly irritated. He had enough on his plate without having to act as a marriage counsellor. "Did you have a quarrel?' he said.

'You don't understand,' she said, irritated at his gross misinterpretation. He ought to know it simply wasn't English to go to the police with a domestic disagreement. 'He's been kidnapped,' she fairly shouted at him.

'Oh, my God,' Isani said under his breath, as he saw his in-tray of cases-pending leap to Merapi heights. 'How d'you know?' he said. 'Is there a ransom note?'

'No,' she said. 'He's just disappeared.'

'Take it easy,' Isani said, handing her the mint-tea that had just been brought. 'Tell it me slowly, step by step.'

'I woke up in bed this morning,' she said. 'I don't remember how I got there. Something happened last night at the reception. I don't remember anything.'

'It happened to us all, Mrs Brownlow. None of us remember.' He saw a small measure of relief on her face, and he told her of the night's raid, and how there'd been a conspiracy to keep the forces of law and order out of action. He was investigating he said. 'But please go on.'

'I woke up,' she said, 'at about nine o'clock, and he simply wasn't there. I looked in all the rooms. Emily was already up, but she hadn't seen him. They were cleaning the suite, but none of the cleaners had seen him either. All his clothes were there, his passport, his briefcase, even his toothbrush. Then the office rang and asked where he was. I know he's been kidnapped,' she was almost crying. 'He would never have walked out, just like that. Why should he?' she shouted at Isani as if he were cross-examining her. 'We were so happy together.'

Isani went over to her chair and touched her arm. 'I'm sure he's all right Mrs Brownlow. If he'd really been kidnapped, there'd be some word from those who took him away. There'd be some ransom demand. Something. It's more likely that he went for a long walk to clear his head.'

'In his evening suit?' she said, annoyed by such a stupid suggestion.

'Perhaps,' Isani said, but with little conviction. 'Your best place now is at the hotel. You must wait at the telephone. I'll send my wife over to be with you. I will see you later in the day. I shall be taking statements at the hotel.' He saw her out gently, then turning to Kapotto, he said, 'Get over to Brownlow's office. Get hold of last night's guest list. And if you can, go through his personal files, discreetly, of course. His disappearance worries me. Of course he didn't take a walk.' Then, almost to himself, 'I hope to God,' he said, 'that he's still alive.'

The whole day was spent checking on the guest list and the staff personnel at the Ambarrukmo. All the guests told the same story. Apart from an afterglow of extreme contentment, they remembered nothing. And none of them was too anxious to talk about it. In the sober light of morning, with all their defences well back in place, they regarded it as faintly sinful that they should have so disported themselves and they did not want such pleasure investigated.

The hotel staff was no more helpful. Those at the reception desk had noted nothing amiss in any of the arrivals, and they presumed that whoever took the lift to the Brownlow suite had been invited. It did not occur to the desk clerk to mention the wheel-chair guest. A wheel-chair was a frequent sight in Djogja, and nothing to comment on. And he had seen them both arriving and departing. Thoroughly respectable.

The waiters at the party had a harder time using the drink for cover. For why, after all, were they drinking in the first place? 'Mrs Brownlow herself told me to join the party,' one of them said, and all then made use of the same hostess licence. At the end of the day, there was no progress. Brownlow had not shown up, and the telephone hadn't rung. It was all beyond Isani's comprehension. He spent the evening with his wife and Belinda, in some vain attempt to comfort her. He noticed that Burhan seemed very much at home in the suite, and he was glad that at least Emily had someone to divert her. She kept asking for news of her Daddy, for Belinda had been honest with her, needing to share her fears with someone as close. As they were leaving, Burhan tugged at Isani's sleeve. He took the boy to one side. 'Yes?' he said.

'I must find him,' Burhan said. 'Tell me go anywhere. You know I know everybody and everything not good in Djogja.'

Isani ruffled the boy's head. 'We must wait,' he said. 'Tomorrow, we *must* hear something.'

But they didn't. Nor the next day. And when, after a week, there was still no word of Brownlow's whereabouts, either in this world or elsewhere, Isani had no notion of where to turn. The contents of what was left of the punch had been analysed, and had been found to contain, not surprisingly, a high content of hash. That would account perhaps for amnesia, but it was unlikely that he could wander about in a dinner-jacket, unnoticed for a whole week. Perhaps he wasn't in Djogja at all, in which case he had been spirited away. But by whom? Isani had the uneasy feeling that he was part of the lorry load of equipment that was taken off in the direction of Merapi. It was the first time that Isani made the connection, and he hastened to share it with Kapotto, and with Belinda too, to nourish her fading hopes. 'We must go all out to find that truck,' he said.

A week later, with still no word from Brownlow, they *did*

find it. It had been abandoned in a paddy field about twenty miles from Djogja. The village children had taken it over, and in the process of using it as an adventure playground, they had covered it with their fingerprints. Apart from a few carved wooden toys, the truck was empty, and all tracks from it had been smudged by the swarming children. There was nothing to do but to take it back to the barracks. It was a humiliating return.

Kapotto still believed that Brownlow had been abducted along with the rifles, but Isani somehow had lost enthusiasm for that idea. And one day, when he was sitting at his desk, he had another thought. And it was a terrible one. So terrible, that he was afraid even to think it to himself. So he took it with him to the club, where he was sure it would prove itself ridiculous.

But the very first remark he heard on reaching the bar assured him that perhaps it was not so ridiculous after all. It's true the remark came from von Henkel, so it was bound to be ill-conceived and malicious. Nevertheless, to have thought of it at all, even out of spite, gave it credence.

Von Henkel pulled him aside as he approached the bar. 'It's very strange,' von Henkel said.

'It's baffling,' Isani agreed. 'It baffles everybody. No note. No telephone call. Nothing. And it's almost three weeks.'

'I didn't mean that,' von Henkel said. 'I meant it's strange. The timing.'

'What exactly *do* you mean?' Isani was nervous at the echo of his own thoughts.

'Well,' von Henkel was working it out, 'a girl gets murdered. No clues, nothing. And Brownlow disappears. Makes you think, doesn't it? Come, I'll buy you a drink.'

'Impossible,' Isani said. 'Brownlow? For what reason?' Now that von Henkel had voiced the same suspicion, Isani saw it as pointless, and he abandoned it happily. He looked round at the Club members. Most of them had been guests at the party. He began to resent them all, to resent their presence, while Brownlow his friend, and probably the most honourable of them all, was nowhere to be found. He decided to leave the Club and go straight to the hotel. Poor Belinda.

On his way out he passed by the billiard-table. Stern was there, playing snooker, and losing to his son. They were laughing together. Father and son, Isani thought, that's how it should be. He remembered how he'd taught Oyung the rules of angling, and how when he was older they'd spent whole Sundays together on the river bank. For some reason, he put his arm round Richard's shoulder, then looking at Stern, he smiled. 'It's tough for fathers to lose their sons,' he said.

He found Belinda seated on the couch close to the balcony. Her hand rested on the phone-table by her side. She did not look up when Isani came in. Her eyes seemed fixed on the phone, willing it to ring. He placed himself in a chair within her eye-line. 'You look tired,' he said. Since Brownlow had disappeared, she had aged considerably. Yet her appearance was flawless. Her dress, her make-up, her hair-style were immaculate. It was is if she wanted to be prepared for Brownlow's return at any time.

'I'm tired,' she said. 'I don't sleep very well.'

'Are you taking something to help?'

'I don't want to,' she said. 'I don't want to oversleep. I want to be awake and waiting when he comes back. Did you come to tell me anything?' she asked timidly.

He shook his head. What could he say to her? What piece of news or stray hearsay that would give her a glimmer of hope?

She looked him straight in the eye. And very calmly, she said, 'I think he's dead.'

'No,' Isani said, because although the same thought crossed and re-crossed his mind, he dared not foster it, for personal as well as for professional reasons. 'I don't believe it,' he said.

'If he were alive, he would have sent a message. Somehow or another, he would have let me know.'

'To my mind,' Isani said, 'as a result of that party, he's lost his memory, and he's wandering about somewhere.'

'But it's three weeks,' Belinda's voice broke. 'Someone must have noticed him. A man wandering about in a dinner-jacket.'

'But he may be anywhere. He may have been given a lift somewhere.' 'Given a lift' had less dire overtones than 'kidnapped'. 'There are parts of Central Java, even around Djogja, where there are no people for miles around.' His voice tailed off, drowning in his own lack of conviction.

'I don't know what to do,' Belinda said.

'Have you thought of going back to England?' Isani said, then
gently adding, 'for a short break, I mean.'

She shook her head. 'No. I'll stay till he comes. If I ever leave
this island, it will be because in my heart I have buried him.'
She began to cry, elegantly and softly. Isani shifted in his chair.
He was glad when the door opened and the waiter brought her
supper on a tray. 'Will you have something?' she said to Isani.
'I don't like eating alone.'

He was not hungry, but nevertheless, he ordered a light
supper.

'What's the next move?' Belinda said.

Isani was silent. How could he tell her? The next move was
scheduled for the morning, when divers would go down to the
river bed on a search. It was a last resort. Anything pertinent
found in such a search would be final, and Isani hoped that
like all his other investigations, it would prove fruitless. 'I have
scouts alerted all over the island,' Isani said, for though it was
untrue, he had to say something.

'What about the television?' Belinda had suggested a television
appeal shortly after Brownlow had disappeared. The publication
of his photo in all the papers, and a plea for people to come
forward with information. But Isani had disagreed. His decision
had been backed by the authorities in Java. They did not want
to overblow Brownlow's disappearance, else it might become a
major political issue, and they didn't wish to reveal to the
possible kidnappers that they'd landed a pretty fair catch. Scot-
land Yard had been kept informed from the very beginning,
and they too had insisted on a low profile of the case. Isani
was in favour of giving time, time. If Brownlow hadn't disappeared on account of the Patricia Forrest affair, and that now
seemed to him more and more unlikely, then the PKI had nab-
bed him, and any media publicity would scotch all hope of his
return. There would be no informers, on pain of their lives, and
the movement, alerted to Brownlow's standing, might decide
that they'd caught too big a fish for their appetite, and would
hastily dispose of it. 'I'm not in favour of television,' Isani said.
'It's still possible that it's a political kidnapping, and they're
taking their time. They have something up their sleeves. The
theft of the ammunition points to that. They could be keeping
him on ice as bargaining power.' As he spoke, the idea seemed

to him more and more feasible. But it required a thorough comb-through of the island for PKI hide-outs. He thought again of Oyung. If only he knew where he was.

The waiter brought his supper, and they ate in silence. Isani heard the bedroom door creak open behind him. He turned around. Emily barefoot, in a nightdress, rocked there half asleep. 'I thought I heard Daddy,' she said.

Belinda picked her up and took her back to bed. Isani shuddered. Only a few nights ago, when he'd had a late caller, his wife had done the same as Emily. 'I thought I heard Oyung,' she had said. He'd helped her back to bed, with the same soothing words that he now heard from Emily's room. They had much in common, he and this English family. The fear, the anger, and the pumping heart, and the still small hours of darkness that gnawed like rats on all one's shrinking hopes. He thought of both of them, Oyung and Brownlow, seeing them both as hostages. He prayed with all his heart that both were alive. That was all in his life that mattered.

Chapter Sixteen

When Brownlow had come to his senses, he was sweating. He had woken in the heat of the midday sun, and his mouth was rough with thirst. He knew he must get some water. He got up, wondering why he was wearing a dinner-jacket, then he looked about him and saw quite clearly that he had never been in this place before. But with acute survival instincts, he shelved all his questions until he could find water. He looked around. The great landmark of Merapi was to his right. All that meant was that he was still in Java, and probably too, in Central Java, in which area one could see Merapi from almost any point. He knew, that due to the mountain's unruly behaviour, there would be little habitation in its environs, but he had learned that at the foot of the mountain, the refugee villagers would return and re-settle, for the lava enriched and charmed the soil. So he strode out in that direction, in search of water and habitation.

The land was flat, a poor omen for the presence of water, unless there were some rice-paddies in the area. But there was no village in sight, so it was unlikely that there was any cultivation. He walked on, not allowing himself to think of anything but his search for water. Once his thirst was assuaged, he would sit down and assess his situation. He listened to his watch. It was still ticking and he was grateful for that, for it would mark for him the passage of time, hours, perhaps days, perhaps even longer. In his mind, with what little thought he allowed himself, he envisaged a long and perilous return.

He'd been walking for an hour, not slowing his pace, when he heard it, the trickling of water piercing the silence. He stopped and listened. It was steady and prolonged. Wherever it was, there would be enough to slake his thirst. His stomach heaved in anticipation.

He saw it almost immediately. A stream, narrow but long, and the water falling generously from a pipe that was buried in the earth. It was the source of an old irrigation system that the farmers had used before the mountain had taken over. Now the Merapi stones formed the stream's bed. He would follow it. It must lead to some form of husbandry. But first he stripped. His excitement at the prospect of immersion and slaking his parched throat easily postponed any thought of his present circumstances. He lay on the bed of the stream. It was deep enough to cover his whole body. The water was cold and clear, and he submerged his head, opening his mouth to drink. Then he rested his head on the bank's side, his body lilting to the stream's flow, and he took stock of his condition.

What he was most conscious of was a feeling of enormous well-being that was only marginally to do with his slaked thirst and cooling body. He had a sense of enormous relief. He recalled how, since arriving in Java, he had, from time to time, been assaulted by spasms of fear. Now that fear had found its cause. He had been kidnapped, or rather abandoned, since he had no guards. That niggling presentment had proclaimed itself. He need not be afraid any more.

He looked at his dinner-jacket, neatly folded on the bank. He must start from there and try to make sense of it all. He'd had a cold shower in his suite, though it was nothing as refreshing as this present immersion. Belinda had laid his suit out on the bed, together with his cummerbund and tie. He remembered coming out of the shower and zipping up the back of her dress with his wet hands. He tried to remember what she'd been wearing. The colour had gone, and the style, and only the long backzip remained. He dressed, then took a glass of milk to Emily's bedroom. She was reading the *Ramayana* story, he remembered, in a book full of pop-up pictures, a present from Burhan. He had promised to take them both to the Prambanam temple, for at least one night of the four performances of the legend, and she was hurrying to finish the book in time. Burhan had told her the story many times, of Rama's search for his beloved Sita whom the wicked King Ravana had kidnapped. Burhan saw himself in Rama's role, rescuing Emily from all perilous paths. Sometimes he even called her Sita, but quickly retrieved the word, for it was frowned upon to use the names of the gods in common parlance. Whatever happens, Brownlow said to himself, I have to get back to Djogja in time for the *Ramayana*.

He remembered then that while he was in Emily's room, the first guest arrived. He heard Isani's voice, and his wife's timid greeting, and he had hurried back to his room to finish dressing. More guests began to arrive, but apart from Dr Boxham, who was brought by von Henkel, he could recall no one else. He'd had a glass of punch with Boxham, and that was all. Just a sea of unknowable faces, much laughter and a sense of care-free enjoyment. Since his last clear thought had been about the glass of punch, he concluded that he must have been drugged, abducted from the party and left in the field. He couldn't remember a car ride or any form of transport, so he must have been well and truly comatosed before leaving the hotel. It was all a mystery. He couldn't imagine why anyone wanted him out of the way, and unless his abductors intended to return to the field, there was no move to hold him hostage. He couldn't understand it. And strangely enough he was not curious about it. It might just have been a schoolboy prank, and all he had to do was to make his way home to Belinda and Emily.

He was loath to get out of the stream. The sun was at its highest, and it was folly to walk around bare-headed. He would use his cummerbund as a hat. He felt almost Boy Scoutish in his adventure. In many ways. he'd never been as happy in his life. He slithered up the bank and stood naked in the sun to dry. Then he dressed, covered his head, and set out like an explorer.

For the whole day he followed the bank of the stream, confident that it would lead him to habitation. Then just as darkness was falling, the stream quite suddenly dried up. For the first time, he was conscious of hunger, but he knew that as long as he had water, he could go for days without food. He was loathe to leave his water supply, and he could find nothing in which to carry it. So he decided to bed down for the night where the stream ended. He would need all his strength for what he now acknowledged would be an ordeal. He pulled some bracken off a stunted tree a few yards distant, and with it he made what he hoped would be a protection from the night air and the morning sun. And within earshot of the water, he lay beneath his shelter and conquered his hunger with sleep.

So ended Brownlow's first day in the wilderness. Or what he

thought was his first day. In fact, it was his third, for he had slept for two days after the party, waking occasionally, but too bleary-eyed to take stock of his whereabouts. He was more tired than he knew. His long sleep, and his exposure to the sun and the present day's march had drained all his energies, and on the following morning when he woke, he could barely stir. He crawled to the stream hoping to revive himself in its cool flow and he did indeed feel a little better. It was still early, and the sun was low. He wanted to make an early start. He had high hopes of reaching the hotel by nightfall. He walked a little way and found an old coconut husk on the path. It was a hopeful sign. There were no coconut trees in sight, so someone, at some time or another, had passed there. He picked up the shell, prising it out of the earth. It had obviously lain there for some time. He went back to the stream and filled it. If he were careful, it would hold a day's supply. But it was an added burden, and Brownlow had to face the fact that he was feeling far from well. He went on walking, sustaining himself with thoughts of Belinda and Emily, of his welcome home, of a cool and long shower, of a small aperitif on the balcony, of a light but savoury supper. And of sleep. It was sleep he wanted more than anything and he had to fight the temptation to lie down and give in to it once and for all. He walked. His watch told him it was midday. Lunch time, he thought. He sipped from the coconut shell, and not daring to rest, he went on his way.

By late afternoon, the path began to thicken, punctuated occasionally by clumps of bushes. Then trees appeared, a small forest interspersed with clearings. It was cool inside, and dark, and Brownlow decided to end his day's march. He sipped once more from his coconut shell, then fixed it securely against a tree. He covered it with his shirt. He was not worried. He was too tired for that. Neither was he hungry any more. When he was a boy, with minor complaints, his mother had always said that everything would be better in the morning. He hadn't thought of his mother for many years. She had died young, when he was still at Eton. At this recall of his schooldays, he heard himself humming the school song. He knew that for some reason, that specific memory was important, that somehow it had something to do with his present predicament. But he was too tired. He would deal with it in the morning.

But when morning came he didn't have the strength to deal with anything. His mind was fuzzed over, and its only areas of clarity were concerned with the primal need of survival. In the growing light, Brownlow saw a round object on the ground. Many of them, obviously fallen from the trees. He crawled towards them. Bread-fruit. Edible. Better cooked, but raw would do. He put it under his foot and stepped on it to crush its rind. And with his fingers he scooped out the pulp. He smiled as he looked round at the rich harvest. His survival was assured. He sipped from his coconut shell and steadied himself on to his feet. Carrying his half-empty water bag, he slowly stepped through the forest. He looked at his watch. Ten o'clock. The sun outside the forest was blazing, but he felt none of it. Only its filtered rays through the branches and their clusters of swollen fruit. All this food going to waste, he thought. In this country where thousands die every year from starvation. Why didn't the UN do something about that, he thought. Teach them to use their own rich resources instead of flooding their land with Coca Cola substitutes. And so he was reminded of his job, and the term, Ponsonby Post, rang a faint and familiar bell. He reflected on his line of thought, and was surprised that he'd never had such ideas before, but even as he tried to recall them in order to take them further, they blurred and lost all thread.

He went on walking. The top of Merapi was covered in cloud, and it seemed no nearer now than it had been when he had begun walking. He looked at his watch. Five past ten. Yet it seemed to him that he'd been walking for hours, for days even, and that perhaps when last he'd looked at his watch at ten in the morning, it had been days ago. He decided he must keep a calendar or lose his mind. He reckoned he'd been on the road for three days, so he made three tears in the front tail of his shirt. He would make a tear each day on waking, and thus time his lonely wanderings. As he walked, he had flashes of anxiety, fears for his health, for his body's endurance, and for a split second, whether he would survive it at all. But they lasted only moments. For the most part his light-headedness induced by hunger, gave him a sense of near-euphoria, and from time to time, he even sang snippets of long-forgotten songs. His old school song was one of them, and again he sensed it was an important lead to some past event, but he couldn't associate it, like some well-known quotation whose context is on the tip of one's tongue.

He was out of the forest now, and the sun beat down on his cummerbund head. He wanted water, but he saw that his stock was very low. He had enough instinct to save it, but the going was slow now, very slow, and the sweat was sticking to his body. He thought he should undo his top trouser button so there was no constriction at his waist. But as he undid it, he felt no change. His trousers had left his shrinking waist-line with inches to spare. Well, he thought, I needed to lose a little weight, and for no reason at all, he thought again of his mother. She was sitting in a deckchair on the Promenade des Anglais at Nice. That's what she loved best, during their summers, to sit reading and looking about her on the promenade, while his father took him into the sea. He'd often seen her in a bathing-suit, but it was never wet. She would sun herself by the hotel pool. She was full of oils and sun-smells and dark glasses and white towels. He felt her very close, and he stretched out his arms to hold her. As he did so, he dropped his coconut shell. He stood still, and watched the water spill over his shoes, following each vital drop of it, until they exploded on the heat-racked soil. He tried to quicken his pace, but he felt his legs weakening. He was determined to go on until darkness fell. He had to get to the Ambarrukmo. There was a man there, a visitor. What was his name? He'd come a long way to see something special. Boxham. Who was Boxham? He walked on. Suddenly he was convinced that if he walked a little longer he would reach his club in time to have lunch with Featherstone. And perhaps they could spend the afternoon at Lord's. Yes, he must hurry, he thought. Mustn't keep Featherstone waiting. And he hurried, in a zig-zag path, his steps unsure, his mind wandering.

It was still light when his body surrendered. His legs simply refused to take him further. He dragged himself on his belly to a clump of vegetation and in its almost laughable shade, he slept till morning. When he woke, without trying to remember his name, he knew he had forgotten it. He saw himself in wide open spaces, but he had no notion of where they were. It was hot, so he thought it must be summer. And that was all.

He was thirsty. There was only one thing he had to do in his life, and that was to find water. He shook his legs to order them to work. And miraculously they held him as he shuffled onwards. He wondered why his shirt was torn, and considered it ill-mannered for a man to be seen walking abroad in such shabby attire. He didn't know what the world was coming to. It was none of his business anyway. His only business was to find water.

His legs carried him on, but he did not feel them as part of his body. In fact, all his limbs seemed to have achieved a separateness, and all he felt responsible for was his parched mouth. When the dark came, his eyes demanded sleep, and at daybreak, his legs took him off again. He walked and he slept, and he slept and he walked, guarding his craving mouth like a precious jewel. Once, when his legs began to carry him, he thought it was still dark, and for many many hours the light only came in flashes. And sometimes his eyes would insist on closing and he could have sworn it was still daylight. He wondered what all his body-parts were up to, and sometimes he laughed at them because they were so incompetent. Still he obeyed them, as long as they let him take care of his mouth.

And for four days, he watched his legs and listened to his eyes, until he knew that the farce must surely be drawing to its close. He put his hands to his face. He tried not to think again of his mother, because he knew that her bright vision could only be a prelude to his own demise. With his fingers he felt the soft growth of hair on his chin, and the strange crusts that had formed on his cheeks. He thought he was already dead, fossilised, and possibly had been for some time, and that this place was limbo, or a dress-rehearsal for hell. He looked down at his tuxedo, and he was glad that he was dressed for the occasion.

Then he saw just in front of him in the fading light a strange shape. Two triangles soldered together, the one slightly shorter than the other. For some reason the shape pleased him. He thought it would serve him well as a tomb. He managed to reach the small triangle, and he lay in the shade of its massive hulk. But he had lain himself down on a slope, and with no strength to hold his body firm, he slithered downwards, rolling, rolling and slowly easing to a stop. He considered that he had taken an overlong time to die, and this, he prayed, must surely be the end. Then a strong light shone into his face, and he thought that he had entered heaven.

Oyung called a companion and together they carried him inside. They laid him on a bunk, and the others gathered round and looked at him.

'What shall we do?' one of them said, mindful, as they all were, of the dangers of having a stranger in their company.

'We'll save him first,' Roschun said, 'and then we'll think about it.'

Siswamarto got water and put it to his lips. Another gently peeled the clothing from his body. There were suppurating sores on his feet, and open sun-wounds on his face. But despite all that, he had the look still of a gentleman. They looked for signs of identity in his pockets. A silk handkerchief monogrammed with an 'H' was all they could find. Apart from that the pockets were empty. The label on his dress-suit jacket said 'London' so they presumed that he was English and probably a tourist. Meanwhile they treated him as best they could. Their first-aid equipment catered for battle injuries. They had nothing for sunburn, exposure and possible amnesia. So they washed him and let him sleep. They took it in turns to watch over him, aware that they were saddled with a responsibility that they would have to face, and that the way they might deal with it could be as unpleasant as it was inevitable. Some amongst the men hoped that he would die, but despite that, all were intent on his recovery.

When and if he survived, it would be Oyung's job to question him. Oyung's schooling in Australia had given him an almost fluent English, and he was rather excited at the possibility of using it once again. With his fingers, he rubbed a little brandy inside Brownlow's lips. 'You'll be all right, Mister,' he said, and he decided that he mustn't get to like the man, because it was on the cards that they couldn't keep him. Yet he couldn't stop looking at him, and for some reason that he couldn't understand, he was suddenly very homesick. He wished Burhan would come again and give him all the news. He was suddenly anxious for his younger brother and the bike that was too big for him. He tried not to think of his mother, and as he bent down, hiding his face to wipe away the tears, Roschun, who had been observing him from across the room, put an arm on his shoulder. 'What about a game of dominoes?' he said.

He brought the counters over to the side of Brownlow's bunk.

They played silently for a while. Then, 'What will we do with him?' Oyung said.

'We must wait and see.'

'Perhaps he'll join our army,' Oyung said, his eyes sparkling with a possible solution.

'It's not his struggle,' Roschun said.

They went on playing. Occasionally they put water or brandy to Brownlow's cracked lips. 'What will we do with him then?' Oyung insisted.

Roschun said nothing. He looked at his dominoes, then made a determined move. 'Your turn,' he said.

'For god's sake,' Oyung shouted, 'why don't we do it now?'

'We must get him well,' Roschun said.

Oyung stroked Brownlow's brow. It was cool. He's getting better, he thought, and he looked at him with enormous pity.

Chapter Seventeen

Over the next few weeks, many things did not happen in Djogja. No clues were forthcoming on the Forrest murder. The sabotaged plane was still a mystery. The raid on the barracks had reached stalemate, and the Brownlow case likewise. Isani's in-tray was a nagging pile of negatives. Every day he went to his office and put out the odd lethargic feeler of investigation, but over the weeks he had lost his appetite for all the unsolved mysteries. Except for the Brownlow affair. That unaccountable disappearance nagged at him day after day. He didn't know any longer where to turn, what avenues to investigate. He got up and paced the room. Staring at his feet, it struck him that his boots were very dirty, and it was a good enough reason to go and see Burhan.

He found him at his stand. The boy smiled less and less nowadays. Emily cried a lot and it hurt him to see her so pained. But when he saw Isani's boot, his face lit with hope. 'You have news?' he said.

'None. That's why I'm here. What am I going to do?'

It was a strange question from a Chief of Police to a mere boy whose whole life-style was a complicated operation that steered rigidly clear of the law. 'I don't know. If I could find something for you ...'

'I think it must be drugs,' Isani said. He bent his mouth to Burhan's ear, while Burhan polished the legal boot with fury. Isani straightened. 'I'm not asking you for names,' he said. 'I want . you to go to him, whoever he is. I want you to find out if what I think is the truth.'

'I will need money, sir,' Burhan said.

'How much?'

'The ticket to Djakarta.'

It was an awful lot of money to pay for a shoe-shine, but

Isani gladly handed it over. As he walked back to his office, he noticed that one boot was still dirty.

Burhan went straight to the Ambarrukmo. Emily would be there. For the last week or so, she had stopped going to school. He found her sitting with her mother at the telephone table. He told her that he would be away for a few days, and by now they knew better than to ask why or where. But by the sharp and hopeful glint in his eye, they assumed he was going on Brownlow business. He told them that he knew everything was going to be all right. He hesitated before leaving, then he ran to Belinda and threw his arms around her. She embraced him and he disentangled himself quickly, and not daring to look at her, he fled.

Isani hoped he'd done the right thing. But even if it wasn't right, it was better than doing nothing. It had often occurred to him during the course of his police duties, especially when he was working in the Drug Squad, that a diplomat would make a superb smuggler. Immune from Customs search, he could import whatever he wanted, and in whatever amount. It was a long shot, he knew, but it was vaguely possible that Brownlow had been taken for this very purpose. It was true his passport and diplomatic papers were still at the hotel, but he could, under threat, be forced to apply for others on some pretext, so that he might travel on UN business. Between Djakarta and Bangkok, via Singapore, there was a known cocaine run. It was just possible, he tried to convince himself. If anyone could find out, it was Burhan.

That night, Burhan caught the Surabaya express on its return to Djakarta. At Djogja station, he acted as a porter, loading tourist bags into freight. Just one carrying job in order to get on the train. Then lodged between two large cases, he travelled unseen and freight, patting the wad of money in his pocket. When he got to Djakarta, he would buy a present for Emily.

During the journey he thought about Isani's idea. It didn't seem very probable to him. He knew his Djakarta friend used runners. And some, it was true, were diplomats, but Embassy and UN underlings were two a penny in Djakarta. Had he exhausted all possibilities there that he had to draw on his old hunting-ground in Djogja? He was looking forward to seeing him again. It was over a year since he had seen him last. He knew it was a year because he'd left just after the kite-fighting championships. He'd been promoted to Djakarta, and Isani, who had then been his deputy, had profited too from his move. In those days, the police department often called upon Burhan's underground services. But under Isani's rule, he had been dropped. Isani must be pretty desperate, Burhan concluded. He had no notion of whom in Djakarta Burhan was going to see. Isani would have crumbled if he'd known it was his erstwhile boss. And jogging along between the cases, Burhan thought that the world was a very strange place indeed.

At Djakarta, he portered his way out through the ticket-barrier and made straight for the Central Police Station. He'd never been to Djakarta before and it frightened him. To be able to walk for a whole half hour without meeting a familiar face, or giving a friendly greeting, made him feel like a foreigner. In the market, he bought a short skewer of cooked meat and a paper bowl of rice, and walking along, he ate his breakfast. He didn't know where the station was, and he was loathe to ask anybody for fear of drawing attention to himself, and as a result, perhaps jeopardising the status of his contact. His role was so well known in the streets of Djogja, he couldn't imagine that his repute had not spread to the capital. He knew the station must be in the centre of the town and he made his way to Simpang Square. He was fortunate to arrive as the policeman on point duty was being relieved. Swinging his baton, he strode fearlessly through the traffic and Burhan followed him. And as he expected, he led him straight to the police station.

He went up to the desk. 'I want to see the Chief,' he said. The policeman on desk duty peered over to gauge the height of the visitor. Small, unarmed, barefoot. No threat.

'What for?' he asked,

'I've got a message from his sister in Djogja.'

'What's your name?'

'Burhan.'

The man conveyed the information through a telephone and then directed Burhan to a door on the right along the corridor.

Burhan knocked, as was fitting. Matoredjo himself came to the door. He ushered him in with little greeting. He seemed nervous. The sudden appearance of Burhan could only mean a warning. 'What's gone wrong?' he said.

'Isani's on to you,' Burhan gave him for openers. During the train journey from Djogja, he'd cooked up a feasible tale for Matoredjo, and now he spun it out with innocent concern. 'He knows you've got Brownlow, and he knows what you're using him for. He doesn't want to get you into trouble. So he wants him back quickly and quietly.'

'I don't believe you,' Matoredjo said. He knew Isani well enough. The man, with his Australian training, was incorruptible. If he had the slightest evidence of his former boss's shenanigans, he would issue no threats, no warnings, he would offer no deals.

'It's true,' Burhan said. He'd been prepared for Matoredjo's incredulity. 'If it were anyone else, he'd shop you, but Brownlow's a friend and a very close friend, and he wants him back and he wants him alive.'

The sweat poured from Matoredjo's forehead. Burhan was glowing inside him. He felt sure that Brownlow was within his grasp. But Matoredjo's sweat had nothing to do with Brownlow. 'Who told him?' he shouted.

Burhan shrugged. He was not prepared for that line of inquiry. Matoredjo walked over to the window. He was frightened. For almost a year he'd had it good. Almost too good. Under his superb law-cover, he'd set up a regular run between Bangkok, Singapore and Djakarta, and there was a growing possibility that he could get into the Hong Kong route too. He needed another six months at the most. Then he'd have enough money to emigrate with his family to America. If Isani were truly on to him, it was the end. '*How* could he know?' he asked Burhan again. And again Burhan shrugged, hoping that he wouldn't persist with the question, or worse, perhaps suspect that Burhan himself was the informer. 'If I go down, you're going down too, Burhan,' Matoredjo said.

'He didn't get it from me,' Burhan was very angry. 'You know that I never say anything. Never. Not a word. Not a name, not a date.'

'I know,' Matoredjo came over to him. 'I'm sorry.'

'In any case,' Burhan said, wanting to get the business over and done with, 'he'll say nothing about it. Just let Brownlow go.'

'Who's Brownlow?'

Burhan swallowed. 'The man you're using.' He stressed every syllable.

'Who is he?' Matoredjo said. 'I don't know a Brownlow.'

'The UN man,' Burhan was patient. 'Hugh Brownlow. He disappeared from Djogja nearly three months ago.'

'I haven't got him,' Matoredjo said, and he was clearly telling the truth. He laughed. 'I don't need to kidnap anybody. Djakarta's swarming with diplomatic volunteers. If they're not working for the CIA they're working for me. Sometimes they're greedy and they work for both.' Just as Burhan had originally thought.

'Have you any idea who might have taken him?' Burhan pleaded.

'Not one of our lot,' Matoredjo said. 'You ought to know that. Kidnapping's another business altogether. It's usually political. Poor old Isani,' he mused. 'If the PKI have got him, you can write him off. There'll be no informers on that one.'

Burhan got up. There was no point in staying any longer. He would take the express that evening.

'How's my sister?' Matoredjo said.

'I don't know. I haven't seen her for ages.'

'You going back tonight?'

Burhan nodded. Then Matoredjo took a wad of notes from his pocket, and peeled off a number for Burhan. 'This afternoon, you go to the cinema,' he said, 'and buy yourself some supper.'

Burhan took the money and went to the door. The whole journey had been a fool's errand. All he'd made out of it was money. At the door, he turned. 'Isani doesn't know,' he said. 'He doesn't know anything about you. I made it up so you wouldn't mess me around with Brownlow.'

Matoredjo peeled off some more notes. 'You're a sly one,' he said, stuffing them into Burhan's hand. 'But I'm proud of you. You were always my best pupil. When I go to America, you can come with me and work for me there.'

Burhan shook his head. 'I want to go to England,' he said.

'Why England? There's nothing for our kind there.'

Burhan shrugged. That's where he was going to go whatever anybody said. He knew that Brownlow would never come back, and eventually Belinda would take Emily home. He patted the wad of money in his pocket, and he wondered how much was the fare to London.

He hung around the station for most of the afternoon, and

when the Surabaya express began to board, he portered down
the platform. And there in the middle, with no pickers-up, were
three large waiting cases, and a pair of lady's thick legs between.
As always, Burhan's first eye-contact was with shoes. He stared
at them, trying to recall where he had seen them before. Not
only were they familiar but they seemed to speak to him of some
personal involvement. It did not occur to him to look at their
wearer for a clue. That would be cheating. He wanted to find
out the hard way. He knew the shoes so intimately, yet he also
knew that he had never cleaned them. He knew their colour,
their shape, their size. He'd measured them. That's right. He
jumped with glee at the recognition. He'd measured them in the
corridor of the Ambarrukmo Hotel long long ago. Then he
heard someone shouting his name and a pair of strong fat arms
enclosed him. He struggled free, and took in an eyeful of
generous bosom. Then looking up to her face, he saw that
Hildeborg was exactly as he'd remembered her.

'Come with me,' she said. 'I take you to Djogja. I will pay
everything.'

He could have gone for nothing, he knew, as he had come,
and saved her the price of a ticket. But all his life he'd wanted
to sleep on a train and in a proper bed and go to see the film
they showed on every trip to Surabaya. He picked up her cases
and humped them into first class.

There were two beds in the cabin, with enough room between
them to walk in single file. He lifted the cases on to the rack.
He looked down the corridor and saw her giving money to a
steward. Back in the cabin he sat on the bed, and rubbed the
white sparkling sheets between his fingers. He wished he could
tell Emily about his adventure.

Hildeborg was in high spirits. Even before the train pulled out
of the station she was pumping him for news of Djogja. He
played along as best he could, enlarging some items and invent-
ing others, because he didn't mix in her diplomatic circles, and
knew little of their gossip. But he spun out the Brownlow story
and non-developments in the Forrest affair. She was greedy for
news and swallowed each item with relish. She did not ask him
what he was doing in Djakarta, neither did he inquire why she
was coming back. 'The shoes are good,' he said, smiling.

'The best pair I ever had.'

She took him into the dining-car. After dinner it would be cleared and used as a cinema. But for now he was her guest, and mindful of the great favour he had once done her, she was going to do him proud. She ordered a bottle of wine immediately. Burhan had never drunk wine before, and he was anxious to try it, as much as he was looking forward to lying between the white sheets. He had to learn to deal with both, to grow accustomed to them, for both were symbols of his future life with Emily. He was conscious of the differences between them, and colour was the least of them. He knew with absolute certainty that one day he and Emily would be married, and for the first time in his short life, he wished he knew his family name. Suddenly this lack of a patronymic became the only impediment to their eventual union. He would have to invent one and spread it around, drop it on all occasions with flippant familiarity, as if he had lived with it all his life. When he tried to devise a name, he did not think of it in conjunction with Burhan. It was 'Emily what?' that preoccupied him. It had to be a gentle name, melodious, and full of love. For some reason he suddenly thought of Oyung. Oyung was warm and gentle and loving, and if he took his name, he too would be part of his life for ever. Emily Oyung, he tried under his breath, and he heard that it was good. He would launch it on to the streets of Djogja on his return.

In front of him was a high-piled plate of sati. Hildeborg was well into her portion, and the bottle of wine was already half empty. During the whole meal she could be relied upon to open her mouth only to shovel in food, so Burhan was free to dwell on his new-found identity. He ate his food slowly, using the white table napkin between each mouthful. Quite a little gentleman, Hildeborg thought as she looked across at him. She clinked her brimming wine glass to his. 'To the future,' she said, and Burhan saw himself at his wedding. 'Hurry,' she said through his thoughts. 'I want my pudding.'

He put Emily out of his thoughts and concentrated on eating. By now he was pretty deft with a knife and fork, having put in a good deal of practice at the Brownlow suite. But they were still a novelty to him, and he was happier with his fingers or chopsticks.

The pudding was a white custardy affair and very sweet. Hildeborg had two helpings while Burhan still struggled with his first. Then as a favour, she finished it off for him. What with the wine and the food, and his lack of sleep the night before, he was suddenly very tired, but he was determined to keep awake for the film. She insisted that he have some coffee. 'That will wake you up,' she said. 'They're showing a cowboy picture, and you really will like it.'

The waiters were hastily clearing the tables. A screen was erected at the end of the car. The blinds were drawn down and the music blared. Hildeborg drew her chair to Burhan's side and they settled down stretching their feet on the table rungs. During the course of the film, Hildeborg placed her hand on the back of Burhan's neck, her fingers exploring his hair and ears. Burhan wondered whether she was acting a mother role, but having had no experience of such a part, he wasn't sure. She was certainly old enough to be his mother, his grandmother even, but his experience also told him that she was old enough to need a young boy for reassurance. Suddenly he had no appetite for the white sheets. He was too worried about her fingering to concentrate on the picture, but his fatigue was so overwhelming he worried about that too. If he were to fall asleep he would be completely defenceless against her amorous approaches, maternal or otherwise. He propped his eyes open with his fingers. He wished the film would finish. He'd not been able to concentrate on the story-line because of his neck diversion, and all the picture seemed to consist of was horses going one way over a mountain, and other horses, or perhaps they were the same, going in the opposite direction. Occasionally there was a woman on the screen kissing somebody, and Burhan thought that even if he'd understood it all, he would have found it very silly. She was kissing someone now in a close-up that got bigger and bigger, and the music grew louder, and the people in front of him began to put on their jackets. It must be near the end, he thought, and he was glad of it, until he felt her fingers again, and he wished the film would go on for ever.

The screen was taken away and the passengers filed out. In the corridor outside their cabin, Hildeborg waited. 'You get into bed first,' she said, 'and shout when you're ready.'

He obeyed. He rather wished it was the other way round, then he could have called the tune if tune there would be. He stood by the bed, frightened to take off his clothes. He decided to sleep fully dressed, as some form, however useless, of protection. During the night, when all was clear, he could undress under the covers. He let some time elapse before he called, then he screwed up his eyes and pretended to be asleep. He heard her movements beside the bed. He had no desire to look at her, if that's what she feared. In any case, he had turned his face towards the wall. Then to his horror, he felt her warm body rubbing against his back. He sat bolt upright.

'This is *my* bed,' he said, with the loud proprietary tones of one who had paid for it, or could have, had he so wished.

'But it's comfy together,' she pleaded. 'We could have a little fun.'

'I've got the pox,' he shouted with sudden inspiration.

She leapt out of the bed, her naked flesh dripping. Then settling into her own, she said, 'You naughty little boy. But you are a good boy to tell me.' She lay down and very soon was snoring. Burhan smiled, hiding his head under the sheets, so she wouldn't hear him giggling. He took off his clothes and felt the sheets cool against his skin. 'Emily Oyung,' he repeated to himself, and it acted as a lullaby.

They reached Djogja at three o'clock in the morning. It was too early for him to go to the hotel or to report back to Isani. So he humped Hildeborg's cases into a *betchak* and drove along with her. As they neared her home he noticed that she became very nervous, fingering her clothes, and scratching imagined itches on her face. He felt vaguely sorry for her. When they reached her house, he thanked her for the journey's treat, and would have kissed her, had he not labelled himself untouchable. He carried her bags to the porch and went quickly back to the *betchak*. He didn't want to witness her home-coming. Her tail was obviously between her legs, and the consequences of such a bearing were private. He took the *betchak* back to the station, and waited there till it was daylight.

When von Henkel heard his front door bell, he was just getting into bed. He'd had a late night at the Club. There'd been a party for a new arrival, a middle-aged man from England, who had been sent out with no specific briefing and whose sudden appearance sparked off rumours that Brownlow had been written off and that the new arrival was a possible Ponsonby. Von Henkel had left his hat in the *betchak* that he'd taken on his way home, and he thought that this must be the driver bringing it back. He threw on his dressing-gown and went downstairs.

He didn't know whether he was pleased when he saw her, or downright disappointed. He'd never envisaged that she would return, and he'd grown used to being without her. But she gave off the sour smell of defeat, and that pleased him. He was fairly hostile. He kept her on the threshold. 'What do you want?' he said, though it was plain from the three large pieces of luggage at her side that what she wanted was a home and security.

'Can I come in?' she asked timidly.

He opened the door wide enough for her to enter, but he made no move with the luggage. She stood facing him in the hall. His hospitality clearly did not stretch beyond the foyer. So she came straight out with it. 'Hermann,' she said. 'Will you forgive me? Will you take me back?'

He thought about it with very little thought. The prospect was exciting, he realised, but he had to make his own role clear from the start. '*If* I do,' he said, 'and I'm not saying that I will, but *if* I do, there'll be conditions.'

'Anything, Hermann, anything you say.' She was tired and she wanted to go to bed. She wanted home comforts, food and clothing. She was prepared to pay whatever he would ask. She knew her Hermann. He was too small a man to have too high a price.

He went to the door and dragged her cases inside. 'Sit down,' he said, and he rapped it out like an order.

She went into the living-room, and sat with some kind of victim-instinct on a hard-backed chair, positioning herself for the expected interrogation. Von Henkel followed her, switching on all the bright lights, the questions, relevant and otherwise crowding his mind. But she needed no questioning. Even before he sat down, she was well into her confessional.

'Oh, Hermann, it was terrible,' she said. 'He was a swine. He beat me, Hermann, would you believe. I should never have left you. You're much too good for me.'

He listened and relished every syllable as she gave a recital of her battered life with Stanislav.

'I told you so,' he kept saying, whenever she left sufficient gap in her torrent of self-abuse and self-pity.

'He threw me out, Hermann,' she said, indignant. 'And d'you know what he called me?'

Von Henkel could think of any number of names that would have been applicable, but he held his salivating tongue.

'D'you know what he called me,' she repeated, 'that ugly Russian swine?'

Von Henkel licked his lips. Better and better. 'What did he call you?' he said, relaxing in his armchair and not bothering to hide a smile.

'He called me a fat German pig. All you Germans are the same. Scum, he said. Oh, Hermann, forgive me,' she blubbered.

He got up and grabbed her shoulder. 'Come to bed,' he said.

So it was that von Henkel had his revenge. And whenever he wanted it, and what was more, and much better, in whatsoever manner he wanted it, whether or not she was willing. And he would have other women, too, he decided, and even, goddamit, Ingrid, if he so wished. He rolled off her sweating pink flesh. Hildeborg trembled. Her husband's price was going to be a lot higher than she had ever thought possible.

When daylight came Burhan reported his fool's errand to Isani. Isani took it well. In truth, he'd had little hope of it from the start. He asked no questions. He just accepted Burhan's negative report. Now he faced yet another day of accumulated nothings. He told Burhan to go and get some sleep. But Burhan went straight to the Ambarrukmo.

He found them both at breakfast. They jumped up when he came into the room, fully expecting some news at such an unaccustomed hour. He shook his head sadly, and his voice was lame. 'I'm sure he's all right,' he said.

Emily started to cry. 'I don't want to go home,' she said.

Burhan's stomach heaved. He looked at Belinda.

'It's nearly three months,' she said, and there was clearly no need to say any more. She offered him some coffee. He drank it simply to do something, because he could think of nothing to say. Then, after a while, 'Are you really going?' he said.

Belinda nodded.

'When?' he squeaked.

'Two weeks. Perhaps three. There are many things to do.'

'No,' he shouted, jumping up from his seat. 'I'm going to find him. I'm going to find him.' His voice grew louder with his growing desperation. 'I will,' he said to them both and he coughed loudly so that he wouldn't cry. 'I will,' he said again, walking towards the door, having no idea where to go or what to do. Perhaps if he willed it enough, it would surely happen.

He went straight to his shoe-shine stand on the Square. He felt at ease there, and it was a good place to think. It was the only place too, for him to pick up information. He would not leave his stand all day.

While he was dealing with his first customer, an old man, with the peasant jacket of a farmer, crossed over the Square. He carried a paper bag. On his feet were a pair of thonged sandals, hitched between the toes. On reaching Burhan's stand, he slipped off one of his sandals and put on a town shoe that he took out of his bag. This newly shod foot, he placed on Burhan's stand.

Burhan looked at the shoe, but failed to recognise it. Not a regular customer. He looked up at its wearer. It was the medicine-man from the village of Harbobingangun, paying his formal respects to Burhan's calling. Burhan smiled and set to polishing. The old man bent down and whispered in Burhan's ear. Then he paid him with a written note which Burhan stuffed into his pocket. The medicine-man took off the shoe and put it back in the paper bag. Then, sandal-shod once more, he trudged across the Square.

Burhan watched him go. For some reason he was suddenly happy. Matoredjo had said that Brownlow's was a political kidnapping. His friends in the mountains had something to do with politics. He would ask them about Brownlow. They would surely know. Perhaps the letter that the medicine-man had given him for Roschun had something to do with Emily's father, and for the first time in his life he wished that he could read. He decided to leave for the mountain immediately. He had two, at most three, weeks, to find Brownlow. There was no time to lose.

Chapter Eighteen

Over the first few days after Brownlow fell amongst the partisans, he slowly regained his strength. They bathed his wounds and watered and fed him, and the joy of being alive, and the peace of non-pain blunted his curiosity as to the nature of the men who had rescued him. He did notice though that they whispered a great deal, and they argued too; that was plain from their tone and gesture, though he could not pick up the matter of their disagreements. And they were disagreeing, especially one of them, a young boy who spent, he thought, much of his time beside his sick-bed, feeding him and occasionally smiling. In the next few days, Brownlow concluded that they must be arguing about himself. Which indeed they were.

The men were divided. Most of them wanted Brownlow out of the way, quickly and painlessly. And as the days went by, they argued more fiercely, because each added day of his presence made dispatch more difficult. He was a danger to them. The location of their hide-out, which for so long they had kept secret, and from which they had made many successful sorties, dare not be put at risk. And no matter what promises a man would make, they could not be relied upon. The alternative was to hold him, to gain his sympathies perhaps, even to convert him to their cause. But that was a remote possibility, and they could never fully trust him. As long as he was alive, he was a burden. But Roschun took a different line. He'd obviously been influenced by Oyung. Roschun was the acknowledged leader of the band, and his word was law, but since he was so heavily opposed, he allowed discussion. He knew that if he killed Brownlow, Oyung would leave the mountain. And Oyung was a good soldier, and had already organised pockets of agrarian revolt in the villages scattered on the mountain-side. He didn't want to lose him. The boy was attached to Brownlow in some uncanny way. Perhaps he thought of him as a father, and to kill him would have brought the rebellion too close to home. Besides, Roschun was too professional a fighter to be a killer, and he thought the band could somehow or other contain their un-invited visitor. So they argued until it was agreed to hold him, on the promise that should a crisis occur, Brownlow would be summarily disposed of. The nature of such a crisis was not defined, so it was an unsatisfactory non-decision.

Meanwhile, Brownlow's condition improved daily, and after a week, Oyung was delegated to question him.

In view of the whispering which Brownlow had earlier con-nected with his presence in the hut, he made it immediately clear to Oyung that he knew a little Indonesian. The men had saved his life, and he wanted to be honest with them. When Oyung passed over this information, the men were more guarded than before. Thereafter they confined their talk to the furthest corners of the cave. Prompted by Roschun, Oyung questioned Brownlow about his background, his family and his job. They had assumed he was a lost tourist, so they were surprised and a little disconcerted to find that a larger and much more incon-venient fish had slipped inadvertently into their net. The argu-ments began again, and once more Roschun held sway.

In the course of the questioning, Brownlow asked Oyung his name. He gave it to him directly. It was a common enough name on the island and Brownlow would have given it no more thought had the boy not looked uncannily like Isani. 'Where are you from?' he asked him.

'From Java,' Oyung said.

Brownlow understood that he must not enquire further. From the boy's looks and his Australian accented English, he knew that he must be Isani's son. He was frightened of such knowledge, knowing that they would regard him more dangerously if they suspected his conclusions. He determined never to refer to it again, and even to deny any acquaintance with the Police Chief of Djogja if such a question were ever asked.

Oyung asked him about his family, and Brownlow was happy to talk about them. He spoke mostly about Emily, about how happy she was to live in Java, about her school and her friends. Oyung had already in his own mind made the connection between Emily and Burhan, and he prayed that Brownlow would not mention Burhan's name for fear the others might see him too as a threat. Oyung skirted his questioning away from Brownlow's family, and on Roschun's instructions, he asked him of his life in England. Roschun wanted a key to his political leanings, but when Brownlow described his English town and country life-style, it was clear that he was no material for conversion. So they let it be. Brownlow, on the other hand, was eager to talk with them and to learn from them the meaning of their struggle. He was able now to walk around, to eat with them at table, to share their games, but he was not allowed out of the cave. He did not have it in mind to escape. He was so grateful for his deliverance that he was prepared to wait indefinitely for a reunion with his family.

Over the weeks he grew very close to the men, admiring their spartan way of life, their dedication, and their joyful humour. He knew they could not be evil men, and he began to wonder about the nature of that law that forced them to work outside it. He assumed that they were members of the PKI and he wondered why they felt that a change in the *status quo* of their country was so desperately necessary. He wanted to learn so he asked many questions, and when they were sure that his only motivation was a genuine pursuit of knowledge, they told him of their hopes and ideals. There were many areas of their argument with which he was in full agreement. They bitterly opposed the westernisation of their country. Patiently they explained to Brownlow how Indonesia was a puppet of the West. How in the disguise of aid agencies, their culture and inheritance were slowly being eroded. They gave him specific examples, and he felt slightly ashamed of his calling. But when they presented him with their political alternative, his natural English conservatism was assaulted. But he did not argue with them. He knew that the regime they were fighting for differed from the present one only in political allegiance. It was a choice between being a puppet of the West or a puppet of the East, but puppet they would be withal.

But he understood their discontent. In his period with the UN he had, with sickening monotony, seen and read of aid projects, which because of changed political allegiance, had been withdrawn. In parts of Africa, universities stood half built because government loyalties had switched. New agricultural projects had been halted half-way because a rival aid-giver had undercut the price of fertiliser. In Central Java itself, the fluctuating price of rice, determined by a capitalist economic system, militated against any lasting success of the introduction of fertiliser, pesticide and new rice strains. When aid was politically tied, it was as black-mailing as charity. Yes, they had cause enough for frustration.

Over the weeks, the men kept less of an eye on Brownlow, and Brownlow was less aware of being a stranger in their midst. He felt an air of expectation amongst them, as if they were waiting for an important piece of news. They were sometimes restless, and a group of them would make short-lived sorties from the cave. They had nothing to report on their return, and Roschun would calm their impatience with invented games and story-telling. Then one night, when it was growing dark, they heard a whistle from outside the cave. A collection of coded notes, and they all froze where they sat. Roschun darted over to Brownlow and quickly escorted him out of sight to the back of the cave. He delegated some men to stay there with him, and motioned to Oyung to bring in the messenger.

Burhan wondered at the delay. Normally Oyung appeared before the echo of his whistling had faded. It was not possible that no one was at home, yet the medicine-man had said it was urgent, and he feared that it was late and some emergency had driven them out. He whistled again, and he was relieved when he heard footsteps.

Oyung, as usual, was glad to see him. They embraced, and when they entered the main body of the cave, Roschun rushed forward for the message. He opened the paper, reading it as he walked amongst the men. He smiled. 'Yes, yes,' he said to their inquiring glances. 'Yes,' he said. 'When the moon is full.' He turned to Burhan. 'Are you ready to eat?'

Burhan nodded. He was ready to eat, but he was not hungry. More than anything else, he was tired. For the last two nights he had slept fitfully on a train, the first night discomforted in a freight van, and the second, fitful and on guard. But before he slept, he had to ask Oyung if he knew anything about Brownlow. Privately. And if Oyung knew anything they could keep it between themselves.

One of the men brought Burhan a dish of food. He noticed an unaccustomed silence in the cave, and the silence was broken only by whispering as if they feared eavesdropping. There wasn't

the usual open-hearted welcome, and he felt an outsider. Oyung
came and sat beside him. 'You look tired,' he said.

'I can't eat all this,' Burhan said. He wondered why Oyung
didn't ask about Emily. That should have been his very first
question. His own mind was occupied with little else, and he
wondered why it was not everybody's priority. Burhan had shared
with Oyung his closest secret, and it was as if Oyung had forgotten. 'You remember I told you about Emily,' Burhan whispered.

Oyung nodded guardedly. 'Of course,' he said. 'How is she?'

'Her father's disappeared. They say that it's a political kidnapping. I've got to find him Oyung, or Emily will go back to
England.'

'Why d'you ask me?' Oyung said.

'Well, you know about politics. All this here, it's all politics,
isn't it?'

Oyung laughed. 'Politics is a big word,' he said, 'and it's
spoken all over Java. I don't know. Kidnapping's not our business.' Oyung knew the vital importance of keeping the Brownlow
presence from Burhan. It was a secret no one could expect him
to keep. It would be too great a burden for him. 'Go to sleep,'
he said. They were close and dear friends, but for the first time,
Oyung would have been glad to see the back of him. He walked
Burhan over to his bunk. It wasn't his usual bunk, Burhan
noticed. It was in the far corner of the cave. He knew there was
something unusual about the whole visit. There was no comradely
welcome, no treats for his supper, and now the bunk away from
all the others. He was so disturbed by these irregular details,
that tired as he was, he found it difficult to sleep. He tossed and
turned on the narrow cot and he had an uneasy feeling that
everybody was watching him. He decided to leave as soon as it
was light, and get back to Djogja and his shoe-shine stand, his
only possible source now of information. When he thought of
Emily, he pictured her crying, and in a fitful dream, he saw
Brownlow floating in a lake of green water, his body slightly
below the surface. He woke up swiftly. He was sweating. He
thought it must be morning, but the men were still up, talking
louder now, and playing dominoes. He heard a laugh that he
thought was familiar but he couldn't place it. So he turned over
and tried again to sleep. He saw himself back on his shoe-stand,
polishing Brownlow's shoes, with Emily's reflection floating in

the leather. He saw them walking off together across the Square, and he heard them laughing. Yes, he heard them laughing. Even here he could hear them. He woke again, but instinctively he knew that if there were knowledge for him in this cave, it must never be known that he knew. He turned over on his other side, his eyes shut, and feigning a gentle snore. Again the laughter. Unmistakable this time. He was itching to open his eyes, but he knew he must not be seen to be awake. Yet he had to open his eyes, because he thought that after all, he may only be dreaming, but when he tried to open them, he couldn't. He had fallen asleep again, and he dreamt that he had dreamt he'd heard Brownlow.

When he woke again, it was light, and the men around him were still sleeping. He recalled his dream. Quietly he sat up on his bunk and looked around the sleeping figures. He recognised them all. But the laugh kept echoing through his head, and he knew that something was different in the cave, and even though he might regret it, he had to discover what that difference was. He lay very quiet, his eyes half open, and he waited. Very soon there was a stirring. One of the men got up, stretched himself, and came towards Burhan's bunk.

Burhan shut his eyes and began to snore slightly. He felt the man standing over him, and he hoped he couldn't hear his heart pumping. Then a blanket lightly covered his face, and he heard the man walking away. He waited, then turned his head, so that the blanket slipped sideways, giving him a slight chink for viewing. The man was not to be seen, but he heard noises coming from the back of the cave. Then the man reappeared, this time, guiding another. Despite the man's inelegant shuffle, and the growth of almost a ginger beard, Burhan knew him for Brownlow. He wanted to cry out with joy, and he clenched his fists round his knees to stop them trembling. The man led Brownlow through the cave and out into the air. As they passed his bunk, Burhan had a close and full view of him, and he shut his eyes tightly, because he couldn't bear the joy. They would shortly be back, Burhan knew, and he kept his chink clear. Shortly they returned and it was a back view Burhan had of him this time. And he saw him again crossing the Square with Emily and he heard their laughter. He slipped his head back into the blanket, and he waited.

He had much to think about, but he wanted to postpone it,

until he was alone and on the mountain. So he waited, trying to think of other things, and he was glad when Oyung pulled the blanket from his face and told him it was morning.

He ate two bananas, with a cup of buffalo milk, and as if everything were absolutely normal, he laughed and joked with the men. Roschun had no further messages for him, and Oyung accompanied him to the mouth of the cave. 'Keep an eye on my little brother,' he said, as Burhan was leaving. He watched him till he reached the twin-triangle rock, before he disappeared down the other side, and Oyung, like all the other men in the cave, breathed a large sigh of relief.

Burhan ran. He counted aloud to a hundred, then he reeled off the days of the week, and the names of the months, over and over again, hurling them against the wall of humid heat, deafening himself with his voice so that his thoughts could be postponed. He knew exactly which spot he was making for. High above the village of Harbobingagun, just before the downward slope began, there was a stray, lone, unsired coconut tree. There in its shade, not far from the spot where he and Richard had viewed the crashed Piper, he would sit and begin to gather his thoughts. For he had to know by the time he reached Djogja, what he was to do. When he'd exhausted over and over again the months and the days of the year, he began to sing, and though it was a joyful song for he had cause for celebration, he wondered why he didn't feel happy, and as he approached the coconut tree, whose top branches he could already see, he slowed his steps, unwilling to come to terms with his terrible dilemma. But the tree loomed closer, and he dragged his steps towards it as if it were the gallows. And like an old mountain guru, he sat in its shade and he meditated.

Whether he was aware of it or not, he'd already made his decision. He had made it in the first split second of Brownlow's appearance, and perhaps even earlier, in the recognition of his laughter. Brownlow's presence in that cave was a secret, that must never, in any place, or to any person, be divulged. For that would also mean the disclosure of the headquarters of his friends, and there was no question in his mind that he would die sooner than reveal the one fact and at the same time conceal the other, for both were part of the same conspiracy. To keep Emily in Djogja meant the betrayal of his friends, and from his political hearsay, of his country perhaps. It was impossible. Other men perhaps would have been faced with a choice, and the only point in his sitting under the coconut tree was to lament the fact that for him there was no choice at all. He tried to think of ways and means in which he could reveal the Brownlow facts alone, without implicating his friends. He could go to Isani or Belinda, and he could say that he had seen Brownlow, but neither would be satisfied with that simple fact. They would both want proof, and proof meant betrayal. His friends in the mountains had certainly done their best to keep Brownlow from his sight. They had not wanted to burden him with the holding of yet another secret. But if he had seen him, openly, and they had known, they would still have trusted him, as they always had. They had kept him from Brownlow for his own protection, and it would be a double betrayal if he informed on them now. But the prospect of Emily returning to England was an appalling one. He didn't know how he could live without her. He was fearful too for Brownlow's safety. He was bound to be a handicap to his mountain friends. He wished he knew what they intended to do with him. For a moment he toyed with the idea of going back to the hide-out, of confessing everything, and insisting on their telling him what they were going to do. But they loved him, he knew, because he trusted them implicitly, and never asked any questions. He knew what he was going to do, and it was the hardest thing of all. In short, nothing. He was going to keep his mouth firmly shut. He was probably the only person in Djogja who knew with absolute proof that Brownlow was still alive, and he shuddered with the burden of his discovery.

He got up and started to walk down the slope to the village road. He didn't know what to do with the day and the days that lay ahead. There was no point any longer in going to his shoe-shine stand. He had enough money for a while, and he no longer needed any source of information. He did not trust himself to be with Emily or Belinda. He could not listen to their home-going talk, without loosening his tongue. There was no point in going to Isani, for whom he had no more questions. He didn't even want to go riding with one of his *betchak*-driver friends, a pastime he often indulged in his pre-Emily days. He had too much danger-ous knowledge to be with anybody, and he thought he might simply go back to the baker's shop on whose floured floor he usually slept, and curl up in the courtyard and go to sleep. Yes, he would do that, he decided. It was the safest thing for him to do.

But when he reached the outskirts of Djogja, he wanted desperately to see Emily, and swearing to himself he would say not a word, he made for the Ambarrukmo.

But as he walked up the driveway, he thought of Emily in tears, and he realised how stupid he would be to avail himself of such temptation. He would go and see Isani. Just for something to do. At least Isani wouldn't be crying.

He found him huddled at his desk. 'I only polished one shoe,' Burhan said as he came in, as an excuse for coming to see him at all. Isani looked up and smiled sadly. 'I thought you were coming with news,' he said.

Burhan shook his head so violently, his ears began to throb. 'Nothing,' he said.

Isani stared at his in-tray. 'I think he's dead, Burhan,' he said.

'You mustn't think that.'

'Why not?'

'Because then you'd stop looking.'

Isani's phone rang. He picked it up lethargically. He'd lost all appetite for police work. 'Isani,' he said into the receiver with little conviction.

Burhan saw his face pale, and he was trembling. 'No,' Isani was saying and his voice was quite hollow. 'Is it him?' There was a pause. 'I'll come straight away,' Isani said. He put the phone down, but he made no move. He was shivering. 'I think I was right about Brownlow,' he said softly.

'What's happened?'

'A body's been washed up on the river bank.'

'Who is it?' Burhan asked with little concern.

'They don't know. It's been in the water a long time.' Then, rising wearily to his feet, he said. 'Come with me, Burhan. It must be him.'

'No, it isn't,' Burhan fairly shouted. 'I know it isn't.'

'Why are you so sure?'

'I'm not,' Burhan said, tempering his conviction. 'I just go on hoping.'

'So do we all.' He put his arm on Burhan's shoulder, as if the boy were his guide, and together they went down to the river bank.

A crowd had already gathered. A body in the river was an uncommon sight in Djogja. Drowning was a frowned-on form of suicide. Water was sacred. It was for rice or buffalo. It was a ferry to survival, not a cheating conveyance to death. And so the crowd were angry. Even though the body was totally unrecognisable, they knew it could not be one of their own people, and they were bitter that a stranger had come amongst them and defiled their life-giving source.

The body had been dragged on to the bank, and it was covered with a blanket. Isani pushed his way through the crowd. He understood their anger, so he did not order them to disperse or to go about their business. For this was as much their business as his own. He pulled the blanket back. The man was wearing the remains of khaki shorts, and his build was thick and non-Asian. 'It's a foreigner,' he said, turning to the crowd. They grunted their disapproval. 'He's somebody's son,' Isani said, trying to placate them. His mind was on Oyung, though the man, rotted as he was, could well have been somebody's father.

There was a medallion about his neck. But it was green and encrusted with river-life. Undecipherable. He covered the man again and ordered the police to take the body to the morgue.

Burhan sat by his side in the car that followed the ambulance. 'It could well be him,' Isani said.

'No.'

'What makes you so sure?'

'He's too fat for Brownlow,' Burhan said.

'A body blows up in the water. Did you ever see a medallion on him?'

'No,' Burhan said without trying to remember.

'We'll have it cleaned,' Isani said. 'There's bound to be something on it.'

They followed the body to the morgue where the medallion was removed. Isani took it to the laboratory, and while it was being cleaned, they sat side by side on the bench. Isani was nervous. He had already made up his mind that the body was Brownlow's and he was planning how to break the news to Belinda. 'How am I going to tell her?' he asked Burhan.

'I'll tell her,' Burhan could afford to be generous. Isani put his arm around him and it crossed his mind to adopt the boy.

'There's something here,' the technician said from his bench. He held the cleaned medallion to the light. Isani took it from him. Only one side had been cleaned, and the cypher on it was clear. A serpent, wound around a rod.

'What does that stand for?' Isani said.

'The wearer is allergic to penicillin,' the assistant said.

'Then there must be some identification on the other side,' Isani said.

The technician went to work again and Isani turned his back to him. He could already see the letters of Hugh Brownlow engraved in the silver metal and he considered how sad a handicap it was to be unable to respond to a life-saving drug.

'Here it is,' the assistant said. 'It's as clear as it'll get.'

Isani held it to the light. 'Peter Weiner,' he read aloud, and he jumped for joy.

'I told you it wasn't him,' Burhan couldn't help saying.

'That's the man from the airfield, isn't it?' Isani said. 'Poor devil. The German. He lived with the Schmidt boy, the one who was killed. I wonder . . .'

He took Burhan back to the morgue. A cursory report on the body gave suicide. There were no marks of violence or of struggle. Isani looked at Burhan. 'You remember the crashed Piper?' he said. It was as if he'd taken the boy on as assistant, as confidante, as a sounding board.

'Perhaps he left a letter,' Burhan said.

'Let's go back to our office,' Isani said, as if Burhan were already on the payroll. 'He lived somewhere by the airfield. Richard would know. The Stern boy. He was friendly with that lot. Yes, that's an idea,' he said, almost to himself, happy that this was a simple problem that would require concrete and logical investigation. 'I'll get him to identify the body.'

Burhan tagged along behind. He didn't want to be at the office when Richard arrived. It was bad for his image to be found by Richard, or anybody for that matter, hobnobbing with the law. He told Isani he had to get back to his stand. 'I might pick you up some information,' he said.

'I'll come and see you later,' Isani said. 'You can clean the other shoe.'

As Burhan walked down to the Square, he passed by the river. Usually there were fishermen there, or water-buffalo, with naked children hopping from buffalo-back to back. Now the banks of the river were empty, as they would remain till *Ramayana* time, when the moon was full in the sky and the river would be cleansed.

Chapter Nineteen

When Richard heard Isani's voice on the telephone, his knees melted with fear. 'Could you come down and see me?' Isani said. 'I'd rather not talk on the phone.'

'Of course,' Richard said. Even in his sick fear he realised that not to go would cast further suspicion on him. 'I'll come down now,' he said.

Normally he would have stolen the nearest open car to get to the police station, which was on the other side of the town from where he lived. But he decided to walk. He needed time to prepare himself for all eventualities. Was it possible Weiner had talked? They hadn't seen each other since the night they had abandoned Brownlow. There'd been no need to communicate. They hated and trusted each other from a cold distance. Had someone seen Brownlow perhaps? It was impossible that he had survived, and even if he had, he could have had no recollection of the plane ride or his fellow travellers. He walked very slowly. He was terrified of confronting Isani. Crossing the Square, he saw Burhan at his stand. It occurred to him suddenly that Burhan might have talked about their abortive mountain trip. Burhan wasn't busy, so he crossed over to his stand. 'Seen Isani?' he said casually.

'No. Why?'

'Nothing. Just wondered.'

Burhan was glad to see Richard frightened. He didn't like Richard any more. He had almost made him take him to his mountain friends. He didn't know what Richard was frightened of, or what at the time he was running away from, but running away he certainly was, which was why a call from Isani so unnerved him. 'Where you going?' Burhan teased.

'Nowhere. Just walking.'

By the time Richard reached Isani's office, he was shaking

143

with fear. He stiffened outside Isani's door, trying to control his tremblings.

Inside, behind his desk, Isani was daydreaming. He imagined that in Peter Weiner's rooms he would find a written note in which he confessed to the murder of Patricia Forrest, the sabotage of the plane, the kidnapping and whereabouts of Brownlow, the organising of the raid on the barracks, and even, if he were feeling suicidally generous—though Isani mustn't be greedy—to the theft of a pair of lady's shoes from the Ambarrukmo Hotel. Richard's knock startled him into the reality of his mounting unsolved in-tray. 'Come in,' he said.

'It's very humid today,' Richard said as he came into the room, wiping the sweat from his forehead that had nothing to do with humidity.

'Well, I'm used to it,' Isani said.

Richard sat down. 'What is it?' he said. He had prepared nothing, no answers, no excuses, for he was uncertain of the charge. But charged he would be. Of that he was sure. Suddenly, he didn't care any more. Anything was better than the sickening waking moment each morning. Anything was better than the load of his bitter knowledge.

'D'you know Peter Weiner?' Isani said. He put it in the present. It was his way of breaking the news gently.

'Yes,' Richard said, trying to keep his voice straight. There was nothing incriminating in knowing the man, but it was clear to Richard that his name could come up in only one connection.

'I've got some rather bad news,' Isani said.

This is it, Richard thought. He's told the whole story. He resigned himself. 'What's happened?' he said.

'His body was found in the river. Looks like suicide.'

Later on, Richard was to wonder what exactly he felt at that precise moment. It should have been relief. It should even have been joy. But it was neither. Rather it was a heavy sadness, not because the man had died, but that he had left him to bear the burden totally alone.

'Was he a good friend of yours?' Isani was saying.

'Not really,' Richard said tonelessly. 'I knew him. I went to his place sometimes.' Then suddenly Richard was afraid. Had anyone been to Weiner's place? Had he left a note? Had he left a terrible confession?

'I'd like you to take me there,' he heard Isani say. 'Perhaps he left a note or something.'

'Yes, of course,' Richard said, grateful for the god-sent opportunity.

'But first I need an identification of the body,' Isani said.

Richard shuddered.

'He doesn't look very pretty, I'm afraid. But it won't take long.'

It took in fact one second, but it was long enough to remain with Richard for the rest of his life. He stood in front of the blanketed hulk and steeled himself for the unveiling. The morgue assistant eyed him first, gauging his readiness. Then, like a magician, one, two, three presto, he whipped off the blanket. Richard's heart stammered, not with recognition of his partner-in-crime, but with the total incredulity that such a putrid mess could once in a life-time have passed muster as a human being. And all that he could think about was that this object, in the past, had made love to him. It had straddled him and rubbed him, flesh of my flesh, he thought, bone of my bone, and he smelt a rancid filth on his own body that he knew no amount of bathing would ever erase. The body was by any standards unrecognisable. Weiner's mother, standing there, might have felt a faint stirring in her womb as a sole act of recognition, but Richard's bond was more tyrannous, for he looked at Peter's naked body and knew him by his putrified manhood. He turned away, and he wondered how thereafter, he could face his own father.

In the car to Weiner's village, they were both silent. The last time Richard had taken this road was with Weiner, the coma-tosed Brownlow in the back seat. He had been fearful of ever coming this way again. For a moment he envied Weiner who had bequeathed his worldly goods together with the Brownlow ghost they both had so fitfully shared. Now that ghost was his true and very own. He did not think of Patricia Forrest. That ghost did not haunt him. He was sorry that she had to die, but he had killed her for his mother's sake, and he saw it as an act of love. But Brownlow's abandonment was a wilful and selfish act, and had been committed on no one's behalf, but his own frightened self.

'Are we nearly there?' Isani said.

'It's left at the bottom of the road.' Richard was anxious to
enter the house first. He knew the front door was always left
open, and if that had blown to with the wind, the garden doors
were unlockable. As Isani pulled up, he made to get out of the
car. 'I may have to climb through a window,' he said.

'I'll wait out at the front,' Isani said.

Richard passed the front door, and was relieved to see that
it was firmly shut. He took his time to the garden, then, once out
of Isani's sight, he streaked through the doors and into Peter's
bedroom. The blankets and sheets were neatly folded on the bed,
signal to the next tenant. Two large strapped-down suitcases were
piled on the table, and on top of these was a letter. On the sealed
white envelope, it said simply, 'From Peter Weiner'. Richard
stuffed the letter into his pocket, and went to open the front door.

Isani came in. 'Is there anything?' he said.

'Not in this room,' Richard said, indicating the living-room
that gave out on to the garden. 'I haven't been in the bedroom
yet. It's over there.' He followed Isani.

'Obviously suicide,' Isani said, after a cursory examination of
the room. 'He's left everything in perfect order. Packed and
ready to go.' He started to open the drawers. They and the cup-
boards were empty. 'I don't see a note of any kind,' he said. He
opened the cases. They were neatly packed, as if by a woman's
hand, each item of clothing interlaced with a piece of white
tissue-paper. 'I think we'd better take the cases,' Isani said. 'I'll
get his details from the German Embassy in Djakarta.

They took a case each, and loaded them into the car.

'Sad,' Isani said. 'Very sad. Why did he do it?'

'He was often depressed,' Richard said.

'But he was so young,' Isani said, convinced that the two states
were antithetical. 'His poor father.'

Isani dropped him off at the police station. 'Thank you,' he
said, as Richard got out of the car. 'You've been very helpful.'

Richard hailed a *betchak*. He was too close to the seat of the
law to steal a car, and he needed to get home quickly to read,
and if he had the courage, to burn Weiner's last will and
testament.

He went straight to his room. He had a mean feeling of victory. He had managed to cheat Weiner the informer. Now his
silly death would have served no purpose at all. He was sure

that Weiner had confessed to the Brownlow kidnapping, and even perhaps to the sabotaged plane. He was curious however to discover whether the Forrest murder which was none of his doing, had been disclosed as well.

Carefully he unsealed the envelope. One white folded sheet. The message was short, and the handwriting impeccable.

'If my body is ever found, I would like it returned to Germany for burial'

There was no signature. It was as if he had already died when writing it. He had seen his body as something quite separate. It was an 'it' for him. 'I want it returned to Germany,' as he might have taken his hair to a barber and said 'I want it short back and sides.'

Richard was overcome with shame, and he resolved that whatever happened, whatever the consequences, he would see to it that Peter's body went home. He was alarmed to find himself crying.

Chapter Twenty

The moon grew fuller. Burhan was visiting Emily every day, and for the past two weeks, no word had been spoken about leave-takings. The temptation to betray Brownlow's whereabouts was thus modified. He continued to express his total conviction that Brownlow was still alive, and offered as his only proof that had he been dead, his body would have been found. 'No news is good news,' he kept saying, repeating a phrase he'd picked up from Isani, who used it hopefully in connection with his missing son. Only a few days ago he had asked Burhan if he had heard or seen Oyung, his first public admission that his son was missing at all. Burhan had no problems in denying any knowledge of him, but with Emily and Belinda there was the overhanging threat of leave-taking. Then one evening when he walked into the Brownlow suite, there was actual evidence of departure. There were two open half-packed cases on the floor, and a wooden crate in the corner full of newspaper wrappings. He swallowed. 'You don't have to go,' he said simply.

'There's no reason any more to stay,' Belinda said. Then coming close to Burhan she said, 'He won't come back any more.'

Burhan walked to the balcony, looked down over the pool, clenched his little fists, and held his tongue. He tried to estimate the value of his friendship with Oyung and the men in the mountains. He tried to put some kind of price on it, to compare it with the cost of Emily's departure from his life. But no matter how much he loved her, how empty his life would be without her, he would never forgive himself, if, in order to keep her, he would have to sell his friends. For a moment he hated Oyung, and he cursed the day when Zein from the barracks had first sent him up the mountain-side. He was worried too about Brownlow's safety. Something was afoot in the cave. That had been clear from Roschun's reception of his last message. 'When the moon is full,' he'd said, and that clearly pointed to some event, and perhaps, he shuddered to think, the end of Brownlow's days on earth. He looked at the sky. A week to go perhaps, before the moon waxed to ripeness. He turned back into the room.

Belinda had laid out some of Brownlow's suits on the couch. 'I'm sure he'll come back,' Burhan said lamely.

'Not any more,' Belinda said, as she gently slipped the suits from their hangers. It was a terrible act of burial. He could do nothing and there was nothing he could say.

'Could you lift that case for me please,' Belinda said, 'and put it on the table?'

He hesitated. He did not want to assist their departure, and it would have been fraudulent for him to take part in any of her funeral arrangements. He knew that Brownlow was not dead, so how could he possibly bury him? 'Wait till the moon is full,' he said as a last desperate stand. 'In Java, many things happen at the full moon. It's a magic time,' he said, and he started to cry.

Belinda had never associated tears with Burhan, and Burhan himself was surprised by this unaccustomed display of emotion. She held him in her arms. 'I think you too have lost a father,' she said. He'd never known that kind of maternal embrace, and it embarrassed him. He struggled free. 'You must promise to wait till the moon is full,' he said.

'But we're waiting in any case,' she said. 'We're all going to the *Ramayana*.' In that moment, she'd made the decision. If her husband were there, they would automatically, the four of them, have gone in a party. Emily had read the story over and over again, and Burhan, though he had grown up with the tale, had never seen it performed. Now Belinda would take them both. It would be by way of fulfilment of Brownlow's wishes.

That gave Burhan almost a week's grace, but given a month, a year even, he knew there was nothing he could do to profit by it. He took Brownlow's suits and one by one, he put them back on their hangers and carried them into the bedroom, hanging them singly and lovingly back into the wardrobe. Belinda watched him. Though his actions did not give her any hope, she was ashamed of her own lack of faith. For the first time she realised how dependent Burhan had become on them as a family, and it crossed her mind that perhaps she should take him back to England. But to adopt him when Brownlow was alive might have been a proper undertaking; to do it now, and alone, was a tourist and sentimental pursuit, and she dismissed it quickly from her mind. She, and Emily too, would learn to get over him.

'Burhan,' Emily called out from her room. She had woken. 'Did you find Daddy?'

They went to her room. 'We're going to wait until the moon is full,' Belinda said, trying to catch some of Burhan's optimism. 'Burhan says it's a magic time, and we're all going to the *Ramayana*.'

'And Daddy?' She was excited.

'You must wish very hard,' Burhan said.

'No.' Belinda was adamant. 'There's no more wishing. Daddy's gone, Emily. He won't be coming back, any, any more.' She ran to Emily and held her close, both crying for each other's comfort.

Burhan watched them, helpless. 'Perhaps you're right,' he said. If he said it loud enough and often enough, he thought, perhaps he could come to believe it himself, and that would be an end to all his heart-searchings.

'We can't go to the *Ramayana* without Daddy,' Emily said. 'It wouldn't be fair.'

'No,' Belinda said, rocking her. 'You're right. We'll go back home.'

'But you promised to wait till the moon was full,' Burhan pleaded.

'We will,' Belinda said gently. 'And we shall leave on that day.'

Now he wished that it would come quickly, that they would go away and be done with it, and he could go back to his business and stop caring. But he knew that when they left, it would be much worse.

They heard the door again. Isani called from the living-room. He was making his regular evening commiserating call. As always, he was glad to see Burhan there. He could use him to share the load of consolation. Sometimes he irritated Burhan with his naïve incompetence, but he was also very sorry for him because of his nagging worry about Oyung. It struck Burhan, that here and now, and with one short sentence, he could bring such joy to these three people, and he felt almost criminal in holding his tongue. 'I must go,' he said quickly, as he trusted himself less and less. If only he had somebody in his life to whom he could confide. Someone who had no personal involvement in the complicated story, someone who loved him well enough to give him guidance. I wish I had a mother, he said to himself. Or a father. Or anybody, for that matter. Just one single person in the whole wide world that he could tell.

'Wait a while,' Isani said. He didn't want to be left alone with them. 'We'll walk home together,' he almost pleaded.

And so they sat, the three of them, with Emily wooed back to sleep.

'We're leaving on the thirtieth,' Belinda said after a while. 'It will be exactly a year since we arrived.'

Isani felt he had no right any longer to dissuade her. He didn't know whether Belinda was aware of it, but Brownlow had been unofficially replaced. The new Ponsonby man was sitting it out patiently at the other end of the town, waiting for Belinda's final surrender. It was only a matter of weeks, days perhaps, that Brownlow would be officially written off, and his successor officially installed. Isani's in-tray was, of its own accord, emptying itself. That day, the wrapping-up inquest on Patricia Forrest had pronounced murder by a person or persons unknown. The sabotaged Piper had officially been taken out of police investigation. Now, all that remained was the stolen pair of lady's shoes, and even that trivial offence defied solution. It was in a way, the end of a very sad chapter, littered with at least three bodies, and a fourth lying God knows where, in the wilderness of Java. And somewhere, in some other wilderness of the spirit, his son. The moon brings changes, he thought, always, at every fullness. It can only be better for us all.

They sat in spasmodic silence for another hour, when Isani felt that they could, with adequate decency and courtesy, take their leave. Belinda would have been glad to see them go earlier. She wanted very much to be alone, and for the first time since Brownlow had gone, to mourn him. The paraphernalia of death, she thought, could be very painful, but at the same time it served to punctuate the process of one's sorrow. She would have been glad of a ceremony of burial, of a body as proof, of a total irrevocable acceptance by all her friends that she was now undeniably a widow. Now she could only bury him in her own sad heart, and she had to do it alone, without mourners, now and for ever.

She went to Brownlow's wardrobe and folded the clothes into the case. Then his underwear and his shirts. It was the only practical way she had of burying him. The shoes were the worst, those shells of life and mobility, and she was tempted to shut the door on them, like skeletons in a cupboard, but she knew that they too were essential to the finality of her ceremony. Gently, and with as much care as if they were to be worn again, she laid them on the white tissue. Then she closed the case. She stroked the leather with her fingers, then, crouching by its side, she wept long and loud into the night.

Chapter Twenty-one

And long into that same night, Mantoni's wheel was spinning. Louisa had given her regular soirée, and the men at the gaming table in Mantoni's loft had well and truly earned their throws. For they had sat and listened to, or rather could not help but hear Louisa, who, with her perilous notes stalked her ever-shifting prey. Few of them had hit the target. It had been the most unmusical musical evening in their memory. So they felt they'd earned their pleasure.

The usual crowd were playing, with the addition of the new-comer. Henry Thwaite, from Swindon, England, had been lured from the civil service to refill the Ponsonby Post. While waiting in the wings, he was availing himself of the UN social life in Djogja, which he fitted as to the manner born. He was much more to the men's taste than Brownlow. The last thing he wanted to do, or rather, was capable of doing, was to interfere. He was happy to let things be, to defer to what he accepted as others' larger experience, to sign the odd form or two, and to try to keep everybody happy. He was the kind of UN official, who in the terms of the Ponsonby Post, was totally redundant. Thus he was one of the boys, and they welcomed him.

He'd just made a killing. He'd covered the 8, *cheveaux* and *carrés*, and his number had come up. He'd doubled and it came up a second time. In the space of three minutes, he'd collected more than two months' salary. Mantoni lost like a gentleman. With his metal scoop he pushed the pile of winnings towards Thwaite with the cool confidence that during the course of the evening, he would scoop it back. And with interest. Which he did. So that by the end of the evening, Thwaite had mortgaged his salary for almost half a year. He tried to take it like a man. He laughed with painful and exaggerated heartiness and he wished that he were alone, so that he could have a good cry.

The other men played carefully, mostly on the even chances, and sometimes Mantoni was irritated and bored by their meanness. During every gambling session, he made the decision to give it all up. To leave his boring, gushing and off-pitch wife, and return to his farm in Tuscany. To pick up Proust for the seventh time and really work his way through it once and for all. To eat the prosciutto and drink the rough wines of the region. And to have a young boy or two, simply as companions, he stressed to himself. If ever that senseless Thwaite took over Brownlow's job, installed in the Ambarrukmo with official UN blessing, he would pack his bags and go. Inside himself he felt it was a safe enough bet. He believed profoundly that Brownlow would return. Somehow or other, in whatever condition, he would make his way back. There was no concrete evidence to the contrary.

But in this conviction he was alone. The others had written Brownlow off. Von Henkel thought he'd wandered off during the Boxham reception, and drugged as he was—as they all were for that matter, but people like von Henkel knew how to hold their liquor or whatever it was—he had walked off into the night, and fallen off a cliff or into the river. Sooner or later his body would show up.

Henderson thought he'd been kidnapped by mistake by the PKI, who were probably after Dr Boxham, and that when they realised they had the wrong man, had probably buried him somewhere in the mountains.

Stern, too, thought he was dead, not that he wished it, but simply because it was easier to think that way. He had too much on his mind to give it much thought. Besides, he feared that Brownlow's disappearance was somehow connected with his own terrible guilt. Since Patricia had died, no word of the matter had passed between himself and Richard. Neither had dared to conspire with the other, to tally each other's stories. They were both lost in their own wilderness of shame. Yet over the past few months, he and his son had been closer than ever before, but the poor girl's death had been a high price to pay for their reconciliation. If reconciliation it was. Rather it was a negative peace between them, in which neither did nor said anything to provoke the other. It was a situation they knew could not last for very long, and any day it might explode. Sometimes Stern was very frightened.

Henry Thwaite thought Brownlow dead, simply because he had to. While waiting in the wings, he was only on half pay, and if he was going to enjoy the night-life of Djogja, he was going to need cash and quickly. He decided to bet again, and once again on the 8. Mantoni made a small bet with himself. If the 8 comes up, he thought, Brownlow is dead. He spun the wheel. 26. The pleasure he felt in Brownlow's survival was only slightly off-set by the receding dream of bachelor joys in Tuscany.

Downstairs the women were gossiping. If Brownlow ever did show up, or if his body were found, there would be a desperate scratching around in the European drawing-rooms of Djogja for a new topic of conversation. The women, who had hardly let it go since he had disappeared, were still at it, each with their own pet theories. Hildeborg thought he was dead, because Hermann said so, and Hermann was always right. The other women felt sorry for her. Anybody who could think that von Henkel was always right was bound to be simple-minded. Besides, Hildeborg was looking very poorly of late, and her usual vacant look was even more cow-like and submissive.

Louisa, unlike her husband, thought that Brownlow was dead. He'd appeared to her in a dream and told her to look after Belinda. Threes said nothing, though privately she thought he had been killed by her own people, and she was ashamed. The others understood her feelings, and didn't press her for an opinion. And this needled her more than anything, for they had no right to link her with a possible accused.

The Brownlow theme was inexhaustible. Between them the women dragged the rivers, excavated the soil, speculated on poor Belinda and the child, assessed the amount of UN compensation, estimated the character of that man Thwaite, his successor, and when all tangential aspects had been picked to the bone, they started again with the central theme. And they knew better than to let it go, for if they had, captive audience as they were, Louisa would have started to sing again.

An hour or so passed in this way until the men came down and coffee was served. Only Hildeborg was silly enough to ask her husband whether he had won or lost. The other women knew that all gamblers were liars, and that it was impossible to lie with witnesses present.

'You don't ask such questions,' von Henkel said with the unspoken rider of 'wait till I get you home'.

Poor Hildeborg quivered. An ever-so-slight flutter of rebellion stirred inside her. But what could she do? Where could she go?

As usual, all the women were solicitous with Stern, serving him coffee and cake, inviting him to their houses. Richard was included. Before the Forrest affair, Richard was not considered a good house-guest, but now they noticed that the two had become very close, and it was like inviting a married couple.

'He should be here soon,' Stern said. 'He said he'd pick me up.'

'I gather Weiner's body is going back tomorow,' Henderson said.

They were glad of a new topic. With Weiner they were altogether on surer ground. Here was a body, pretty unrecognisable, it was true, but a corpse withal, a matter somewhat more tangible than the Brownlow ghost.

'Poor boy,' von Henkel said. 'Wonder why he did it.'

'It can get pretty depressing stuck out in a village,' Mantoni said.

'Probably a girl,' von Henkel offered, for whom all answers were simple. 'A broken love-affair.'

'They say he was upset about the Piper crash,' Stern said.

'You don't think he had anything to do with it, do you?' Hildeborg actually contributed to the conversation, if only to lodge an inquiry.

'They seem to have hushed it up,' Mantoni said.

'Like the Forrest business,' von Henkel said.

'There's plenty more coffee,' Louisa almost screamed in an attempt to change the conversation.

'It's all right,' Stern said, moved by her concern on his behalf. 'I'm learning to live with it.' He was grateful to hear the door-bell. It would be Richard and they could both go home, and leave von Henkel and the rest to their speculations. 'I'm ready,' he said, as soon as Richard came into the room. Although he preferred to be with Richard in company, for he was uneasy with him alone, he wanted to avoid the turn the conversation was taking. He wondered why none of them ever spoke about

their work, and why the problems and excitements of Third
World development did not interest them outside office hours.
He realised that apart from Brownlow, who was always willing
to discuss and learn about projects that had worked or that had
failed, there was no one he could seriously talk to. Patricia had
once filled that role in her dedicated missionary way, and he
missed her terribly. He began to miss Brownlow too.

Once they were alone in the car, Stern felt Richard's edginess.
His jaw was taut and he was silent.

'What's the matter?' Stern asked timidly.

'Nothing. What should be the matter?'

'You're so quiet.'

'What's there to say?' He was bitter and sullen and obviously
spoiling for a fight. Stern dreaded the explosion, and he wished
he'd stayed longer for coffee. Now he was anxious to get home,
to make some excuse to go to his room to avoid the confronta-
tion that Richard was so obviously manoeuvring.

When they pulled up at the house, Stern made to open his
door. 'Wait a minute,' Richard said.

Stern put his hand on his lap, clenching his fist. He knew he
had to keep cool. Richard was seething and would soon boil
over, and it was clearly his intention to embroil his father in his
own eruption. Stern waited. There would surely be a measure
of relief when it was all over.

'I've got to tell you something,' Richard said, without looking
at him. 'It's not going to be easy for you to hear.'

'We share a murder together,' Stern said softly. 'What on
earth is there left that you *cannot* tell me.'

'You remember the crashed Piper,' Richard said. 'Peter
Weiner did it. He screwed up the plane.'

'How do you know?'

'He told me.'

'But why? Why, in God's name?'

Richard couldn't answer. His courage, such as it was, had
petered out.

'What is it?' Stern said, unable to bear the silence any longer.

'Let's go,' Richard said, opening the door.

Stern put his hand on his son's arm. 'No,' he said decisively.
'We'll have it out, whatever it is, once and for all.'

Richard closed the door and stared through the windscreen

into the darkness. He took a deep breath. 'Father,' he said, 'I'm a homosexual.'

'So Peter was jealous of you and Klaus,' Stern said, making the simple connection.

'Father,' Richard shouted, incredulous. 'Did you hear what I said? I'm a homosexual.' He turned to face him. 'Your son's a homosexual,' he shouted.

'I know,' Stern said, with utter simplicity. 'I've always known.' He put his arm round Richard's shoulder. 'And it doesn't pain me at all.'

Then Richard sobbed uncontrollably. His father's reaction was so loving, so tender, so utterly removed from the horrors and the recriminations that he had expected, that he had in a strange way hoped for so that he could spill out the whole story as an act of filial punishment. But now he loved his father too well to tell him about Brownlow. He couldn't burden him with that knowledge. That he would have to bear alone.

A great weight was lifted from Stern's heart. The expected explosion, such as it was, was over. Perhaps, he thought, and with a most fearful joy, that from this time onwards, his son would trust him enough to love him freely. He took Richard's hand. 'You'll get over Klaus,' he said, 'and you will love again. There's no shame about grief, and no shame about love, whatever and whomsoever the cause.'

They sat silently for a while, then simultaneously they opened their doors. On the way to the porch, Stern said, 'I miss Brownlow, you know. I wonder if he'll ever come back.'

'No,' Richard said. 'He's gone. We must mourn him too.'

Chapter Twenty-two

Once again Richard and Isani took the same road out of Djogja for the airfield. This time, they followed the hearse with Peter Weiner's body. There were just the two of them. It was as if for the UN officials, death had lost its novelty. Richard had had no trouble in organising Peter's final resting place. His mother had cabled from Frankfurt insisting on a home burial, and the German Embassy had paid all expenses. But Isani had allowed Richard to make all the arrangements. He was impressed by the boy's sense of loyalty, and to one who, he had himself admitted, was not a very close friend. He had even offered to accompany the body alone, but Isani had insisted on going along, if only to acknowledge on his country's behalf, the debt that they owed to any aid-giving programme. He was rather disgusted that the UN personnel had made no attempt to hold a memorial. It would have been different if Brownlow had been around.

'What do *you* make of Brownlow?' Isani suddenly said.

Richard shivered. He was not reassured by the conversation-like tone of the question. 'How should I know?' he said shortly.

'Everybody's got their own theories. I thought you might have one too.'

'He's dead, I think,' Richard said more calmly. 'He must be. He was a good man. We could do with more of his kind.'

'Your father's a good man too,' Isani said. 'You get on pretty well, don't you?'

Richard nodded. 'He's very understanding,' he said.

'Have you ever met my sons,' Isani ventured, slowly breaching an inquiry concerning Oyung.

'No,' Richard said.

'I've got one almost your age,' Isani said. 'He's away at the moment. Have you never met him?'

'No.'

'Have you ever *heard* about him?' Isani pleaded.

Richard turned to him. 'What's the matter?' he said. 'Is there something the matter with your son?'

'I don't know,' Isani said. 'I'm afraid to speak about it.'

'You can tell me,' Richard said. He was genuinely anxious to help. On Isani's face he saw traces of his father's former bewilderment, his helplessness in the face of uncontainable love. 'Perhaps I can help you.'

'It's so heavy a secret,' Isani said. 'But I have to share it with someone. Can I honestly trust you?'

'I would tell nobody,' Richard said. 'Not even my father.'

Isani looked around the car for possible eavesdroppers. 'It's my son,' he said. 'He's run away. I think he's with the PKI. I don't know where he is, so I can't protect him, and if he's ever caught, they'll shoot him. That's the penalty.' Isani shivered at the prospect.

'What can I do?' Richard said. 'I'll do anything.' And he meant it. For the rest of his life he would be looking for avenues of expiation.

'Nothing,' Isani said. 'There's nothing anybody can do. It's been a kind of relief though to tell somebody. Sometimes I think I should get out of my job, then people would trust me more and perhaps give me news of him. Sometimes I dream that he's already dead.' A tear rolled down Isani's cheek. At that moment Richard would have given his life to find his son. 'Forget all that,' Isani said suddenly. 'No one must ever know. But you have friends in the villages,' he went on. 'You could talk to them. About the movement, I mean. Gain their confidence. But they're tight-lipped. All of them.'

'He'll come back,' Richard said lamely.

'D'you know,' Isani said, 'it's a funny thing but I think that if Brownlow's dead, Oyung's dead too. In my mind, they're somehow connected. That's why I believe Brownlow's alive. I've simply got to, or I shall go mad.'

The words of a full and total confession gathered in Richard's mouth. It was not cowardice or self-protection that held him back. In his heart he was ready to confess, and above all to this man who so truly trusted him. But Isani was relying on Brownlow's return to perpetuate his faith in his son's survival.

Richard swallowed the words. There would come a time for their airing.

They pulled up at the airfield and the waiting plane. Weiner's successor came forward to greet them. He was astonished at the poor turn-out, and lack of ceremony, and he wondered why the notion of suicide should be found so offensive. For that could be the only reason for the lack of respect. He was angry. He was a fellow German, and he took it as a personal and national insult that a compatriot should be so coldly and almost dishonourably dispatched. He went forward and helped with the coffin. Then, as they reached the plane, he ordered the carriers to set it down on the ground. He was determined to send a dead comrade home with some form of ritual. Had he had a trumpet handy, he would have sounded the last post. But in the circumstances, he stood to attention by the coffin, and saluted. Then, in a thin unsteady voice, and all by himself, in the middle of that desolate field, he sang the German national anthem, proclaiming to his astonished listeners the irrefutable superiority of his homeland. He sang it all the way through, even repeating the final reprise. Richard and Isani felt they should both start clapping, for it was so patently in the nature of a performance. The singer scowled at them, and ordered the body aboard.

Richard and Isani waited until the plane took off. Richard tried not to think of the last time he'd stood on the airfield. He recalled the school song that Brownlow had been singing, and his own impatience to get it over and done with. He forced himself to think of Brownlow's fate. He prayed, but with little hope, that howsoever it was, it was swift and painless. But the vultures kept bothering him.

On the way back to Djogja, Isani kept reminding him of the vital necessity of keeping the secret between them. Perhaps he was already regretting having taken Richard into his confidence. 'It's not because I mind losing my job,' he said. 'But if it has to go, I want to move out of it of my own free will.'

Richard kept reassuring him. He was determined to find out about Oyung. And his first move would be to ask Burhan.

When he got back to Djogja, he went straight to his stand on the Square. But Burhan's place was empty, and according to his neighbours on the stand, he had not been there for some days, and they jokingly suggested that he had retired.

But Burhan was sadly sitting it out in the Brownlow suite watching the packing and paraphernalia of departure, and bravely holding his young and tempted tongue. He felt he was sitting at a loved one's death-bed, hoping against all hope for a recovery.

Chapter Twenty-three

The thirtieth of September 1970 marked three anniversaries in Djogja. It recorded the end of Brownlow's first year in the Ponsonby Post; it also marked the 400th performance of the *Ramayana* at the Prambanan Temple. It was, too, the fifth anniversary of the abortive September 30th coup when the PKI had attempted to overthrow the government.

In the days approaching the anniversary, Siswamarto thought continually of his son, and prayed that his deliverance was near. And he talked about him too, re-telling old stories of Wan's boyhood, the tears welling in his eyes, as he feared that deliverance might already be too late. Brownlow and Oyung were his constant and faithful listeners. In Brownlow, he saw a father like himself, and in exchange for Wan stories, Brownlow gave him Emily. In Oyung he saw a son, just like his own and he loved him like a father. But he feared for Wan. There were terrible stories about the Djogja prison. Stories of men who had broken under torture, stories of murder and suicide. One image haunted his dreams. The vision of Wan in *diplentong*, a system of torture in common use against political prisoners. It was a form of nail-less crucifixion. The prisoner's right wrist was chained to his left ankle, so that he could neither lie nor stand. In this state he was left for months or even years, and at night, when Siswamarto struggled for sleep, it was this hooked vision of his son that scalded his eyelids. Brownlow had tried to keep his mind away from such nightmares, and for days now, they had been playing chess. Siswamarto was a good player, and he rarely lost to Brownlow. This time, Brownlow prolonged his game, giving openings to his opponent, complicating moves, so that by the night of September 29th, the game was into its fourth day, and still unfinished.

And on that night, the mountain men prepared to leave their

hide-out. All day they had postponed the Brownlow decision. They had argued amongst themselves, but the general and overall verdict, though unspoken, was that Brownlow must die before the sortie. This decision, unspoken as it was, had the air only of a formality. The men reckoned that that was what they were supposed to do. That was what the movement expected of them. They should have done it long ago, before he was well, before he was able to talk to them, to tell them about his family, his love of paintings, and his simple pleasures. They should have done it when he was insensible and at death's door, then they would not have cared for the grief of his bereaved. But now they knew so much about him, his childhood in the English countryside, his schooldays at an English public school, and his days at Cambridge, that they were now expected to extinguish not only a human breath but a whole way of life. Nevertheless, it was their duty to get rid of him. That they had decided. But strangely enough, nobody seemed to be doing anything about it. Brownlow himself was aware of their dilemma, and he was certainly frightened. He knew the nature of the partisans' work. He even knew the purpose of their present sortie. He understood that his continual presence in their midst was a danger. He understood too that they couldn't let him go. Why should they be expected to trust him not to reveal their plans and whereabouts? He wondered what he would have done if he'd been in Roschun's shoes. He was aware too that they were loathe to dispatch him, but he didn't want to play on that. If you blackmailed via affection, that affection was quickly assailable. Most of the day he said nothing. He helped them with their preparations. He strapped their packs, he cleaned their guns, he helped make up food packets, and he filled their water bottles.

His game of chess with Siswamarto stood unfinished on the home-made checker-board. Brownlow had taught the men the game, and they had taken to it with a natural and joyful aptitude. Some were even hooked on it, and played well into the night. The unfinished game lay in Brownlow's favour, but he didn't suggest finishing it. He didn't want to remind them of their affection for him.

Brownlow was not afraid of death, but he was sad that it might possibly come to him at such a time, when a new and such a rich horizon was unfolding. For since he'd been with the partisans, he'd learned so much about Java and the East-West dilemma, the ambivalent nature of the UN and its sometimes myopic programme making, much more than he could ever have learned closeted in his Ambarrukmo suite. And in a strange way, up in these mountains, away from all the ham-fisted projects and hot-potched aid, he'd done more for the Ponsonby Post than ever poor old Ponsonby had dared to hope. He wished they would trust him. Enough to let him go, and never in a life-time to say a word. He wanted so much to see Emily and Belinda again. Yet he felt he could not even talk about them any more. Any revelation of human emotion could now be counted as blackmail.

The moon was rising as they completed their preparation. Suddenly there was nothing more to do. Now the only unfinished business was Brownlow and the game of chess that would be left unmated in his memory. Roschun motioned Brownlow to the far end of the cave, out of ear-shot, and he gathered his men around him.

They sat in a circle and were silent. In their shame, they were unable to look at each other, so they stared at the floor. Even Roschun seemed unwilling to break the silence. Then quietly, he whispered, 'He must die.' He had meant to say, 'We must kill him', and though he knew their hands were the only means of Brownlow's sudden demise he couldn't bring himself to associate his men with such a monstrous act.

'How?' one of the men dared to ask.

'Who?' another risked.

It would have to be all of them, together, until twenty or so simultaneous shots would annihilate him, and no one could ever be personally blamed. But shooting was out of the question. It would have drawn attention to their whereabouts, which they needed now, more than at any other time, to hold secret. There was no other communal means of killing a man.

'One of us must strangle him,' Roschun said.

They shuddered and were silent again. Each man recalled his own private bond with Brownlow. How could you kill a man who had compared his mother with your own. How could you kill a man who had taught you chess, and whom you had taught Malay checkers. Who could kill a man who had swapped you the Arthurian legend for the *Ramayana*, and exchanged for 'Saya Cinta Badamu', 'I love you'. How could such a tongue in all conscience be stilled.

'We must draw lots,' Roschun said.

Yet nobody moved, and they felt Brownlow listening fearfully to their silence. Then almost to a man, they shouted, 'I'll do it.'

'Let Oyung do it,' Roschun said, and the men were glad because Oyung knew and loved Brownlow best, and he could be trusted to do what all the volunteers would have done, quietly, secretly and in their own way.

Oyung went to the far end of the cave. He put his arm in Brownlow's and walked him to the gathering of men. Here he stopped. He knew the men wanted no farewells, but for Brownlow's sake there had to be a formal leave-taking. Oyung gently touched him on the arm, and by the sad silence in the cave, Brownlow knew that he was to die. He was no longer afraid. It was just the sheer pity of it all that overwhelmed him. He wanted the touch of each one of them. 'Goodbye,' he said. It seemed silly to thank them for saving his life when they were now on the point of killing him. Yet he wanted to thank them if not for his life, then for the *Ramayana* that he would never see, for their village games that he would no longer play, and for the sharing of their linguistic loves. 'Goodbye,' he said again, 'I'm sorry. I'm sorry for us all.'

The men watched him go, then they busied themselves, each one at a quickly invented task, silently though, so that none of them would miss the strangled cry in the moonlight.

Oyung guided Brownlow out of the cave and up the slope to the twin-triangle rock.

'The moon is almost full,' Brownlow said. It seemed to him an appropriate time to die when the wheel in the sky had come full circle. The need to talk about Emily now overwhelmed him, and he was free to do it now, close as he was to his end. But what came out of his mouth had nothing to do with Emily at all. 'Oyung,' he said, turning to him. 'I know you for Isani's son.'

They embraced. He had spoken about Emily after all. They sat down against the rock. 'I am here to kill you,' Oyung said. 'That is the official decision. As far as we are concerned, you must be dead.' Brownlow was not sure he understood him.

'None of us can kill you,' Oyung said. 'Not even Roschun. We all volunteered so that we could set you free. Roschun chose me, because he knew I spoke for them all.'

Brownlow clasped Oyung's hand. He was not ashamed that he was weeping.

'We ask only for your silence,' Oyung said. 'You must invent a story to tell. You lost your memory perhaps. The farmers fed you. You don't know where. You wandered many weeks. You don't remember anything. Stand up now,' he said. 'We must make noises of killing. Then I shall return to the cave. Wait here awhile. It would be better if you waited for the morning light. Djogja is about five miles away. You take the track that points south from the base of the big triangle.'

They held out hánds to each other. Oyung put his around Brownlow's throat, and motioned Brownlow to do likewise on his own. They pressed their fingers on each other's flesh, gently like a gesture of love. Then in unison, they let out a strangled cry. Then their hands moved and they clasped each other, holding each other's head in an embrace beyond the language of love. 'Help us if you can,' Oyung said.

'I will. I promise you.' He watched Oyung's silhouette as it faded down the slope, and he knelt at the rock and thanked God for his deliverance. After a while, he heard footsteps of men, marching steps, and though he could see nothing, he heard them out of sight. Then he went back to the cave. He noticed that the chess game had been finished, and that he had mated. It had been Siswamarto's gesture of trust. He picked up the wooden piece of the king and put it in his pocket. He would leave him the queen, and he would know it as a sign for his victory. And if Wan were rescued, it was victory for them all.

He looked at his watch. It was nine o'clock. He would wait there half an hour, he thought. That would give them time to be well on their way. Then by the light of the moon, he would find his way to Emily.

Chapter Twenty-four

It was the sight of the brand new but totally inaccessible poly-clinic at the foot of Mount Merapi that finally triggered off poor Ponsonby's anger and led to the writing of his report. One of Brownlow's first undertakings when he arrived in Djogja was to organise the building of a road linking the hospital to the villages at the foot of the volcano. He had also managed to ease out the largely American staff and replace them with Indonesian doctors and nurses. There was now no reason why the clinic with its comprehensive programme of planned parenthood, maternity and child care, and general hospital services should not become a vital and beneficial centre of community life. But it remained largely idle and empty. Few village women availed themselves of family planning. A large family was part of their cultural tradition. They knew that if they had ten children, only half of them stood a chance of survival, but their attitude to death was culturally different, and those do-gooders who came from the so-called developed world preached to them on the assumption that their ways in the West were the right ways, and anyone else's were wrong. 'You have to cut down on your families,' the gospellers said. 'There's a world shortage of food.' But the village women were not conned by that one. There was plenty of food, and in their own country too, and much of it was rotting in the go-downs, while the owners waited for the market price to rise. They'd heard too on their transistor sets that they were burning coffee in Brazil, and burying tomatoes and apples in England, and destroying grain in God's own country even. 'It's not our many children, thank you very much,' they told the hot gospellers. 'It's your rotten system.' The men from the mountains had tutored them well.

The maternity wards too had a pathetic turnover. The women preferred to have their babies at home. The midwife would come with her herbs and talismen, and the village women would crowd into the hut as was their custom, and soothe and bless and urge the baby's debut, attending the mother as in the court of the queen. Outside the hut, the men waited in the clearing, fed by the occasional bulletin, and when it was over, the new child, minutes old, was presented to the elders of the village as proof of fertility and regeneration. One or two of the village women had regrettably risked the maternity ward, and had a different tale to tell. There were white sheets and never-ending silence, and strange contraptions that put you to sleep so that you couldn't even feel the baby coming. And there was no one to sing or gossip by your bedside, and nobody waited outside the ward. It was the silence and secrecy that was the worst part of it. It seemed to endow the glory of birth with a terrible sense of shame.

As for the other departments of the clinic, those for general care, the villagers preferred their medicine-man. Their fathers and grandfathers before them had been treated and cured by village medicine. So all in all, the polyclinic was a bit of a white elephant until the medicine-man from the village of Harbobingangun hit upon a way to put it to some use.

On the night of the full moon there was going to be bloodshed and the injured men would need hiding and attention. The polyclinic was an obvious god-given choice. There were ample medical facilities and the staff were sympathetic and no military or police boot would dream of entering a lying-in ward. The irony of his choice was not lost on the medicine-man. The clinic had been built with American money as part of their aid programming in Indonesia. Their involvement was not however altruistic. It was, like much aid, politically motivated as part of their determination to keep Communism out of the archipelago. Well, thanks very much, the medicine-man said to himself. It will come in very handy.

He sat in his clearing waiting for Roschun and his men. From hide-outs all over the mountains, the men were gathering. The lorries were ready, hidden in the clearing behind the *Lurah's* house. As far as the *Lurah* was concerned, they'd been ordered to take the villagers to the *Ramayana*. The medicine-man was content. He had done all that had been asked of him.

Now he could only pray for victory. If it came, there would be singing and dancing in the village and much rejoicing.

The men arrived in small groups, four or five of them from different hide-outs. They were to spend the rest of the night and the following day hiding in the village homes, and at full moon they would follow Roschun out of the village and prepare, if necessary, to lay down their lives. The medicine-man knew few of the men personally, but it was enough that they were joined together in a common struggle, for him to offer his large hospitality. His wife had prepared food, and as they arrived, they passed through the clearing into the hut and took refreshment before they were billeted. The last to arrive were Roschun and his men, and the medicine-man was joyful to see them for he knew each one of them and he shared their private griefs. With Siswamarto, he feared for his son, with Oyung, he feared for his father, and with Roschun he feared nothing and nobody but his own fragile vulnerability.

The band of fighters was now complete, and in little huts all over the village, they gathered sleep and strength for the onslaught of the full moon.

Chapter Twenty-five

Brownlow picked his steps over the mountain. His watch showed ten o'clock. If he didn't lose his way, he would see Emily by midnight. He was in no hurry. He had waited and he had prayed for so long. Now was the time to savour the waiting. He rehearsed how he would greet them. He was acutely aware that they would be deeply shocked on seeing him. They had surely written him off for dead. He would forgive them that. They had been given no cause to expect his return. Somehow or other he must cushion the shock.

Belinda would probably be in bed, and Emily would certainly be sleeping. He would knock quietly on the door of the suite and he would wait. Belinda might call, 'Who is it?' and how could a presumed ghost announce himself through a wooden door? She would be too frightened to open it. She would think she was dreaming. Then he thought he might just walk into the rooms and present himself. He hadn't looked at himself for many months. There had been only a small shaving mirror in the hide-out, but he knew that he looked very different. He had a bushy red beard and he had lost a lot of weight. He knew that, because his trousers would have fallen had they not been secured round his thighs with a piece of string. He looked down at himself, and it occurred to him that the night-porter at the Ambarrukmo, at the sight of him, might well turn him away. He was still dressed basically in his dinner-jacket. The cummerbund and the shirt had disintegrated, and underneath his jacket he wore a white cotton vest. The suit was dirty and shabby and hung about him with little contact or familiarity with his body. For shoes he wore toe-thonged sandals which Mohammed had cut for him out a piece of old rubber tyre. Not exactly Ambarrukmo *haute couture*. He began to worry that he might not even get past the foyer. Then another more terrible thought occurred to him. Belinda might have done with waiting and, in widow's weeds, gone back with Emily to England. He began to hurry with the illogical notion that he could catch them in time.

The moon was one night short of fullness. He thought about his mountain friends. He knew it was unlikely he would ever see them again, and he wondered how many would have survived when the moon began to wane. He would never forget them, and though their aims did not agree with his political thinking, they had taught him much about their people and the mismanagement of the powers he represented. He was going to make a lot of changes when he got back to work. He was going to involve the villagers in all policy-making decisions. Especially the women. And he was going to weed out all the dead rot in the administration. He would take them out of their air-conditioned offices and send them out into the field. He would make von Henkel and his ilk go to the villages and live there for a month so that they could understand how little their reports to head office had to do with the flesh and blood of the problem. He was going to make himself pretty unpopular, but in his own way he would also make a small revolution.

He heard a trickling of water, and he knew he must be near the rice-paddies that bordered the road out of Djogja. The hills began to level out. He could not be far from the road.

He began to think of what story he would tell to explain his prolonged absence, and he rehearsed it aloud. 'I don't remember anything. I wandered about in the heat and I was very thirsty. I was with a farmer for a while, and his wife fed me. But I don't know where it was. Then they took me in a cart to another village, and I began to remember where I was. I remembered the Ambarrukmo Hotel, and I kept repeating it, but they didn't understand. I heard them say I was "amok", and they were almost right. Then I started walking over the mountains. I seem to have been walking for ever.'

He tried it again, laying more emphasis on his amnesia, but however he said it, it sounded a lame tale indeed. It was almost silly, so silly in fact, that it was patently a lie, and Isani would no doubt privately probe him further. At the thought of his friend Isani he was much cheered, and he wished he could tell him about his son. He wondered how Burhan was, and whether he and Emily were still close friends. The excitement of seeing them all was more than he could bear, and to take his mind off it, he rehearsed his silly speech once again.

He had reached the road, the smell of the tobacco plants was almost tangible. They must be fully open he thought, in their pungent ripeness. Though Merapi that night was invisible in a misty haze, he knew it was to the left of him. So he turned right in the direction of Djogja. Occasionally on the road he recognised landmarks; the corrugated iron shed, where Boskaro, the *Lurah's* handyman, kept and trained his fighting-cocks, known as champions all over the island; further down the road, the wooden studio of his sculptor friend Sanjoto. There was a light in the upper window, and he was tempted to call on him to try out his silly speech of explanation. He was nervous, so nervous that he wanted to delay his return. He hesitated, and as he made to walk up the path to the house, the light was switched off. The decision was made for him.

Now he began to run and he heard the flip-flop of his sandals beating the silence like a metronome. There was no one about and he was glad of it. He had so much explaining to do, and so few and silly words to do it with, that he had to keep them all for Belinda to make what she would of them. He was just hoping that she would be so overwhelmingly pleased to see him back that she would not question his story. She would sniff out his need for concealment, and she would respect it. One day, when it wouldn't matter any more, when they were back in England, sitting one winter's evening before a log fire, he would tell her the whole story. That is, what he could remember of it. The days before his sojourn in the hide-out were still a complete blank for him. They had gone, and he didn't care whether or not they returned.

In the driveway of the Ambarrukmo there were two *betchaks*, their drivers asleep at the wheel. The hotel mini-bus that nightly took passengers to the station to catch the Djakarta express, stood outside the entrance. Its driver too was asleep. Brownlow walked into the foyer with as much dignity as his tramp-apparel would allow. There was mercifully no one at the reception desk but he heard the clerk's voice on the telephone in the cubby-hole behind. The lift was waiting. He pressed the button for the fourth floor.

His excitement and apprehension was now so intense that he

suddenly and badly wanted to relieve himself. He went to the cloakroom at the far end of the corridor, deliberately avoiding the mirror over the hand-basin. Then he walked to his own door. He made an automatic movement to straighten his tie, and his hand clutched his neck and dirty white vest, and he made a resolution that though his garb was threadbare, he would keep each piece for ever. He put up his hand to knock. He heard voices, a man and a woman's and he dropped his hand. He thought that Belinda might have moved to another room, and again he feared that she might have gone back to England. He put his ear to the door.

'I'd like that too,' he heard, and his heart leapt as he recognised Belinda's voice.

'Are you ready then?' This time it was a man's and the voice was familiar. Isani. What in God's name was Isani doing in his wife's room with such conversation and at this hour of night? With a rush of fury and jealousy he burst in through the door.

Belinda and Emily had their backs to him. They seemed to be packing a case. Isani was strapping a large trunk. He too had his back to the door. Only Mrs Isani faced him, and after a second of silent unabsorbed shock, she let out a scream of fear, joy and total amazement. Isani turned and looked at him, but Brownlow was looking at Emily. When she saw him, she made an impulsive step forward, then withdrew. She wasn't absolutely sure who he was. Slowly they moved towards one another, trembling. Brownlow realised how radically he must have changed. The next move was clearly his, and he had no idea of what to say. At that moment, Burhan came out of the bedroom carrying a case. He saw Brownlow, dropped the case and ran straight into his arms.

'Where are you all going?' Brownlow said, and hearing his voice, they knew it was he, and in his large and throbbing embrace, he clasped all five of them. He held on to the laughter, their joy and their utter incredulity. And their silence too. Not a single question. It was so obvious to ask where he had been, but now it seemed so irrelevant. All that would come later. They were giving him his own time for explanation.

Burhan broke the silence. 'I told you he could come back,' he said, and he picked up the case like a little commercial traveller with his load of samples, and took it back into the bedroom.

'We were leaving tonight for Djakarta,' Belinda said. 'I'd given up hope.' She was ashamed to admit it but it had to be said. 'Oh my God,' she whispered. 'How good to have you back.'

Then Emily, who felt they'd had time enough to get over the initial shock, and for whom the long and hopeless waiting time was now completely forgotten, said, 'Where have you been, Daddy?'

He looked around the room and he saw Burhan staring at him. He was shaking his head furiously, and in his eye was a look that could only be seen as a challenge. He could almost hear the boy's heart beating. Suddenly he remembered the boy's sudden and unexplained absences, and he made the very natural connection. He smiled at him, hoping to convey that he too could be trusted. He realised what it must have cost Burhan to keep his little mouth shut and what tremendous courage and loyalty filled that adult childish frame. 'I don't know,' Brownlow said simply. 'Most of the time, I lost my memory.'

Burhan's face broke into a large smile, and he went over to the couch and sat by Emily. Then Brownlow gave his rehearsed little speech. It was clear that nobody in the room believed him, but it was also clear to them all that it was not to be questioned. 'You're back,' Belinda said, her face ashen with the shock of it, 'and that's all that matters.'

'Now we can go to the *Ramayana*,' Emily said, jumping with excitement. So it was arranged. That night, the first of the full moon, they would all go in a party, and afterwards they would celebrate his return. Together they made a great performance of unpacking and cancelling the cars, train and plane, and when it was time for the Isanis to go, Brownlow embraced them both. 'I thought of you a lot of the time,' he said. 'After my family, I missed you most of all.'

'Now he'll come back, you'll see,' Isani said to his wife as they were leaving. In his mind, Oyung and Brownlow were connected, and he was filled with hope that one day, and perhaps very soon, he would see his son again.

Chapter Twenty-six

Burhan was singing at his stand. Never in his short life had he been so happy. For the first time that morning, after many months, he'd woken up without fear. Emily would not be leaving Djogja. He rubbed away at his client's shoes, telling everybody that he was going that night to the *Ramayana*, and that Brownlow had come home. But since most of them were unaware that Brownlow, whoever he was, had gone away, they were not unduly interested in his return. But Burhan wanted everybody to share his joy.

During the morning, while the Brownlows were still sleeping, the news spread around Djogja of the miraculous return. Isani went himself to the UN offices and announced it to the staff, and all of them began to catch up on work that had been neglected. Of them all, Stern was the most pleased. In his heart he had feared for Brownlow's life, with an instinctive yet unsupported fear that Richard was somehow involved in his disappearance.

But Richard was a late riser, and it was midday before he crossed the Sultan's Square, unknowing. Burhan saw him, and shouted out to him, beckoning him frantically with his arms. Richard walked quickly towards him. Burhan had news, and news from Burhan was always worth hearing.

'He's back,' Burhan shouted, even before he reached the stand.

'Who's back?' Richard said.

'Brownlow. He came back last night.' Burhan saw how Richard trembled. He was shaking so much that he had to lean on Burhan's shoulder.

'Where had he been?' Richard said, wanting to know his sentence without delay. 'Who took him away?'

'He doesn't know,' Burhan laughed. 'He lost his memory. He doesn't know where he was. Honestly,' Burhan repeated, because

Brownlow's feigned amnesia was in the interest of his mountain friends too, 'he doesn't remember anything. He just walked across mountains and came home.'

'I don't believe it,' Richard said.

'I saw him,' Burhan shouted. 'He's at the Ambarrukmo.'

Suddenly Richard was lying at his feet, sprawled across his stand in total black-out. A small crowd gathered. Some fanned him, and another brought water. Burhan did nothing. He eyed the figure on the ground with utter contempt, for from Richard's strange reaction there was no doubt in his mind that for some reason or other, all those months ago, he had taken Brownlow away.

When Richard recovered, he stood up unsteadily. 'It's the heat,' he said, by way of explanation.

'It's like this every day,' Burhan said with disdain, and he went back to his customers.

Richard never called in at his father's office, but Stern was not in the least surprised when he came, pale-faced, through the door. Richard suspected Burhan of laying a trap, and he'd come to his father for confirmation or otherwise. If it were true, his father would tell him right away. But Stern first wanted to know why he had come.

'Just passing,' Richard said, caught off his guard. There seemed to be no startling news about. Burhan had simply tricked him. But why?

'But you've never been before,' Stern said.

'I was just passing,' Richard fairly shouted.

Then Stern knew it was about Brownlow he had come, and he didn't want to know. He didn't want to know anything about anything any more. What was most important to him was a continued relationship with his son, and he must not threaten that. 'Have you heard the news?' he said.

'What news?'

'Brownlow's back.'

Richard feigned astonishment. 'How? Where'd he been?'

Then his father repeated what Burhan had said, and Richard began to believe it. If it was true that he remembered nothing, then he himself was in the clear. But did memory ever come back? Could a sight or a sound trigger off the memory of some event that had sunk deep into the unconscious. He was very uneasy. 'Have you seen him?' he asked his father.

'There's a small party tonight at the Ambarrukmo. We're all going there after the *Ramayana*. Will you come too?'

'Yes,' he said. He would go. He would brazen it out. He would stand face to face with Brownlow and dare him to total recall. Then, should he be accused, he would deny it, claiming that amnesia was closely linked with delusion.

But in spite of his fears, he was deeply glad that Brownlow was still alive, and he wished that Weiner could have known sooner.

Chapter Twenty-seven

The Hindu Temple of Prambanan reaches 130 feet into the sky, and its floodlit towers could be seen long before they entered the temple grounds. The Isanis and the Brownlows sat in the back of the large official car, and Emily and Burhan were up front by the driver. All along the sides of the roads, people were walking towards the Temple, and there was a general air of festivity. Very little traffic was coming in the opposite direction and the car was free to use the width of the road. Until three lorries loomed in the distance and the car swerved sharply.

'What are those?' Belinda said.

'Vegetables for the Djogja market,' Isani said, with the assurance of one who knew these parts. Instinctively Brownlow put his hand on Burhan's shoulder, and Burhan, in full understanding of the gesture, smiled back at him.

They parked some distance from the Temple and joined the crowd going into the amphitheatre. They could already hear the gamelan band, and as they entered the arena, the followers of Rama, red and black-masked, strode on to the stage to herald the arrival of their leader. Their dance was by way of inviting the audience to settle, and it was not until the arena was full, that Rama himself made his spectacular entrance. It was a leap that seemed to have come from the highest tower, and Emily drew in her breath with wonder. Burhan was a little frightened, and he held on to her hand for protection.

'They'll be tired tomorrow,' Isani touched Brownlow's arm.

'It doesn't matter,' Brownlow said. 'Tomorrow they can sleep. It's a national holiday.'

Suddenly Isani was uneasy. It was indeed a holiday the next day. And everything would be closed, including the vegetable market. Then what were those lorries carrying to Djogja?

*   *   *

179

Three-quarters of the police force of Djogja were patrolling the grounds of the Prambanan Temple. And while on the floodlit stage, Rama and Hanuman, the monkey king, were preparing to invade the kingdom of Ravana, Roschun and his men made ready to scale the prison wall. From inside information, they knew that the *tapols*, or political prisoners, about a hundred of them, were housed in a separate building to the right of the main block. Lowokwara prison, on the outskirts of Djogja, was known as the worst torture centre in the Archipelago, worse even than the Kalisosok at Surabaya. The Indonesians had their own time-honoured methods, and variety was provided by Japanese and Dutch refinements, to which dissidents on the island had been subjected during the various occupations of their country. But even though the country was no longer occupied, and considered itself a freedom-loving state, certain methods of torture were still widely in use. It was known that over the five years since the September massacres, thousands of the *tapols* had been tortured to death, or in their abject despair, had somehow or other contrived to end their own lives, for suicide was a forbidden luxury. The figure of one hundred rotting in the Djogja gaol was approximate and varied from day to day. Roschun's contact in the prison was a guard, who that night would be patrolling the inner wall. Another contact, Ani, the guard at the main entrance, was from the village of Harbobingangun and a friend of the medicine-man. A handful of guards within the prison blocks were prepared to join the mountain men once they were inside, but the majority of them would amount to a formidable opposition. Thanks to Zein, and the raid on the barracks, the men were well armed, but it was going to be a tough battle.

Roschun had sent two of his men to the watch-tower. They were the twin brothers Capurro, farmers from one of the Merapi villages, who had been agents for the partisans since they'd moved into the mountains. They were young, agile and inseparable. In conjunction with Roschun, they had worked out their own strategy. Dodging the beam of the searchlight, they cut the barbed wire of the outer fence. Then they crouched hidden in the long grass. Almost immediately, the raucous sound of a brass band broke the prison silence. Roschun had hidden a hand-cranked gramophone in a ditch and a powerful microphone sprouted from the grass like an enquiring toad, spreading the trumpet blare over the compound. The watch-tower beam swung quickly trying to locate the source of the sound, while the Capurro brothers crept under the darkness to the foot of the tower. They counted five, and as they expected, the music cut out abruptly. Now, wherever the beams cared to travel, they were safely out of their angle of light. They crept to the tower stairway. A free-standing iron spiral led to the top of the tower, and they climbed it stealthily. There were two guards at the top, as they expected. They took one each from behind, and as they slit their throats, the beam hesitated, but within seconds, the brothers had maintained its swinging course, spotlighting their comrades, who by now, had reached the inner yard, and guiding them to the *tapol* block. Once inside, they switched off the beams, and scrambled down the stairway.

Inside the block, they met their first opposition, and within seconds of their entry, six of their men lay dead, riddled with the angry and astonished bullets from the warders. Roschun retreated, holding his men back. It was a fatal move, for it gave the guards time to take up their positions so that the invaders would be covered from all angles. From the corner of the stone outer wall, Roschun understood the price of his hesitation, and he wondered now whether he should call it all off and save his men from further massacre. He heard himself praying for guidance. His men waited for his orders, but already they feared that the battle was lost. Then Mohammed took out his flute, and loud and clear, he played the song of the Revolution, the song to which the *tapols* had marched to Merdeka Square and the song to which thousands of them had died. And the men behind the bars listened, and dared not believe the sound. Some thought that it was a final signal to their own madness, that this song, which for years was confined, on pain of torture, to the inside of their skull, had now escaped and would damn them for ever. So what the hell? They would try the words for size. And out of the grilled bars came the hesitant sound of men's voices, four, five, that swelled to a glorious choir, louder and louder, till the men knew that it was true and that freedom had come. And to this symphony of freedom Roschun made his charge.

He had about sixty men, but the prison guards dropped from the walls like bugs. About thirty of them, Roschun gauged, and he realised that there must be many more prisoners than his information had led him to believe. He was glad. The cost might be high, but the returns would be manifold. His strategy was to disarm, or annihilate if necessary, enough guards to risk opening the cell doors, thus increasing their own man-power. It was much to the credit of Roschun's men that they were not trigger-happy. Sharp as their appetite was for victory, and long as they had waited, they did not rush to attack. Instead, they spread out under cover of the lower gallery, and to their horror, they saw one of the warders start to open the cell doors. They were going to use the cells as cover, and pick off the enemy from inside. Or perhaps they would let out the prisoners, so that they would be caught in the cross-fire. Roschun had no choice. From behind the wall, he waved a white handkerchief and called the warders to hold their fire. Then he stepped out alone to address them. 'We are all Indonesians,' he said. 'We are all one people. We have lost enough men in our wars, and we want peace. No more need die here. We ask for the peaceful release of our prisoners, and no one will be harmed.'

The chief warder fired into the air for an answer. 'Throw down your guns,' he said, 'and surrender. Then no one need die.' The warders, in their confidence that it was all over bar the shouting, formed themselves into a solid block, to bar any possible entry to the upper gallery. Roschun fired through the centre of them, and his men rushed into attack. There was little cover for either side, until the mountain men rushed the gallery and were able to fire the locks of the cells and take cover. But the warders were doing likewise, and shortly there was only sporadic sniping in the block, each combatant having fired from his own shelter.

Roschun peered through the bars of his cover. Even within his narrow vision, there were countless bodies on the gallery and most of them were in uniform. The block was uncannily silent. Occasionally a dying groan rattled through the gallery, and a young and useless protest, and he shivered with the pity of it all. He pulled back into the cell, and for the first time witnessed its prisoners. He drew in his breath. It was a horrible sight. Most of them were naked and covered with running sores. The bones stuck through the starved and shrivelled skin, and he wondered from which part of their bodies had come the strength to mouth their song of freedom. And loudly mouth it too. Now they were exhausted, but their eyes were fever-bright, and hope and tears had moistened their lips. Roschun smiled. How else could he hold back his own tears? As he looked at them, he heard the silence and he realised that some minutes had passed without a single shot. He put his revolver through the grille and fired. There was no response. 'Come out,' he shouted, 'and throw down your guns.' Again silence. Then a warder, his uniform immaculate, as if for a dress parade, walked out of a cell on the far side of the gallery, his hands above his head.

'Call your men to surrender,' Roschun shouted.

The warder clenched his fists above his head. 'It's all over, officers,' he said with dignity. 'Come out with your hands up.'

There was no movement. Roschun ordered the officer to walk over to his own cell, and when he arrived, Roschun slipped out, and with his gun in the man's back, he used him as cover. Then he called to his men to follow him. As they trailed out of the cells, he wondered how many of them he had lost. He saw Oyung amongst his followers, and Siswamarto and Mohammed grinning, his flute sticking out of his vest pocket, and he was suddenly homesick for the cave in the mountains, for the chess and the songs, and the good, good fellowship. He told them to group into fours and to go into each cell and weed out the resistance. He himself went with his prisoner before him.

He kicked open the door of the first cell, and thrust the warder in before him. Three warders lay dead on the floor. He noticed with some curiosity that one of their throats was slit. None of his men carried knives, except the Capurro brothers, and they had been ordered to the waiting lorries. He looked round at the prisoners. The cell he himself had used for cover was, by comparison, a paradise. There were six prisoners, whose age could in no way be guessed at, and all were in *diplentong*, their wrists chained to their ankles, and propped against the wall, and staring vacantly. They could have been dead, yet sound was coming from them, an aged hum, an ingathering of all their corporate failing strength, and the hum spelt out the sol-fa of steadfast revolution. One of them held a knife in his free hand. It dripped blood which had spattered to his elbow. He was smiling. Roschun wanted to be sick. 'Unlock them,' he said.

The warder went from prisoner to prisoner with his keys, and the chains clattered on the floor. Yet the men did not straighten. None would risk what would surely be a general breaking of bones. All they could do was to wave their free hand in a gesture of victory.

Amongst them was a young boy, young, Roschun knew, from his unwrinkled neck and taut clear skin. 'What's your name?' he said.

'Wan.'

'And your family name?'

'Siswamarto.'

'Come with me,' Roschun said. 'I'll take you to your father.'

The boy let out a small wail of joy. He staggered to his feet, but his body was fixed in its tortured U-bend. Roschun gathered him in his arms. 'They're all dead,' the call came from Oyung, and there were cheers in the gallery. Roschun came out of his cell. 'Where's Siswamarto?' he called. Then the men heard him calling for his son, rushing from cell to cell, fearing that deliverance was too late.

'He's here,' Roschun shouted.

Siswamarto stumbled over the bodies, his hands reaching out for his son. He took the bundle from Roschun's arms, and rocked it in his own like a baby. Miraculously Wan was able to put both arms around his father's neck. Neither of them spoke. They would go back to the mountains and slowly learn to know each other once again.

Roschun called his men to order. 'There will be time for celebration,' he said. 'Now take our men away.'

And the long rehearsals they had had in the mountains, marshalling imagined groups of fragile men, down the stairs, over the compound yard, through the gate and into the waiting lorries, would now begin to bear fruit. They went to work. Roschun kept one group of men behind to count and to carry away their own dead. Siswamarto stayed by Roschun's side. Now for the first time in the whole battle, he was frightened. Now it seemed that he had so much to live for, and he feared that the dangers were not wholly past, and he lurked with his bundle in Roschun's shadow for his protection.

Within ten minutes the prison block was empty. Almost two hundred prisoners had been freed. Roschun had lost twenty-two men, a third of his entire force. He put his arm round Siswamarto. 'Come,' he said. 'Now we must start all over again.' In his mixed sadness and exhilaration, he had forgotten his one and only prisoner, who now, slowly from behind, picked up a stray gun. It was covered with blood. His hand trembled as he pointed it. Then, moving forward to steady his aim, he pushed against a body, which, to his horror, began to groan. Roschun turned quickly around, but the warder in his terror, had already fired, and Siswamarto lay sprawled at Roschun's feet. Roschun screamed, firing a single shot to the man's head. Then, with sick and heartbroken rage, he emptied his gun into the warder's body.

He turned Siswamarto over, and took Wan from his arms. Then Wan spoke, softly and with unused speech. He touched his father's face. 'You gave me life,' he said, 'and you gave me freedom.' Siswamarto clutched Wan's hand. 'And you give me good words for my dying,' he said.

He went quickly and without pain. Roschun hoisted his body over his shoulder, and he made his way out of the courtyard, cradling the weeping Wan in his arms.

Back at the Ambarrukmo, the party was in full swing. Richard had placed himself squarely before Brownlow, and there had been no flicker of recall. Brownlow was genuinely pleased to see everybody, so he did not feel too badly about the rigorous changes he was going to make in their routine. He looked at von Henkel stuffing a chicken wing into his mouth, and wondered how he would make do on dog in a village, and what sauce he would concoct to smother its taste. There was a great deal of joking talk about the last party held in the Ambarrukmo, and Richard donated his own personal remembrances in the style of a drunk's invention. Yet nobody talked of the aftermath, and no questions were asked about Brownlow's amnesic journey. It was a good and friendly party. Emily and Burhan were allowed to stay up, and in the corner, they were re-living the *Ramayana*, step by step. And as Isani was raising his glass to toast the miraculous return of his dear friend, Kapotto, that time-honoured bearer of bad news, burst into the suite. Isani looked at him and thought again of the lorries.

Kapotto took him to one side, and spilt his dire tidings. The others, sensing that something had gone radically wrong, were silent, hovering. Only Brownlow was unconcerned, and in the corner, Burhan. Brownlow lifted his glass in his direction and drank a toast to Roschun's victory.

Isani was spluttering with rage. His in-tray, except for that silly pair of lady's shoes, had gloriously emptied. Now he saw it rising high. 'Find them,' he thundered. 'Take every available man. Comb through every single one of the villages. Drag the bars and doss-houses for information. Scour the mountains. Every inch of them.' He was like a general going into battle. He almost saluted the company as he took his leave. Mrs Isani muttered an inward prayer. Burhan came over to Brownlow. 'What shall we do?' he said.

'I'll do what I can,' he reassured him. He went over to Isani and took him quietly into the bedroom, away from everybody. 'Isani,' he said slowly. 'Listen to me. Look where you like, but call your men off from the caves around Merapi.'

Isani stood in silence, listening again in his mind to what Brownlow had told him. Then tears started in his eyes, and he held Brownlow in a close embrace. 'How is he?' his voice was muffled.

Brownlow stood him at arm's length. 'He's well,' he said. 'And he's beautiful.'

Isani wiped away his tears. 'I must tell my wife,' he said.

Brownlow watched him go, and saw how his shoulders were rigidly humped to contain his sobs. He resolved to find his way once again to the mountains, and persuade Oyung to the occassional and secret family reunion. He would send food too, and through Burhan, he could play them postal chess. None of these duties were, by any stretch of the imagination, prescribed in the Ponsonby Post, but was it possible, Brownlow thought, that by the title of Liaison Officer, that's what poor old Ponsonby had meant after all.